1

It's the same at any job: the person you have to keep happy is whoever's giving your company the money. Call them sponsors, call them partners, call them whatever you want, it doesn't matter — a client is a client, and at the end of the day, if you take their cash, they get to tell you how to do your job.

With some clients that's not a big deal. They give me a brief with a clear, reasonable list of what they want done, then trust me to make my own decisions about how I tick it off. They leave me alone, I get the job done, and we continue to 'strengthen our great business relationship', as my boss Gabby has taken to saying recently.

Some clients, though . . . are not so easy. Take today's, for example. It's bad enough they had the entire job timed down to the minute. I needed to be in the right office at exactly 17.42 to wait for my appointment with a man called Cyril Hargreaves at 17.45. From there they allocated exactly five minutes for chitchat before I could get to the real purpose of my visit. Business taken care of, they'd send someone to pick me up.

Sounds simple, right?

The first problem was getting into the office at all. If you think your commute's a nightmare: trust me, this one was worse. The Dynafreight Logistics building is out in bloody Southampton, two hours and change from where I usually work in North-West London, assuming the journey goes smoothly. It did, despite the rain running in rivulets up the windscreen of my rented car, but I was grateful I gave myself the extra time when I realised what a pain it would be to get into the office itself. I knew it was connected to a warehouse – actually, it squats *above* the warehouse like a redbrick chicken on a particularly ugly nest – but the client's intel had promised a doorway leading straight into the office building from the road. When I got there, I found that door to be padlocked, bolted, and run through with a bike chain for good measure, forcing me to improvise an alternative route through a warehouse full of chemicals in huge plastic tanks, with so many pictograms and warnings stencilled on them that I started to think I should be in a hazmat suit.

But like I said, I'm a professional. I arrived at the right room at 17.42.57 *exactly*.

Only, now it's nearly 6 p.m. and there's no sign at all of the man I'm supposed to be meeting. Which is frustrating – it means I've spent the past twenty minutes sitting in the dark by myself – but also worrying, because now I'm concerned about whether the rest of the client's planning will still line up as it's meant to. For instance, my promised ride home, which for some reason the client is refusing to explain in detail. Any issues with *that* would, at best, be very annoying, especially after I forgot to tell Beth – my best friend and flatmate – that I might not be back in time for our usual Friday night hang with a movie and Chinese takeaway.

2

At worst, though, a failed extraction could spell disaster.

'All right, team, where is he?' I whisper into the mic hidden in the embroidered white cuff of my long-sleeved blouse.

'*No movement yet, Maisie.*' Jason, our tech guy, crackles through the tiny receiver disguised as a piercing in my left ear. '*No sign of him on any of the cameras in the office building — he must still be in the warehouse. I'll let you know when he's up.*'

'OK, no worries,' I lie. Then, almost immediately after: 'Look, can you ask Steph to check with the client what's the holdup with my exit strategy? I don't like not knowing how I'm getting home. It makes me antsy.'

Jason replies after a moment. '*Steph says she's worried the client will get annoyed if she asks again.*'

'And?' I snap.

'*She won't do it. Bad for the relationship, apparently.*'

I can hear the eyeroll in Jason's tone. It's not much, but I appreciate the solidarity. Steph's only been at the company for six months, but already her position as 'client relations specialist' has given her an irritating degree of influence over how we handle things. Irritating to me and Jason, anyway — Gabby seems to think she's doing a great job, for whatever reason.

'Great,' I mutter back. 'I risk my neck, but at least Steph can make sure we have a stellar relationship with the client, whoever they are.'

'*Mind on the mission, Maisie,*' Jason chides gently.

I know he's right, but once something like that gets to me, I find it hard to move on, and not having a face or a name to pin my frustration on isn't helping. Not that anonymous clients are anything new in this industry, of course – some of my favourite clients have been anonymous. But generally our anonymous clients have the decency to stay hands off: being anonymous *and* micromanaging is a recipe for bad vibes all around.

'*OK, bingo*,' Jason says.

'He's moving?'

'*Not quite. But I've managed to crack the cameras down in the warehouse. Someone's cornered him for a signature on something, but he looks impatient to get back to his desk. I can't see him being more than another five minutes.*'

I relax a little.

'*Oops, Gabby's just come in*,' he adds quickly. '*I think she might want to talk to you.*'

'*Good evening, Maisie*,' says Gabby Hawthorne before I can interject. '*Glad to see you right where you need to be, as usual. Trust the plan and you'll be back in time for supper: the client has just confirmed your extraction is ready and waiting.*'

By the way, yes, I do mean *that* Gabby Hawthorne. The one from *QI* and *Springwatch* and the House of Lords, and her bestselling book about the obstacles women still face in the workplace: *Glass Ceilings, Broken Ladders*. I know, I still can't believe I work for her, either. Not that I really knew who she was before I got the job, to be honest, but I was living under a bit of a rock back then.

'*Safe to say, you'll want to leave through the window, rather than going back down to the street. Think that's possible?*'

Somehow, she sounds even posher over the radio than she does in person (or on TV). On someone else her accent might be irritating, but with Gabby I've always found it a confident,

4

reassuring kind of posh – the sort of posh that suggests a safe pair of hands. I feel my anxieties about the mission being kneaded out of me the longer she keeps talking, like an audio massage. 'Of course,' I say, reflexively tucking my hair behind my ear, even though I know she can't see me. I might bicker and gripe when it's just me and Jason, but when I'm talking to Gabby, confidence comes naturally. What can I say – her management style just brings out my best qualities. That, and even after seven years working for her I'm still desperate to stay in her good books.

'That's my Maisie. Just a few more minutes – then give the client what they want.'

'Will do, Gabby. See you on the flipside.'

When Jason speaks again, his tone is all business. *'We've got movement. Cyril Hargreaves is done with his convo and is coming up the warehouse stairs towards your position. He's made it to the gantry, now the office hallway, and he'll be with you in 3, 2, 1 . . .'*

Right on Jason's cue, I hear a door click open and a switch flick on. Ugly white light edges around the door of the walk-in stationery cupboard I'm hiding in. I hold my breath as the floor shifts slightly under the weight of a reasonably heavy man – 101.2 kg at the time of his Bupa medical last January. After a second, the telltale squeak of flexing plastic and the whisper of caster wheels on carpet confirms he has reached the empty chair with its back to the impressive floor-to-ceiling window that I glimpsed when I first arrived in the office.

I count down from thirty in my head to clear my mind and give Hargreaves time to settle. Then I step out of the cupboard and into the room proper.

'Cyril Hargreaves?' I ask, clutching my handbag to my chest.

'Yes? What is it?' Cyril snaps without looking up from his expensive laptop. His loss – if he had, he might have noticed that my entrance to his office wasn't exactly conventional. 'I'm busy. Do you have an appointment?'

'I do, actually,' I say, padding softly towards him. 'You and I are scheduled for a chat about the Accra contract. Do you have a minute now, or . . .?'

That gets his attention. Now staring right at me, the owner and director of Dynafreight Logistics looks almost exactly how he did in our files, only a little older and a little more worn. The worry lines on his forehead are new, as are the crow's feet around his eyes. I wonder whether his stress is the result of his recent dealings with unscrupulous parties, or the cause of it – whether he turned to crime to get out of unfairly earned debt, or to pay for a loved one's experimental cancer treatment.

Unlikely. And don't get me wrong, I still wouldn't have sympathy for him, even if he did. Cyril Hargreaves is, by all accounts, a monster. But we all contain multitudes, don't we?

'No, I don't think so,' he says, pressing his lips together to form a thin white line. 'Who are you? How did you get in here?'

'Fake IDs, mostly,' I tell him. 'Oh, and we spoofed the camera system with an AI deepfake, so as far as the guys downstairs are concerned, you're alone in your room. Any other questions?'

Cyril's hand disappears under the desk, no doubt to call some of the guards I just mentioned.

'No point doing that,' I continue. I shouldn't really keep talking, but my words have a habit of running away with me at times like this. 'Naturally, we've overridden all network connections leading in and out of this room, even the secret ones. Security can't help you. Nobody can.'

As I finish speaking, I slip my own hand inside my pink leather Gucci handbag – not usually my style, but I have to admit it goes nicely with the grey suit the client insisted on – and take out a pistol. It's Russian made, also at their insistence. Not bad, though. It has a nice weight to it.

'Who are you?' Cyril barks, standing up so quickly that he sends his chair tipping backwards onto the carpet tiles with a muffled thud. 'What's this about? Are you one of Charlotte's friends?'

I raise an eyebrow involuntarily. Charlotte is his wife. I'd heard rumours – nothing that put me off taking the job, that's for sure – but for his marriage to be bad enough for him to assume a woman coming after him with a gun was acting on her behalf?

'That's dark, Cyril. Why? Should I be?' I take a slow step towards him as I speak. He's simultaneously edging away from me and glancing about for something to use as a weapon. Hope and disappointment flash across his face in quick succession as he notices the hefty spined cactus on his desk then realises he's already backed away so far that it's out of reach.

He tries another approach. 'You won't shoot me,' he explains. 'Even silenced pistols are incredibly noisy. The whole floor will hear you. You might kill me, but there's no way you could make it out of here.'

That makes me smile. 'Really, Cyril? I've done this before, you know. You think you can mansplain silencers to me because you watched a YouTube video once?'

'No, I—' He looks at the cactus, then at the gun, then back at me. 'Do you want money? I can give you money.'

But I'm looking past him, out through the window at his back. The office isn't high by big-city standards, but it's higher than the other warehouses and dock buildings – high enough to give a clear view out into the bay and beyond, through the tall skeletal cranes, to the ocean, iron grey beneath a torn-wool sky that's just starting to turn pink as the sun approaches the horizon. It's beautiful, honestly. And for once this summer, it's stopped bloody raining.

'Tell me, Cyril,' I say, making sure the gun stays trained on his chest as I take in the view. 'What's the best part about having a window like that in your office? Is it just for gazing out of in quiet contemplation, or does it intimidate your underlings across the table? Or, I know, is it that looking out over the open water gives you a sense of freedom, even when you're chained to your desk by contracts with the sort of people you really don't want to piss off?'

'What?' asks Cyril, not following. He has plastered himself against said window and is edging along it away from me, as if there might be a door hidden somewhere in the glass to offer him an escape. He'll go through it in a minute or two, actually – just not, I imagine, in the way that he's hoping.

I spell it out for him. 'Your business partners, Cyril. Those nice, scarred men from all over the world who *really* want whatever you've got in those big tanks downstairs. Want it so much they're willing to pay four, five, six times the usual price to get it shipped out to Kaliningrad or Accra or Yangon Via intermediaries, of course – you wouldn't want to get your hands *too* dirty. But you know what you're doing, don't you.'

It isn't a question. I know that he knows what he's doing. I wouldn't have taken the job if I wasn't sure about that. Unlike Cyril, I'm not a monster.

'What, agricultural chemicals? Pesticides?' Cyril scoffs. 'Check the whole warehouse if you want, you won't find anything illegal here. How should I know who it ends up with?'

I'm far enough forward by now that I've passed his desk. I move the cactus to one side to perch on the corner. 'OK, first of all, selling any pesticides – or anything at all, actually – to the organisations you are dealing with *is* proscribed by international law. You do know that, don't you? Technically speaking you ought to be in the Hague – not that they bother arresting white British men in suits, most of the time.'

This time, he makes no protestations to the contrary.

'Not that I care much about the letter of the law,' I continue. 'What's more important is how the pesticides you mention will be used. Because they're not all destined for the fields, are they? You know that, I know that, and if you want proof that I know it, I've got some audio files of you talking on the phone to some persons of interest that I'd be more than happy to share with you.'

He swallows, and I wonder for a moment if he plans to keep arguing with me that the sky isn't blue. If he does, I might just lose my top and shoot him before I mean to. The intelligence we received from the client on this case was extensive. I've seen email tranches, cargo manifests, and photographs – endless, horrible photographs of what Cyril's humble inventory is capable of in the hands of a bloodthirsty warlord. Because unfortunately, the new ultra environmentally friendly formula some firms have been using lately is also just one lethal ingredient away from becoming a nerve agent.

When he speaks again, his tone is cold. 'What are you? A vigilante? Fucking MI6?'

I wave my *pistolet* under his nose casually. 'Russian mafia.'

A sharp exhale, almost a laugh. '*You* are not Russian mafia.'

I smile. 'I could be. At least, that's what the police will think. They'll see your accounts and chalk it up to a business deal gone wrong. With friends like those, who'd think otherwise? Play with fire and you always get burned, sooner or later.'

'*Good work, Maisie,*' says Gabby in my earpiece. '*The target is in position. Take the shot.*'

That's Gabby's way of saying stop messing with him and get on with it.

'Give the client what they want, eh?' I reply out loud as I stand up.

I see the wheels in Cyril's head turning as he realises I'm not talking to him. 'Client,' he repeats. 'You're doing this for money. How much are they paying you? I can match it. I can double it. I promise I—'

'You're right,' I say, raising the pistol to his forehead as I cut him off. 'I'm a hitwoman. But it's not about the money. Well, not *only* the money. It's also that you're a really, really, really bad man. Killing you will be priceless.'

Cyril Hargreaves was right about one thing, though: even

silenced pistols are pretty loud. So is his scream as the first bullet cracks into his forehead, shattering his skull and sending a geyser of blood spraying out of him like I just popped the pimple from hell. The second shot I send intentionally wide, making the beautiful Southampton seascape vanish behind a frosting of damaged glass. Then I jump, grab hold of a light fitting, and slam both feet into Cyril's chest with so much force that he crashes hard into the cracked windowpane. It holds him for a second.

Then he falls.

And despite the mush I've made of his brain, his arms windmill as he stumbles backwards into the early evening. He's suspended in the empty air for a moment and then he's gone – a four-storey fall is all that separates him from becoming a twisted wreck on the car park below, which has been closed since the morning due to a spurious gas leak.

Don't worry, we take *extensive* pains to avoid collateral damage.

'*Let's go!*' Jason shouts in my ear. '*Nicely done, Maisie. That speech gave me chills.*'

'*Excellent work,*' adds Gabby. '*The client says they can get you back to your place in forty minutes, and they're sorry for the holdup. I imagine what they have planned will beat getting stuck on the M3. Enjoy your weekend.*'

Forty minutes? Maybe I won't have to flake on Beth after all. It's like Gabby said: trust the process.

'Thanks both,' I reply. 'Debrief on Monday, yeah?'

Then there's a commotion outside Cyril's door. 'Everything all right in there?' somebody yells. 'I heard a banging.'

11

But the noise from the corridor is nothing compared to the noise from outside the building. It's a cross between the sound a washing machine makes when it seems like it's about to take off and an actual hurricane. By the time the door clicks open again behind me, I've followed Cyril's lead and stepped out through the shattered window frame. I toss my Russian-made pistol to the floor as I go, making sure it lands somewhere conspicuous. The newspaper headlines write themselves: a classic story about a businessman who got in too close with the wrong people, until he pissed them off and they made him pay.

Broken glass dances around my ankles in the sudden, powerful turbulence as I step forward, out onto the rope ladder that dangles from the sleek black helicopter hovering dangerously close to the building above me like a hummingbird coming in close to a flower.

OK, I'll give this to the client – they managed to pull some strings where it counts. As I'm hoisted over Southampton in the light of the setting sun, I slip my phone from my pocket and shoot a text to Beth: **Sorry, got held up in the office! Omw now.**

Beth replies almost instantly: **No worries at all hun. I'll get our order in. See you soon xxxxxx.**

2

Beef with black bean sauce. Vegetable chow mein. Special fried rice. A crap romcom, and a glass of wine.

Is there a better way to start the weekend when you're twenty-nine years old, single, and sharing a flat with your best friend? If there is, I just can't imagine what it could be.

'I *needed* this,' Beth breathes as she sets her first empty plate down on the coffee table. We'll both be doing seconds in a few minutes — as is tradition — but you can't eat that much food in one go without a half-time break.

I laugh through a mouthful of perfectly mushy, inauthentic, British-style chow mein noodles. 'You say that every week.'

'I know, but, Maisie — this week I *needed* this. Not needed. *Needed.* You see what I mean?'

It's not the first time she's added the emphasis, either, but every Friday since she started her new job the italics have been leaning a little further. I want to call her on it, but before we sat down, we made a solemn promise not to talk about work. So far, we've managed twenty minutes without an explicit mention but it's hard to talk about anything else when it seems to be hanging over both of us — Beth's job in particular. Even when she tries to talk about something else, her words come out dripping in subtext.

I'm the one to break. 'Still not feeling settled?'

'Settled,' she repeats with a bitter laugh. 'It's been two and half months. When do we accept that it isn't getting settled, it's just how it is? I'm starting to think I didn't know how good writing copy was when I had it. Not that we're supposed to be talking about work.'

'You don't mean that,' I protest. 'Your old job was *literally* sucking your soul. I could see it returning to your body every time you got home.' She rolls her eyes, unconvinced. I carry on. 'However things are now, this move was the right choice for you. Remember how happy you were when they told you you'd got it? How much you wanted to do something that would make a difference?'

That's the thing with Beth: all the time I've known her, since the drunken blur of freshers' week, she's wanted to make the world a better place. She's never been annoying about it, but it's always been there – the driving force behind all of her decisions, the thing that gets her up in the morning. She wanted it back in uni when she was editor of the student newspaper and coordinated a campaign to stop the university from investing in the arms trade. She wanted it when she moved to London to work in advertising but volunteered at a language café for refugee families on the weekend. And she'd wanted it more than ever when she finally got the chance to ditch writing advertising copy for her dream job, researching hard-hitting current affairs documentaries to hold the powerful to account and shine a light on corruption and abuses of power. She might not look like it right now, slumped on our sofa in her Garfield pyjamas, but Beth Walsh is a bona fide hero.

Or she would be, if this was a world that allowed people to be simple, uncomplicated heroes. 'Yeah,' she says. 'I was so happy *before* I knew what the job was really like, wasn't I?'

And what can I say to that? I want to help her, but I just can't accept that her dream job is turning into such a nightmare. 'At least it's the weekend,' I offer with a weak smile.

That, at least, makes her relax a little. 'Thank God. OK, I had to get that out of my system, but from now on – no more thoughts about work for another, what, sixty hours? They don't deserve it.'

I load up a second plate of food and focus on the film. It's a romcom about a San Francisco career woman who wins the deed to a rundown hotel in remote New Zealand in an online competition and then decides to throw her complicated city life away for a simpler one in the country. I catch Beth gazing wistfully at the shots of the rolling green hills and sleepy Kiwi villages, as if she's imagining following in the heroine's footsteps. I'd be lying if I didn't admit to feeling a little of the same pull. I think of the open ocean behind Cyril Hargreaves' desk, the quip I made about him finding peace in the freedom it symbolises – as if I don't sometimes feel the same way. But at the end of the day, I do like my job. Even if I have to kill a lot of people.

'How about you, though?' Beth asks during a lull. 'How's your week been?'

'Yep, it's been good,' I say quickly. 'Gabby's fine,' I add, in a misguided attempt to sound less awkward.

Beth shoots me a sceptical look. Ugh! I hate, hate, *hate* talking to her about work. You'd think I'd be used to it by now, but after all these years, lying to Beth about what my job actually involves hasn't gotten any easier. Lately, it's felt harder than ever. As far as she's concerned I'm still Gabby's personal assistant — after seven years of the same, just with steadily worse hours.

Although, now I think about it, maybe she wasn't even asking about my work. But what else do I have going on? It's not like I have time for hobbies, and all my attempts at dating seem to fizzle out halfway through the first meeting — around the time they ask me what I do for a living, funny enough. I seem to just clam up and shut them out, no matter how well it's been going up until that point. But under Beth's perceptive gaze, clamming up isn't an option.

Instead, I run my mouth. 'No, it's been really good, actually. I was out on my own in Southampton today. Meeting someone important to one of her businesses. It's nice to feel like she trusts me to take those kinds of actions, you know?'

Beth raises an eyebrow. 'Actions?'

'Yeah, actions. Like, terminating . . . a contract . . . for the Hedgehog Project.'

Fuck. Why did I phrase it like that? Why mention Southampton at all? Do I subconsciously *want* Beth to know that I kill people for a living? Considering she's literally an investigative journalist, cryptic statements like that are only going to make her suspicious and could get me caught and put in prison forever.

Well, maybe the desire isn't entirely subconscious. I *do* wish I could let Beth in on my actual job, and tell her why it's not as bad as it might seem. But that can never, never, never, never happen – *especially* not now that she's got her dream job researching documentaries that end up on the bloody BBC.

'Hmm,' she says, glancing at me sideways as I pretend to focus on the film.

★

The ironic thing is, I wouldn't even have the job if it wasn't for her.

It was our final year of university and Beth's life was going great while mine was falling apart. She had already been accepted onto a prestigious journalism MA down in Sheffield, while my postgraduation plans involved begging my boss at John Lewis for a few more hours. Beth had a promising relationship with a sweet boy called Simon, while I'd just been dumped by a dickhead called Josh. Not to mention, her parents were still together and living an hour away in beautiful Edinburgh, while my always difficult single mother had just been diagnosed with a life-changing illness and consequently whisked off to Thailand by her new rich boyfriend, because apparently yoga and meditation are more effective than getting treatment. And then, to add the ultimate insult to injury, the beautiful, sweet dog I grew up with was hit by a car – two weeks after Beth and I took her in. Rest in peace, Maple.

None of this was Beth's fault and even at the time I didn't feel jealous of her, but that's just how it was – me flailing while everyone around me zoomed ahead – and to put it bluntly, I was struggling to cope. I spent most of that semester crying about Josh, when I should have been grateful that he'd gifted me a fantastic way to avoid thinking about my real problems. The downside of doing so was that I missed every deadline and almost failed my degree outright. But the further I sank into my pit of despair, the harder Beth worked to drag me out – and she was damn good at it, too. Some nights she followed me down into the abyss with a takeaway and a shoulder to cry on; others, she stood at the top of the cliff, throwing down ropes and yelling encouragement until I climbed out. Usually, those ropes came in the form of productive distractions, like adverts for jobs or internships she was certain I could get if only my application was good enough. She had an irrepressible faith that all of her friends would go on to achieve great things, if only they believed in themselves. With her own future apparently sorted, she set to work sorting out mine.

'What's that?' I asked, one Friday night, having flicked the kettle on in preparation for cooking my trademark meal of penne pasta and tinned tomatoes. Beth had just come in, excitedly bearing a poster that she'd stolen from a display in the library. It featured an array of women, a couple of whom I thought I recognised, wearing business suits and posing with their heads held high. Above them, text in faux-graffiti font proclaimed, 'WOMEN, WE RISE!'

'It's a mentoring scheme for women at the start of their careers,' she announced. 'Just like you!'

It was a struggle to see myself as at the 'start' of anything except a sleepless night rewatching *CSI: Miami* on Netflix, but that was Beth for you: endless confidence in the potential of those she valued, irrespective of evidence to the contrary.

'Oh, cool,' I said, in a tone that probably suggested I didn't think it was cool at all. 'I'll take a look later.'

Ignoring me, Beth smoothed the poster out on the kitchen table, moving some dirty mugs around to weigh down its corners. 'Look, it's *perfect*! It's all about unlocking your potential – and you have *so* much potential to unlock, I just know it. Plus, you could work with some incredible people, like Gabriella Hawthorne. Do you remember that speech she gave in the House of Lords?'

I look up at her. 'I don't remember a speech *anyone* has given in the House of Lords.'

Beth rolled her eyes. 'Gabby Hawthorne? Gabriella Hawthorne? Her speech went viral for a reason. She's only *the* top female philanthropist in the flipping country. Remember Girls Code? Or the Hedgehog Project?'

I took another look at the poster. Now that Beth mentioned it, the woman with the blonde bob looked a little familiar – and the Hedgehog Project rang a bell too. 'Was she on *Springwatch* or something? I think I remember Mum going on about her at some point.'

Beth nodded, almost proudly. 'Yep. So, are you going to apply?'

I gave it another look. Could I really ever be that kind of woman, who can stand in a suit with their shoulders back like a monochromatic superhero, without feeling totally ridiculous? I couldn't see it. 'I'll give it a look, but I don't really know if this is *for me*, you know?' I said. 'I have literally no idea what I want to do with my life.'

Somehow that only perked her up even further. 'That's *exactly* why I thought it'd be perfect! With a mentoring scheme like this, you'll see every part of one of these organisations, and you can decide yourself where you most want to work. You're destined for great things, Maisie, you just need to put yourself out there.'

She's delusional, I thought, pouring pasta into the hot water. *Millions of people apply for these things. Why on earth would they choose me over anyone else?*

Then I spotted something on the poster that I hoped would end it there and then. 'Well, even if I am the chosen one, it closes tonight and Michelle and Liv are coming round at eight for predrinks. I still need to eat, shower and change. There's no way I'd have time.'

But Beth was not the sort of person to let a little thing like that get in the way of reality. 'What sort of attitude is that? You can drink and write a job application at the same time, can't you?'

I could, as it turned out – as long as Beth kept looking over my shoulder to make sure I was writing fast enough. While my three best friends let loose with progressively louder and rowdier drinking games, Pitbull and Ke$ha blaring from someone's Bluetooth speaker, I was hunched over my laptop in the corner, filling out the application form with one hand, glass of vodka-lemonade in the other.

My only memory of the last few questions was getting a *little* too personal when answering something along the lines of '*In 150 words, write about a time that you maintained composure in a high-stress situation*'. I didn't have much work experience to draw on, but the last conversation with my mum before she moved to Thailand was a high-stress situation so I wrote about that without stopping to second-guess myself.

I had no real hope when I pressed send on the email that my attachment would go anywhere except straight into the recycle bin of whoever downloaded it, but the cheer that went up from the room when I announced I was finished almost made the whole thing worth it. Just getting it done felt like a turning point in scraping myself out of my abyss of despair. For the rest of the night, I managed to enjoy myself in a way I hadn't in weeks, hardly worrying at all about my mum, my chances of dying alone, or the yawning dearth of career options that awaited me in the adult world once I graduated with an inevitably sub-par degree in a subject that was barely employable to begin with.

So I was a little surprised when, a week later, I got a phone call from a woman with a cut-glass accent that twinged something buried deep in my memories of watching family TV.

'Hello, this is Gabby Hawthorne. Am I speaking to Maisie Baxter?'

'Yes?' I replied, suddenly uncertain. It didn't feel real, and the sense of unreality only intensified as Gabby went on speaking. On the one hand, it was just an invitation to interview, but Gabby also stressed that I'd been set aside for a special, exclusive, *secret* shortlist to be mentored by her, personally.

'Why?' I couldn't help blurt out when she told me. I hadn't looked back at my application since I'd hit submit, but in my memories it had transformed from an OK effort considering the circumstances to the TMI screed of a drunk depressive. 'Was my application really that good?'

'Oh yes,' Gabby replied, her tone unreadable over the phone. 'I believe you are exactly the sort of person I am looking for.'

★

'OK, I know we said we wouldn't talk about work, but be honest with me – are you sure you're still happy there?'

Beth's question jolts me back to the present. She's looking at me intently, and I get a sudden, sharp sense of how she has and hasn't changed over the last ten or so years. She's matured, and become a little more cynical, but the love she has for her friends is still real and powerful. Sometimes I don't know if I deserve it.

'You don't have to answer if you don't want to,' she continues. 'And if you say you're happy I'll drop it. But you've been with Gabby for, what, six years now?'

'Seven,' I correct her.

'You never feel like it's . . . time to move on?'

I bite the inside of my mouth, forcing myself to pick my words more carefully this time. 'It's not just managing her schedule and running after her into meetings anymore, you know. There's more interesting stuff, too.'

Now *that's* an understatement. For a while, at first, I really was just Gabby's PA. Back then I used to tell Beth everything – all the celebrity gossip Gabby passed on to me, the surreal encounters with London's finest, the near misses as I learned to balance her hectic schedule and anticipate what she'd need next.

Then the position evolved. Something happened, Gabby

helped me take care of it, and then she showed me how to make sure it never happened again. After that, we got to work making sure it never happened to anyone else. Eventually that work grew into Novum, the company Gabby founded, with me as her first – and, for a year or so, only – employee. Ethical assassins: that was the idea. Hitmen who go after people who deserve it, unlike those working for our main competitor, Removals Inc., who'll kill for no reason at all.

'It's not about whether it's interesting or shows progression or whatever,' says Beth. 'It's whether it's making you happy. I guess that's what I'm realising myself. Maybe all this career stuff is a load of crap and we should just do whatever we enjoy.'

I give her another sympathetic smile. 'It's all work, isn't it?' I say evasively. 'And as it goes, my job's not too bad.'

Then I zone out a little, because they've found an excuse for the hunky handyman love interest in the film to take his shirt off, and suddenly my mind is on other things.

Now *that* is what I really need to be happy, I think to myself. Everything would be a lot simpler if I could find the right man – but what sort of psycho would love a girl who kills people for a living?

3

I'm meant to be in the office at 9.30 a.m. on Monday, but Gabby always has meetings first thing so there's not a whole lot of point. As usual, I find myself tapping my ID card on the electronically locked gate in the garden wall of her who-knows-how-many-million-pound house not long before ten. It's 9.53, according to the time on the little security display. For Monday, I think, that's close enough.

In case you're wondering – no, we don't have a real office. Novum has always been Gabby's scrappy, under-the-table side-project, so we work from her living room in North London, right next to Highgate Cemetery. A little on the nose, perhaps, planning assassinations while gazing out at elaborate headstones poking out from above the bushes, but I find it strangely soothing. The way I see it, we all end up in the ground one way or another; it's just that some people deserve a bit of a push.

I even had my interview here. I want to tell you that before then I'd never seen anything like Gabby's house before in my life, but that wouldn't be true. The thing about insanely expensive houses in London is that they just look like regular upper-middle-class houses in the rest of the country. Where I grew up, Carlisle, in the North-West of England, a successful electrician could buy a house that looked like Gabby's if they owned their own company and got enough work. It's only after you've lived in the capital for a while that you realise that things like 'having their own driveway' mark someone out as a member of the 1 per cent.

I wasn't even impressed by her gleaming Mercedes back then, though I suppose I've never been a car person. My equally black and shiny 'interview shoes' crunched in the gravel of the driveway and pinched at my toes as I walked towards the door. But failing to be intimidated by her wealth didn't mean I felt relaxed about the whole interview thing. As I lifted the heavy metal doorknocker, my heart was in my throat in the way that I now associate with someone unexpectedly pulling out a gun on me.

I knocked. I heard someone move inside the house. Then the door opened.

That's her off the telly, said a little voice inside me, unhelpfully. I might not have known much about Gabby before Beth mentioned her, but I had been bingeing her features and guest appearances on YouTube in what I told myself was interview prep, but really was just half-productive procrastination. Now I regretted it. I hadn't been starstruck when we spoke on the phone, but now—

'Hi,' I stammered. 'I'm Maisie Baxter.'

'Of course you are.' Gabby's tone suggested I'd just uttered the stupidest possible thing you could say when meeting someone for the first time. 'You told me that on the intercom.'

Well, that's that then, I thought. *I can't even tell her my name without it somehow being the wrong thing. I really am a failure.*

25

'Well, yes.' I stuck my hand out awkwardly for her to shake. 'But it's great to meet you, anyway.'

Then Gabby smiled, and it felt like the clouds parting on a rainy day. She took my hand in hers and shook it firmly. 'Well, Maisie Baxter, come on in. Leave your shoes by the door – there are slippers by the mat you can wear to keep your feet warm. Take a seat in the living room, wherever feels comfortable, while I fetch us some tea. And after we get to know each other a little, we'll discuss how you can get started.'

In a daze, I stepped through the doorway. I donned slippers as instructed and let myself be directed towards Gabby's opulent, cream-coloured living room. From the outside, Gabby's house may have been nothing special beyond the staggeringly high value of the land it sits on, but the inside was – is – another question. Before I walked on her carpets, I didn't know carpets could be so soft. They sprang beneath my feet like I was treading on an inch-thick coating of marshmallow. Every other carpet I had ever experienced suddenly paled in comparison.

It was only when I'd fully sunk into the equally luxurious couch that I properly realised what Gabby had said.

We'll discuss how you can get started.

That awkward two-sentence interaction at the doorway had been my interview. Somehow, I was on the programme.

*

Seven years later, I still feel a little out of place in Gabby's living room, no matter how much time I've spent here. I even lived here for a few months before finding my own place in London, and though it technically was home for a little while, it never quite felt like it. Today I'm sitting on the same (reupholstered) couch, my laptop balanced precariously on its wide leather arm. I don't even want to kick my feet up like I do at home – in Gabby's house it doesn't feel right.

You might not think there's much office work to worry about as a hitwoman, but there is – especially now Novum has expanded into a full-blown team. What I should be doing right now is compiling a report about Friday's mission to send back to the client, whoever they are, via Steph, but I'm not. Instead, Steph and I are arguing about the flowers on the table.

'All I'm saying is that if she *does* have a problem with them,' she's saying, 'it's hardly my fault, is it? The flowers are *for* you.'

'Right, they're *for* me,' I tell her, speaking slowly and enunciating every word so there can be no misunderstandings, 'but I didn't take them in, did I?'

Steph is a recent hire at Novum. As such, some of the operational security measures that, as far as I'm concerned, get drilled into our heads so thoroughly that they may as well be tattoos seem somehow to have passed her by.

For instance: as a hitwoman, you start to become a little wary of unexpected gifts from anonymous parties arriving at your place of employment. You *might* think that such presents could be hiding within themselves a nasty surprise, like a listening device or a vial of nerve agent. You might not, when opening the door to find a smartly dressed man from the florist's, holding a bouquet along with a card congratulating someone on your team personally for a job well done, simply accept them with a smile, take them inside, and sit back down at the dining table to work on your laptop. But Steph did. At least, I assume that's how it went down – at that time, I hadn't quite arrived yet.

'It's not my fault you were late, is it?' she says, speaking in a stage whisper that only accentuates her frustration. Actually, we're both whispering, since neither of us want our squabble to be overheard by Owen, who is doing calisthenics in the next room, or Jason, who's outside testing some new tech.

I ignore her, pretending to work. This eventually prompts Steph to change her strategy. 'I'm sorry, Maisie. I thought you'd be happy to know you've made such a good impression on one of our clients. I know I'm always happy to receive positive feedback on my work . . .'

This woman, I think, is a walking LinkedIn post – and not even in the endearing, encouraging way Beth could be sometimes, back when we were in uni. But I guess that's why Gabby hired her. I'd hoped that having her on the team would mean I no longer had to think about client relations, but instead Steph keeps inventing new things we need to do to keep the clients happy, like these damn reports, which mean more time on the sofa with my laptop and less time training or in the field.

I roll my eyes. 'I *am* happy. It's very sweet of them to send them. But you have to think about the possible consequences . . .'

'Something happen?' asks Jason as he clomps in from the garden. Herb, Gabby's rescued greyhound, lollops in behind him.

Steph and I exchange glances. My glance says, *You explain it.*

'Ugh, nothing!' she says. 'Jason, tell Maisie it's not the end of the world that I accepted these flowers from our *client*.'

'Oh, I can help with that,' he says easily, crossing to a teak cabinet in the corner of the room and retrieving an electronic-looking remote that wouldn't be out of place on a *Doctor Who* set. He waves it over the flowers and it gives two happy beeps. 'There,' he says. 'No unwanted cameras, microphones, or anything else that might expose our deep and dark secrets.'

Stowing it away, he settles in on the opposite side of the table from Steph and gets to work. That's Jason's natural environment: behind his laptop, with the screen between him and everyone else in the room. He's a tech guy through and through, and though I don't know enough about that world to know for sure, I think he might be a genius. It's rare that a mission will take me to a building where he can't hack the cameras, or create a fake entry for me in the employee database, or set off an alarm somewhere I'm not to distract the guards. He's an absolute asset to the team; always easy to work with. Try to talk to him about anything outside of work, though, and he goes silent. When I asked him about the stickers on his laptop – some Pride flags, the logo of a game called *Overwatch*, and some other bits I didn't recognise – he told me he helps organise a London LGBT gaming society with a few hundred members. I imagine that must be where he spends his social energy, as it certainly isn't on us: all of my follow-up questions were shut down right away.

The sound of tyres in the driveway makes all of us look

up. Moments later, Owen appears through the door from the gym in baggy black sweatpants and a damp white vest that clings to his well-trained pecs, leaving nothing to imagination.

Owen is the other hitman Gabby keeps on staff, and no, I don't fancy him. At least, I shouldn't. I *really* shouldn't. He's a well-toned himbo who thinks he's James Bond but has the brain of a labrador. He takes on the more *straightforward* cases, shall we say, the ones where all that's really required is brawn, doggedness, and a strong stomach. He could kill almost anyone in a straight fight, but I've seen him dismiss a children's woodland animal crossword that Gabby had left lying around as 'stupid bullshit' because he couldn't figure out how many letters are in 'hedgehog'. Though today, as the room fills with the scent of his gym-bro musk, I'm horrified to find that I actually don't mind the stench. In fact, he smells kind of . . . good.

Shit.

Things are getting desperate.

Forget finding Mr Right who can accept me for everything I am – maybe all I really need is to get laid.

'All right, ladies, look alive, eh?' Owen says, whipping his gym towel towards Jason. As always, seeing Owen actually do or say anything is enough to burst the horny bubble that had been inflating inside me. 'The boss is here,' he adds, as if we haven't worked that out ourselves by the sound of tyres crunching to a stop and an engine cutting out.

The conversation stills, and as we wait, an electric tension fills the room. Then, with a jolt, the front door swings open.

'I am having a *morning!*' Gabby Hawthorne announces as

she sweeps inside. In Prada heels and an elegant berry suit, her dark blonde bob perfectly angled around her perfectly made-up face, she looks like she's just stepped out of the *News at Ten*. She's nearing sixty, but she looks somehow ageless in a way that only the rich can afford to.

'You know, I'm starting to get the impression that the Woodland Trust doesn't even *like* hedgehogs,' she says as she stops to slip into her own pair of fluffy cream slippers. This is how she often enters rooms: already talking, as if we'd all been involved in her conversation the whole time and just somehow failed to realise. 'They make it so bloody difficult for us to help the poor things. It turns out that site in Bedfordshire is on Forestry Commission land, which complicates things, apparently, but what do hedgehogs care about property rights? It's like they're worried the hedgehogs will side with us in the divorce.'

'They might, Gabs,' says Owen, who may or may not understand she is speaking metaphorically.

Gabby straightens and gives Owen a look. 'Yes, well. Owen, would you be a dear and make us all some tea?'

He nods and slopes off without further comment. Whatever else you might want to say about Owen, Gabby has him well disciplined when it comes to making drinks.

'Ah, my stars,' Gabby says once Owen is out of the room. 'How are you all today? *Smashing* work on the Hargreaves case, all of you. We had some hiccups, didn't we, but in the end the three of you were like a well-oiled machine.'

'Thanks, Gabby,' Steph and I say in unison.

But it catches in my throat a little. Hiccups are one thing when you're sitting in Gabby's living room, but not knowing what your exit strategy looks like when you're the one in danger is . . . not great.

Before I can decide whether to raise the issue, Gabby notices the flowers. 'Flowers. Who got flowers? Maisie, are these yours?'

'They're Maisie's, sent from Friday's client,' Jason confirms, before Steph and I start bickering again. 'We've checked them; they're clean.'

Most of the time I respect Jason's commitment to diplomacy, but I do wish he'd let loose just a little bit. Especially when I'm clearly in the right and Steph is just being annoying.

'Well done, Maisie,' says Gabby, with an approving nod. 'Looks like you've made a splendid impression. With the help of Steph and Jason, too, of course.'

Well done, Maisie. Those words always feel that little more special when Gabby's the one saying them.

'Thank you,' I say, forgetting all about the confusion around the helicopter.

But Steph can't leave it well enough alone. 'Though *maybe* we shouldn't be improvising monologues when the client has explicitly told us what we ought to be saying?'

'Oh, leave it be,' Gabby says. 'Pascal sent her flowers, didn't he?'

I glance at Steph, who glances back nervously.

'Who?' I ask.

'Pascal Robertson?' Gabby repeats, as if everyone in the world ought to know who Pascal Robertson is. Though now she mentions it, the name *does* ring a bell. 'The man who you just went and killed Cyril Hargreaves for?' she adds by way of explanation. 'Oh, thanks, Owen, just set mine down on the mantelpiece.'

Owen has just re-emerged with a tray of mugs and is distributing them around the room. I take mine just in time for him to throw himself down onto the sofa beside me, causing the overfilled tea to slosh violently.

'Sorry, Maiz,' he says in response to the dirty look I involuntarily shoot in his direction. Luckily for him, I have more pressing concerns.

'Pascal *who*, Gabby?' I ask. 'Wasn't that client anonymous?'

'Gabby, we haven't shared this information with the wider team yet . . .' Steph trails off nervously as she sees my clenched jaw.

I catch Jason's gaze as he peers over his laptop. He evidently *does* recognise the name.

'Pascal Robertson?' he asks, his tone a little sceptical. 'The CEO of ILS Industries — *that* Pascal Robertson? He was the client?'

'Oh, that's right,' Gabby says, coming back to life like a computer that's finished updating. 'Pascal *was* anonymous, wasn't he? Faceless, nameless, all the rest of it. Sorry, busy morning — bloody Woodland Trust — it's hard to keep track of who knows what all the time. But yes, Jason, it's *that* Pascal Robertson. Really, Maisie, I'm surprised you haven't heard of him. He's only the biggest agricultural innovator Britain has seen since, I don't know, Jethro Tull. Not the band, though you're probably too young to know who they are, aren't you?'

'His company makes chemicals,' Jason adds helpfully. 'Not the most glamorous industry but they've massively taken off; he was doing the podcast rounds after the launch of some new miracle pesticide. One of those guys that works like twenty hours a day; I heard he literally has an apartment in the London office so that he never has to leave.'

Ah. Jason's comment about pesticides makes the pieces fall into place. It's not a pretty-looking jigsaw.

'There were ILS products in Cyril Hargreaves' warehouse,' I say, thinking aloud. 'Most of the pesticides being used by overseas warlords came from ILS.'

'There were,' agrees Gabby, taking a sip of her tea. 'And *that* is exactly why Pascal wanted Cyril Hargreaves dead. Not exactly good for your company's reputation, is it? Especially when he's built ILS around green solutions and saving the planet.'

I exchange another look with Jason, who is thoughtfully scratching Herb's head. He looks like he has something else to say, but Gabby has gathered steam and isn't to be interrupted.

'You know, when Pascal got in touch to ask for a meeting,' she's saying, 'it felt like the culmination of our years of hard work. I started feeling a little sentimental about how far we've come over the past few years. The rest of you weren't around in the early days, when Maisie and I were starting out. But if you could see the girl she was then, straight out of university, no idea what she wanted to do with her life, a little timid – I hope you don't mind me saying, Maisie, but a little all over the place, too. If you contrast who she was then with the woman she's become now – confident, talented, sharp as a tack – I think you'd be so proud of her.'

I feel my face flush, like when I was really young and my mum would embarrass me by being too affectionate in front of the school gate, where my friends might be able to see.

'It's all thanks to you,' I tell Gabby.

'Psh, nonsense. It's just you becoming who you always were,' she replies. 'And the rest of you, I don't want you to think you're any less valued. Jason, your inimitable tech wizardry is unparalleled in this industry. Owen, you've let us take on twice as many clients as we could before, while also giving Maisie a few of her weekends back. And Steph. You help us get the clients, and without the clients we couldn't do all the great things we do.' She looks round at each of us, beaming. 'With every job we take on, the world becomes a better place – for our clients, yes, but for everyone. These are things that the public sector will never do, that the police will never do, that the courts will never do. But they need to be done.'

'Thank you, Gabby,' says Steph, her voice cracking. As always when Steph gets emotional, I have no idea whether she's putting it on. 'That means a lot.' Then her voice turns serious. 'But is Mr Robertson OK with everyone, you know, knowing his name? Shouldn't we . . .?'

Shouldn't we what? All agree to forget that we heard what we just heard? Good luck coaxing *that* cat back in the bag.

'Oh, not at all,' says Gabby. 'Besides, you'll be putting a face to the name shortly. Very shortly, actually. We're going to meet him this afternoon – he has another job for us.'

4

'Isn't Owen coming?' I ask Gabby as we crunch up the driveway towards the white Audi that's just pulled in on the far side of the gate. It's now about 3.30 p.m., and I still haven't made any progress with the report I was supposed to be writing. I don't know what it is about reports, but even when I try my hardest to focus on getting them done, I invariably find something else to occupy my mind. Like how I'd assassinate obscure members of the royal family – just on the off chance it ever came up. Behind us, Jason swings the front door of the house shut, leaving Owen decidedly inside.

'Why would he?' Gabby replies. 'Pascal wants to meet the people who worked on the Cyril Hargreaves job, which in case you haven't noticed, doesn't include Owen.' She leans in conspiratorially as she opens the front passenger door of the car. 'Why, would you rather he came? I thought you said he wasn't your type?'

I feel my cheeks grow hot, glad she said it quietly enough that Jason and Steph wouldn't hear. At one point, Gabby had got it into her head that Owen and I might be a potential romantic item. 'In our line of work, Maisie,' she'd told me back then, 'it can be very difficult to form deep relationships with people who don't understand our priorities. Sometimes it might be better to look a little closer to home.'

'Just wondering,' I say. 'Maybe he'd feel left out.'

Gabby shrugs and steps into the car. 'He's a big boy. He can handle it.'

I slide into the back seat behind her, while Steph makes a show of holding the opposite door open for Jason. 'You're in the middle,' she tells him.

As we're driven towards Central London, Gabby regales us with more tales of the impossible pressures faced by small charities in the present economy. 'What it actually is,' she declares, twisting to look at the three of us between the two front seats, 'is sad. The state won't do anything, because they don't want to waste taxpayers' money on what they see as non-essential. Fair enough, I suppose – you know how the newspapers can be. But they've left so much red tape that the organisations who want to help, *legally* help, that is, need so much more funding than their projects actually cost. You know, my charities spend almost as much on lawyers as they do achieving their goals. On lawyers! It's madness. If things continue like this, I just don't know how much longer the Hedgehog Project can operate.' Then she spots something out the back window and turns sharply to speak to the driver. 'Make sure you take the next turn-off, it'll be quicker. What was I saying? Oh yes, it's like Derek said: once again we're stuck in the position of waiting for the perfect partner to come along, who has enough money to make all of our problems go away without bringing any extra pressures or demands. Ha! And a unicorn, too, I told him.'

I have no idea who Derek is, but I get what she's saying.

Unlike the Hedgehog Project, Novum is not a charity. Legally speaking, it's a private limited company which employs Jason, Owen, Steph and me as 'executive assistants' to assist 'individuals and organisations known to the owner in whatever personal and administrative tasks they require'. But the concern about funding is no different from organisation to organisation. You have what you want to achieve and then you have the people willing to give you the funds you need to do it. It would be nice if we could manage without them, but the reality is, getting shit done costs money.

With the work we do, that can be complicated. Even after you've come around to the idea that murdering bad people can sometimes be ethically viable, it can be hard to trust a client's motives. Naturally, most people don't want someone dead unless they have something to gain – even when their proposed target objectively deserves to be killed. As such, our clients tend to be a little shady: business rivals, business partners, or ungrateful children angling for an inheritance. That's why Gabby and I developed strict ethical criteria for the jobs Novum accepts. On top of that, Owen and I can each veto any job that is brought to us, provided we can give an adequate explanation for why.

Very occasionally, you run into the opposite problem, when a prospective client's case against their target is so strong that you feel bad about taking their money. Back when Gabby and I were starting out we would regularly meet clients in person, many of them vulnerable women who had been wronged by powerful men. The last client we had in this vein was a woman named Skyla Dawn, an up-and-coming pop singer trapped in a *very* exploitative record contract with an utter scumbag producer. She wanted out, in every way imaginable, but he controlled her. I don't want to spell out what that meant.

Skyla was a star, but due to the nature of her record contract, she wasn't rich in the way everyone thought. And our services cost a lot of money. She could just about afford us, but when she told me about her situation I wanted to take the producer out there and then, free of charge.

Seeing where my mind was going, Gabby pulled me into her kitchen, leaving Skyla waiting in the living room for our decision. 'Are you a hitwoman, Maisie, or a vigilante?' she asked. 'Because you know what the difference is, don't you? Hitwomen get paid, vigilantes get caught.'

'It's not that simple,' I protested. 'I know what I'm doing. He deserves it more than anyone. It would be easy.'

'That's not the problem,' she explained. 'It's not a question of knowing what you're doing, it's about resources. If we take the fee, we can fulfil this contract *properly*. We can get the right kind of poison to fake an accidental overdose, make everything look like it should. We can pay off the police, so they don't come snooping around where we don't want them to. And after this job is done, we can continue to expand our operations, so that when the next Skyla Dawn comes to us for help, we can help her, too.'

She was right, of course. She always is. And I knew I was being irrational: I'd had my own run-in with a record executive just a year earlier. That was what led to the idea behind Novum. Looking back, it's obvious that the parallels between Skyla's position and my own were clouding my judgement.

In the end, I took the job and got paid. Within a year, Skyla was living her best life, making enough money that what she'd shelled out seemed like nothing. It all worked out.

So these days, I've got a simple rubric — two rules to decide whether or not to take a case while retaining my sanity.

One: if the world would be a better place with the target dead, they should die.

Two: you need a client. Killing for free is a mug's game.

But aside from providing the cash and sometimes dictating the method, the best clients might as well not exist. Most of the time, I try not to think about them at all. It makes everything easier to compartmentalise. Plus, it's better for the client, too, if they stay anonymous — for some reason, people generally prefer if trained murderers don't know their names, addresses and place of occupation.

Only now, a previously anonymous client has decided to turn around and show his face. Either Steph's new client-centred approach is already paying dividends, or things are about to get *weird*.

★

'I'm terribly sorry for dragging you up here,' says Pascal Robertson from the far side of his dining table.

True to his reputation as the man who literally never leaves his place of work, said dining table is situated in his penthouse above the ILS Industries office, just north of Hyde Park. There ought to be an incredible view through the window behind his head, but all the windowpanes have been replaced by some other material, presumably for safety. Unlike normal bulletproof glass, which is practically indistinguishable from regular glass (but only mostly bulletproof), whatever this material is has a weird distorting effect on light coming in, reducing what should be one of the most beautiful views in London to a hazy mess, like seeing a room through a fish tank.

'Given your line of work, I'm sure you understand why all this security is necessary,' he continues. 'But just knowing *why* something exists doesn't make it any less irritating to deal with, does it?'

I'm not sure what I expected from the CEO of a chemical company with a side interest in agriculture, but Robertson isn't it. At first glance he's got a touch of the ageing rock star around him, with floppy hair, dark blue jeans, and a tightly fitting blazer. But his speech and mannerisms also carry an awkward, self-deprecating air, making it easy to forget he's on the *Sunday Times* Rich List at number fourteen – as Steph helpfully informed me in the lift.

'Oh, not at all, Mr Robertson,' Steph's saying now, flashing him a beaming smile. 'We're just delighted to be here. The security was nothing, really.'

That, Stephanie, was a lie and you know it. Getting up to Pascal's penthouse was absolutely, categorically, not nothing. Even just getting up to his floor took about fifteen minutes of bag scans, metal detectors, pat-downs and more – plus all the usual time wasted in offices waiting for lifts. Then, upon reaching the penthouse suite, we'd had to go through it all over again, only this time some dopey-looking men in stab vests also had the temerity to shake out my handbag full of

Crunchie bar wrappers in full view of my colleagues before, to top it all off, confiscating each of our phones.

'I thought I was boarding a flight,' I say, prompting Steph to shoot me a dark look across the table. Pascal, however, cracks a smile. *Who's the client relations expert now?* I project in Steph's direction.

'Ah, this is the firecracker Maisie I have heard so much about!' he chuckles. 'I hope you liked the flowers – they are a thank you, of course, but also an apology for the hoops I made you jump through on the Cyril Hargreaves case. I know they made things difficult – Gabby and I almost came to blows over some of my requests – but I'm very particular, and I wanted to be certain of a few things before we continued this relationship.'

I'm a little thrown by this. It's not often that a client acknowledges when they're making things needlessly difficult, and I appreciate his candour as well as the insinuation that Gabby stood up for me. But there's a hint of something more serious that throws me a little, and I'm not quite sure how to respond.

'I enjoyed the helicopter,' I decide on eventually.

It seems to be the right thing to say. Pascal laughs outright this time, though his expression quickly sobers. 'You know, it's funny the difference between how people see us, and who we know in our hearts we truly are.' He pauses and nods to Gabby. 'I imagine *you* understand this.'

'Oh yes,' she agrees wryly.

'To you,' Pascal continues, 'I am the controlling client who thinks he knows better than the experts. To the media, I am the man who works so hard he never leaves his office.

To my employees, I am the paranoid in the attic, who makes them pass through a metal detector every time they want to nip out for a smoke. But to myself . . .' He trails off, gives an impotent shrug. 'Most of the time I feel like a scared little boy, forced to hide away in this luxury prison. I dearly wish it weren't necessary, but here we are. Aren't we, Tommy?'

Sitting to his right, Tommy Mitchell looks like an MMA fighter, with his manbun and his muscles bursting through a too-tight suit. Pascal had introduced him ILS's Head of Security, but the vibe I'm getting is more personal bodyguard than corporate protection.

'That's right,' says Tommy. 'Here we are indeed.'

I glance around our side of the table. Steph is nodding along enthusiastically, while Jason seems deep in thought. Neither of them looks as if they are going to ask the obvious question. I catch Gabby's eye and she dips her head in encouragement.

'Mr Robertson,' I say. 'Are you telling us you're worried for your life?'

A dramatic pause. Then Pascal pushes his chair back, stands up from the table, and begins to pace.

'Look at this,' he says, gesturing out at the distorted view instead of answering me. 'Horrible, isn't it? We've had to replace every window in the building with state-of-the-art polymers, just so that we can work without having to worry about snipers blasting our heads off. Because with modern firepower, it turns out, bulletproof glass no longer cuts the mustard.' Finally, he meets my gaze. 'It is a tragedy to have a view like ours ruined by windows like this. But I do it because I must.'

'Who would want to kill *you*?' asks Steph, stressing the final syllable. Not for the first time I'm amazed by her commitment to flattery, regardless of appropriate context. But then, who would want to kill him? I weigh up the options: is Robertson genuinely concerned, or is it an act? Is he *reasonably* concerned, or a paranoid nutcase? It's hard to tell, but I didn't get to where I am without being pretty damn good at reading body language, and nothing about what he's said so far suggests that he's crazy or lying.

Pascal continues his steady pacing back towards the head of the table as Tommy flicks a switch, and a painting above the mantelpiece transforms into a television screen.

'It's not just my life I'm worried about,' he finally says, voice low and a little choked. 'It's everyone here at ILS.'

At this, Tommy presses a button and an image appears on the screen. It displays an ID-style headshot of a young man with light brown hair and glasses, wearing a striped blue and white shirt.

'Despite what my security measures may imply,' he says, tone sombre, 'I pride myself on being approachable and available to all members of staff, whatever their position at ILS. About six months ago, an employee came to me having noticed irregularities in our inventory system — irregularities that always seemed to fix themselves before they could be investigated. This was that employee. His name was Sean Davies: thirty-three years old, recently married — and too curious for his own good. Two weeks later, while out on his morning run, he was stabbed to death in broad daylight.'

The screen now shows an article from a local news site —

the standard lead image of Sean smiling, with his arm around a woman I presume to be his wife.

'Sean's death shook the company. The police said it was a mugging that got out of hand – horrible to think about, but ultimately a straightforward case of wrong place, wrong time. I had no reason to think differently – no reason to make the connection to what he had told me about the inventory issue which appeared to be a simple computer error. Even today, I have no *evidence* that Sean was killed for what he knew . . .'

Another dramatic pause, allowing us to finish his sentence in our heads.

'Regardless, I began to take security more seriously. I asked Tommy to start keeping tabs on a few things. On the off chance that Sean's death was somehow connected to our company, I wanted to be the first to know.'

The image changes to a woman, a little older than Sean, with deep laugh lines.

'A month ago, Sean's manager Helen Michaels met the same fate. She was doing renovations on her house when she slipped and fell two storeys. So the police say, anyway. Again, I can't *prove* anything . . .'

'But it's a reasonable assumption,' Gabby declares, as he trails off. 'Two employees from the same team; anyone would start asking questions.'

Jason finally pipes up. 'So, you want us to find who killed them?'

'Not quite,' says Pascal. 'This is all background for why I've invited you here. It was while Tommy and I were investigating these deaths that we stumbled upon evidence that ILS products were being used in warzones, in ways we could never imagine. I can't tell you how horrified I . . .' He shakes his head, refocuses. 'Tommy followed that trail back to the source, and in doing so discovered Cyril Hargreaves' key role facilitating this exchange. That's when I called you. But Cyril Hargreaves was not acting alone. He was at every step aided and abetted by men I thought I could trust. Members of my own senior team, who are now so well connected to criminal organisations that I'm afraid to fire them without risking retaliation.'

Another slide appears, with a picture of two men shaking hands. I recognise the one in army fatigues – a man the press referred to as the Tyrant of Timora, one of the most inhumane butchers on Cyril Hargreaves' contact list. I *don't* recognise the one in cargo shorts and a Hawaiian shirt, looking uncomfortably sweaty in an unfamiliar climate.

'Everyone,' Pascal says, indicating this second man, 'meet your next target – if you accept my proposition. His name is Archie Henderson: my Director of Sales.'

5

When we finally all re-emerge into the open air, I'm surprised to find it's still daylight outside. According to the clock on my thankfully returned phone, it's only been an hour, but since it's already after 5 p.m. there's no point in going back to work.

'Have a good evening, Maisie,' Gabby says, patting me on the shoulder as we wait on the kerb for our taxis. 'Sleep on your decision, but remember – a good relationship with a man like that would be a valuable thing to have.'

'Sure,' I say. 'But I'll want to verify all the information he provided, given his position relative to, well, you know.' I stop myself from saying Archie Henderson's name: talking openly about targets on the street isn't best practice as a hitwoman. 'I just want to be one hundred per cent sure we're not being led up the garden path.'

To be honest, I already have a good feeling that we're not. Before we even left the meeting, Pascal sent us a great big tranche of evidence which ought to confirm everything he said about Archie Henderson's nefarious dealings with war criminals behind his back. It looked legit, at a glance, but it will need some serious time under the gaze of a trained professional before we can know for sure.

'Of course,' Gabby says. 'Jason!'

Startled, Jason comes over. 'Yes?'

'I'd like to go back with a yes or no tomorrow afternoon, but we'll need to double-check his files before then. Do you think that's feasible?'

He blinks. 'It'll take a bit of overtime.'

Gabby doesn't say anything, just lets the tension hang in the air.

Jason sighs. 'I'll cancel my plans.'

*

The following noon, I'm sitting with Jason around Gabby's kitchen counter, munching sandwiches and drinking tea.

'Well,' he says, 'the good news is, I have no doubt whatsoever that Archie Henderson is exporting ILS tech to illegal military organisations behind Pascal Robertson's back.'

We've been working silently in the living room all morning, him continuing to comb through the data Robertson sent us for any signs of fakery, while I checked that Robertson's big idea of how to take out Henderson – on Saturday morning, during a speech he's giving at an agriculture show – was as sensible as he'd made it sound.

We didn't want to discuss our findings while Steph was around – she has unhelpfully taken the side of an extreme pro-Pascal partisan, making nuanced discussion impossible – but Gabby has taken her off to do some of the grunt work I used to do at one of her charities. With Owen out on a job, we have the house pretty much to ourselves.

'Yeah?'

'Yeah,' Jason says tiredly. Not surprising since he seems to have been up all night, but there's something else in his tone, too – the same uncertainty he had in the meeting. 'The files included video and audio recordings of meetings between Archie and all of the worst war criminals Cyril Hargreaves was shipping to, including several where they explicitly stated that it's all going on behind Robertson's back. I've verified everything using every method I can think of. Nothing is faked, nothing is even suspicious. He's the real deal. And the suggestion that others at the company are involved seems real, too – we just don't have enough evidence to prove who they are yet.'

I mull it over through mouthfuls of tuna baguette. 'You sound almost disappointed,' I say with my hand over my mouth. 'You don't like him, do you?'

Jason feigns surprise. 'Who?'

'Pascal Robertson.'

Jason sighs. 'It's not that I don't *like* him . . .'

'You were unusually quiet in the meeting yesterday,' I say. 'Look, if there's anything fishy about the case, I have to know. Steph has been bugging me all morning about how it's important we let Pascal know quickly if we're going to turn him down, "on the off chance he'll ever want to work with us again if we reject him".'

Which is typical Steph. She has never been a fan of the agency Gabby gives me in choosing whether or not to take a job – she thinks it makes things too unpredictable, that Gabby's word alone should be enough. I've never had to turn down a contract that Gabby thought we should take — our instincts have always been pretty much aligned on these things, and the criteria we run our clients past seems to do the job — but at the end of the day I'm the one doing the killing. I'm the one who has to take it home with me.

'Oh, *that*,' says Jason. 'Ugh, it's nothing serious. He just seems like a bit of a poser, you know? I've seen clips of him on podcasts and he goes on about how he's innovating, changing the world, when he's got no scientific background whatsoever. He never gives credit where it's due — but at the same time, I guess he does really seem to care about the safety of his employees.'

Jason's got a point, but still, he'd hardly be the first man in his position to give off like he knew more than he really did about something. Morally speaking, it's hardly even a grey mark against his record, let alone a black one.

'What about those deaths at the company?' I ask. 'He obviously suspects the group around Archie Henderson, but he couldn't prove it. Did you find anything else?'

'Nothing on that front,' Jason says. 'I could only find what was in the press.'

Odd. But then, Archie Henderson's cabal would definitely have had the means to make these killings happen — and getting away with murder isn't as hard as people think.

'All I know is, everything he said about Archie Henderson is true. *That* man is a real villain.'

Good enough for me. 'Thanks, Jason,' I say. 'And sorry about the overtime.'

Jason rolls his eyes, but laughs. 'Don't worry about it. It's not your fault.'

When Gabby and Steph come back, I tell them I'm taking the mission. Archie Henderson will die on Saturday at the agriculture show, as per Robertson's suggestion. But for the rest of the afternoon, I can't escape the vague, nagging sense that I've forgotten something.

★

For the rest of the week, work is busy but uneventful. Every day, I get up, have breakfast with Beth in our flat in Mile End, then trek over to North London to Gabby's, where I continue to plot Archie Henderson's murder.

The intel from Pascal is comprehensive and easy to work with, which makes sense: almost no one has more access to info on your movements than your boss, especially when your boss is the fourteenth-richest man in Great Britain.

As far as my hitwoman maxims are concerned, I have nothing to worry about. I've looked through the data and I agree with Jason's assessment. Henderson absolutely, definitely, categorically and unquestionably, deserves what is coming to him.

The plan is simple enough. On Saturday, Archie Henderson is set to attend the Royal Wessex Agricultural Show, which takes place every year in a specialised showground near the village of Arpingham, Wiltshire – about two-and-a-half-hours' drive out of London. The RWAS is one of the biggest agricultural shows in the UK, and probably the most forward-thinking. As well as the usual treats of dog, sheep and cow shows, horse trials, and competitive demonstrations of rural skills like blacksmithing and tree surgery, they have a whole marquee dedicated to farming and tech, with panels like 'Putting Cowpats to Work: New Uses for Old Waste' and 'What Mainstream Ecologists Aren't Telling You About Soil Health'.

Henderson's talk is something of a commencement address for the whole stage, taking place at 9 a.m. That might seem a little early for normal people, but for farmers it's practically mid-afternoon, and it's the only moment where we know for sure where he'll be. Killing him on stage in front of three hundred people will be a bit of a challenge, but nothing I've not done before. All it needs is a bit of forward planning — which means renting a campervan so I can get to the showground on Friday evening to rig things up and ensure Archie Henderson's big speech will have people talking all weekend.

I plot most of it out on Monday afternoon, then Jason and I spend Tuesday working together to hack additional data from RWAS's internal systems, so I can check it all lines up. After that, I decide which of my fake identities I'll be for the weekend and start to forge the physical documentation.

I settle on Crystal Gladstone. She's not actually a farmer, just a posh horse girl with a struggling #vanlife Instagram account, for whom we manage to wrangle free entry to the RWAS in exchange for promoting the event on her social media — which I've spent many a quiet day in the office updating, ready for a time like this. The account is also a 'nice to have' in case anyone at the event starts asking questions, though in all likelihood no one will. Crystal won't quite fit in, but that's fine — it's far easier to fake being part of something if the person you're pretending to be is already a faking it a bit themselves — but she's *normal*, and in the popular imagination normal people aren't murderers. Normal women, anyway.

For the rest of the week, I intend to split my time between memorising the plan and training in Gabby's garage gym and underground firing range: two perks of the job are never having to worry about paying for a gym membership, and free access to a vast selection of highly illegal weaponry and a soundproofed range.

Unfortunately, Steph has other ideas for me.

'Oh, Maisie,' she says on Wednesday afternoon, popping her head around the door as I'm practising my back kicks.

I spin around to face away from her, then *Thwap!* My heel connects with the punching bag hanging from the ceiling between us, sending it swinging in her direction. 'What?'

'Sorry to interrupt.' As she's speaking, I spin back around and, *pop-pop!* Jab the bag twice in what should be its kidneys. 'But I was just wondering how you were getting on with the—' *Thwap!* 'With the report you said you'd almost finished?'

'For the Cyril Hargreaves case?'

'No, Maisie, for the one *before* that. The one out in Wiltshire? I've already explained to the client on Friday that we've had to delay it once, I really don't want to have to—' *Pop-pop!* 'Have to do it again, Maisie.'

'I was a little busy on Friday, Steph.' *Thwap!*

'Well, I'm just saying Gabby asked me to remind you, so if you could just get to it when you have a minute, yeah?'

Sure thing, I think bitterly as she leaves the room. As far as

I'm concerned, reports like this are a pointless chore – time spent plugging numbers into a laptop that could be spent ensuring I don't get caught or killed. Though as Gabby says, without our clients, we wouldn't be able to achieve all the great things we do. We definitely couldn't have afforded that helicopter extract on Friday on our own.

But that's the secret truth about the world of employment, isn't it? It doesn't really matter what industry you work in, you'll probably still spend more time than you want to hunched over your laptop, sending pointless emails, making pointless spreadsheets, and probably getting annoyed at your coworkers. Insurance, journalism, television, law, politics, even the police or fire brigade: the ends might be different, but the means are often basically identical.

At least when I'm killing people it feels like I'm accomplishing something, but more and more of this job is just busywork. But Gabby's right, it's the clients that pay the bills. I wait long enough to avoid giving Steph too much satisfaction, then towel off and start writing the report. It'll take the rest of the week to compile, and I can feel the boredom creeping in already.

★

On Thursday morning, Beth says something that echoes my line of thinking.

'Why is it,' she says as she pours milk over her muesli, 'that the more important I think the story I'm working on is, the more Dom finds ways to distract me with bloody busywork?'

Dom is Dominic Waters, Beth's new boss, a card-carrying

member of the Bullingdon Club who'd make sure you know they don't actually carry cards. I wouldn't be surprised if he ends up on my desk one of these days based on what she's said about him.

I laugh. 'God, I know what you mean.'

She shoots me a quizzical look, perhaps wondering which part of running around after Gabby Hawthorne I find so important that I don't want to be distracted from it.

'I mean,' I correct, 'I can imagine. That must be frustrating. Is it really that bad?'

She buys it. 'It's *really* that bad. We've got our big pitch coming up soon, where the company decides which stories they want to take forward into full shows. Every researcher gets to shoot their shot, and I *really* want my idea to be picked up. But I have to be able to back up my claims, and however sure I am that I'm right, it takes forever to build a case strong enough to get past legal. Meanwhile, Dom keeps saddling me with fact checking shows in post-production, so where am I meant to find the time? It's like he's actively trying to stop me from doing my job.' She sighs dramatically and mimes a basketball shot over my head. 'Might as well chuck all my research down the memory hole at this rate, maybe it'll finally see the light of day in twenty years.'

I follow her gaze to the 'memory hole', a literal hole – or well, gap – between the kitchen counter and fridge. Soon after moving into the flat, Beth had confessed she was still holding on to a Valentine's card from her ex of three years ago, and thus a new tradition was born: whenever one of us has something we never want to see again, but also can't quite bring ourselves to chuck out, it goes in the hole –

like postcards from my mum, Polaroids where one of us is looking super hot but the other decidedly not, and tokens from romantic entanglements we (mainly Beth) have had over the years. Sort of like an emotionally charged time capsule, for whichever unsuspecting soul finally renovates this flat in 2050 or whenever.

'I'm sure you'll get it through legal eventually,' I say. 'What's the story?' *Nothing about former* Springwatch *presenters running killer-for-hire agencies, I hope?*

She winces. 'Can't tell you, sorry. To be honest, I've already said too much. These NDAs are tight.' She forlornly scoops a spoonful of muesli. 'I'll probably have to work this weekend, but we're supposed to meeting Michelle's new guy on Saturday, and I just don't know how I'll fit it all in.'

Ah. So that's what's been nagging at me.

Michelle's been going on about introducing this guy to us for so long that I forgot it was actually going to happen. I control my expression to stop any glimmer of surprise from crossing my face. As much as I like to keep my work and social life separate, there are times when my hitman skills come in useful.

'Oh yeah,' I say, expertly casual. 'That'll be nice, though. What time were we meeting them, again?'

Despite my composure, it's as if Beth can read my mind. 'Maisie, *you're* not thinking of ditching it for work again, are you? We already cancelled last time. If either of us bail, she'll never forget it.'

'No!' I exclaim, running through my timeline of Archie Henderson's murder in my head. 'It's just, I've got a little business trip with Gabby on Friday night, but I'll be back to

London on Saturday morning. Unless — we're not meeting for breakfast, are we?'

'It's a brunch.'

Fuck. My mental calculations are not looking good. Henderson's on stage at nine, so even assuming everything goes to plan and I extract quickly, getting back to London before the afternoon will be a rush.

Beth's checking her phone for the finer details. 'Well, a late brunch. At twelve, she says.'

'So . . . more of a *lunch*, then?'

'Yeah, but with like, eggs and stuff.'

OK. I'm still not convinced that'll be doable, but it's too late now to do anything about it. Maybe I can rearrange things with Archie to have him meet his fate a little earlier.

'So you'll be there?' Beth asks.

'Yeah, of course!' I say. 'No worries at all. And you?'

Beth mimics me good-naturedly. 'Of course! No worries at all.'

6

I'm still feeling worried about the brunch situation as the steward waves my rented campervan towards my allocated part of the RWAS campsite, at around 6 p.m. on Friday evening. The field is already filling up with visitors – mostly rich farmers in dormobiles like my own, though generally bigger and more expensive-looking. Almost all of them are wearing some variation of smart jeans or chinos with checked shirts in a few different shades of blue, pink or yellow. Of course, I've dressed to blend in perfectly: light blue jeans, riding boots, and a crinkly M&S shirt. The evening is warm and still fairly light, so I sit on the stoop of the dormobile to watch people pass through the cars and tents beneath the sunset.

I had planned to have a quiet night in, but I can hear bassy music from somewhere and a group of women nearby are talking excitedly about something called the 'Young Farmers' Night'. Maybe it's the nostalgia of feeling like I'm at a festival, maybe it's the horror of a night ahead without Wi-Fi, but something compels me about the idea.

Why not, I think. I have the evening off, don't I?

★

As it turns out, the Young Farmers' Night takes place in a marquee that looks and sounds like a slightly low-rent festival dance tent, if you replaced everything around it with a seemingly endless grid of single-occupancy animal pens. On my way to the marquee I pass enclosures with banners advertising the award category each animal is eligible for, from BEST BELTED GALLOWAY to EMU AGILITY TRIALS. None of the creatures I pass look particularly excited about their chances.

Inside, the setup evokes barnyard hoedown by way of the Ibiza strip. There's a DJ area at one end manned by a muscular guy in shades and a black V-neck, but the bar at the other could have been lifted from the set of a Western. Along both sides, the canvas walls are lined with hay bales to give the attendees somewhere to sit when they're not dancing. It's not even nine yet, but already a few of them are occupied by people too drunk to stand, about to throw up, or heavy petting enthusiastically enough to get thrown out of a swimming pool.

Someone shouts in my ear: 'Welly-bombs, anyone?'

I spin around to see an athletic-looking man whose blue checked shirt is unbuttoned so far that you can see the dark hair at the top of his firm, flat farmer's belly. My eyes wander, and not to the tray.

'Miss?' he asks when he sees me looking, and I drag my eyes up towards his dozen shots of strangely coloured liquid.

I shake my head in a polite but firm no, enjoying the way his gaze lingers on me. Before I can change my mind, the glasses are snatched up by nearby members of the crowd, who link arms as they drink, jumping and cheering once they've swallowed it all down.

Wouldn't see that in London, I catch myself thinking. Though to be honest it's been so long since I've had a proper night out that I've lost track of what clubs in London are like. Who knows, maybe house music is over and Mumford and Sons have made a spectacular comeback.

I take a look around to decide how I feel about that idea, and you know what? As much as this isn't my usual scene, there's an uninhibited energy, a sense of freedom here that's making me nostalgic for the carefree nights I had with Beth and our other friends back in uni. I don't want to get drunk, I decide, but one beer can't hurt. And if more of the men are as handsome as the guy with the shots, I'm certainly not complaining.

Getting to the bar proves to be a challenge. I press past groups of girls in Oktoberfest-style sexy lederhosen and skirt the edge of an impromptu wrestling ring that has formed around two burly men in polo shirts and luminescent safety trousers, who are pushing into each other with their shoulders locked like stags competing for a mate, while spectators whoop and cheer for them. Then there's the queue itself, which feels more like a scrum in a rugby match. And then, worst of all:

'We're out of beer,' says the barman when I finally get the chance to ask for a Heineken. The clock behind his head reads 9.05.

'*All* beer? Already? Are you about to close?'

'No, not until three. We've got spirits, cider, and WKD. Which is it?'

I go for the cider, which turns out to be the wrong call. It's the strongest, driest-tasting cider that has ever passed through my lips – and believe me, I've drunk some strange things on jobs before. The effect is so powerful that I lose all control of my face muscles, and wince so hard that it attracts the notice of a guy leaving the bar with a plastic cup of his own.

'That bad, is it?' he says as he catches my gaze. As he speaks, his face transforms into an achingly sincere, slightly bashful smile, as if he's a little surprised to hear the words coming out of his mouth. He's dressed to fit in, but even at a glance, this man stands subtly out from the crowd. His hair is a little too styled, his checked shirt a little too unwrinkled, and his muscles a little too gym-toned and regular to be the result of a childhood spent hauling hay bales into tractor-trailers – though there is absolutely no doubt in my mind that he *could*, if he ever needed to.

'Oof,' I splutter, lifting up the glass to performatively inspect its contents – and to stop myself staring. 'It may be a *bit* of an acquired taste.'

He moves beside me with an apprehensive look. 'Well, I've got it now. May as well give it a try, eh?'

He lifts the cup to his lip and takes in a respectable sip – more than I would have advised, that's for sure. At first, he manages to hold back his reaction. Then an involuntary twitch of his left eyelid gives the game away.

'It's a cider-lover's cider,' he says after finally forcing it down. 'With notes of lemon peel and just a hint of paint stripper.'

His voice is lovely, slightly gravelly and softly accented.

I realise we seem to have drifted together away from the huddle around the bar, towards one of the quieter spots near the edge of the marquee.

'Or a farmers' cider,' I say, testing him slightly.

'I wouldn't know,' he says – and I knew it. 'By the standards of this marquee I'm a city boy, if you can forgive me.' He makes an apologetic face, and even though it's a joke, his smile is still absolutely gorgeous. Though the effect is ruined by the way he winces after giving his drink another curious sniff.

'I'll get over it,' I say, and my accent seems to have slipped a little from the one I'd chosen for Crystal Gladstone. Evidently, I've decided that it isn't too late to soften the edges of my false identity into something I can more convincingly flirt in. 'But only if you tell me who you are, and what you're doing here? Perhaps starting with your name.'

He laughs and takes a step closer. 'Well, I'm Will. And I'm a contractor, so just here for some networking – hoping to bump into a potential business partner who's speaking tomorrow, actually. Which means tonight, I'm at a loose end. How about you? Any prize animals in the show?'

'A pig,' I say. 'She's called Tricksy, she's about yay high, and she's *very* intelligent. She can do tricks – hence the name. We're hoping to wow the judges with a rendition of "Good King Wenceslas".'

He whistles. '*Very* impressive. Landrace or Duroc?'

Will might not be a farmer, but he knows his pig breeds at least. Fortunately, I do, too. 'Saddleback, naturally,' I tell him. It's always important to prep thoroughly for a mission: you never know when information will come in handy.

He raises an eyebrow. 'Pretty small for a saddleback, no?'

Is it? Crap. I might be joking about Tricksy, but that's still something I should know. I laugh to hide my dismay. 'OK, you got me – I'm not a farmer and Tricksy isn't real. Sorry.'

'Damn, I was planning on ditching work to follow her UK tour. So what *does* bring you to this wonderful marquee, if it isn't a singing pig?'

I start giving him the prepared spiel about Crystal Gladstone and the #vanlife community, but I cut it short when his eyes start to glaze over. Glazed eyes is, of course, the intended effect of the spiel – but there's something about this man that makes me want to keep him interested.

'How's the cider now?' I ask, noticing that he's still drinking it despite his initial reaction.

He laughs and takes another swig. 'You know what? It's actually starting to grow on me.'

I take a sip and am surprised to find that I agree. Over on the dance floor, the first bar of a recognisable song sends up a whoop of appreciation. Around us, people pull themselves up from the hay bales, starting a mini-stampede as they rush to join in. Suddenly, I want nothing more than to be in there with them.

Will is looking at me.

I step a little closer. 'So, if you're here by yourself, and I'm here by myself, I think we should look out for one another. And I'm in need of a dance partner.'

Oh God, did I really just say that? How strong is this cider, anyway?

But he just flashes that wonderful smile of his. 'I can help with that,' he says, taking my hand and leading me into the crowd.

I don't know where things are going with this handsome stranger at the Young Farmers' Night, but whatever it is, he seems as up for it as I am. What I am sure of is that this is the most fun I've had on a dance floor in, well, a long time. It's just not been the same since I started working full time – even if I find time to go out, there's always something hanging over me, some anxiety about relaxing a little too much and revealing something I shouldn't. But here, whether it's the Crystal Gladstone persona, being out of the city, or the way everyone around us is no-holds-barred *going for it*, it's all too easy to get swept up in things.

And if things go any further – well, maybe that would be the solution to my Owen problem.

The song changes, and our eyes meet in a moment of recognition. I almost burst out laughing: it's too perfect. It's too loud to talk, so I have to stand on my tiptoes and lean forward to reach his ear, his stubble rough against my cheek. 'Oh my God,' I shout. 'Are they really playing "Cotton-Eye Joe"?'

Somehow his hands end up on my waist as he leans down to shout back: 'Why wouldn't they? It's a classic!'

'A classic at primary school discos!'

And at Young Farmers' Nights, apparently. Around us, the crowd is roaring in appreciation. Out the corner of my eye I see a topless man standing on a table and swinging his shirt around. As the beat hits, Will links his arm through mine and pulls me into a mad, hopping, spinning, uncontrollable reel that almost has me careening into the group next to us.

'Sorry!' I shout as we whirl on by.

After a few more spins we lose the rhythm of it and become tangled, slowing, somehow falling into each other. Then, before I know it, his hands are gripping me tightly and mine are behind his head, my fingers digging into his hair as he pulls me closer, his chest pressing into mine as our lips brush. When I stand on my tiptoes to kiss him deeper, something desperate twists in the bottom of my stomach. He gently cups my face and I can feel myself tensing at the contact. It has been so, so long since I've wanted someone like this.

'I have a campervan,' I tell him, surprising myself again. Because I'm never normally this bold – honestly, I'm not. Not when I'm off the job, which I'm telling myself I technically am, at least for the next few hours.

Tonight feels different, though. Or maybe it's Will that's different. I don't know what it is exactly, but I feel relaxed around him in a way I so rarely am around men. I don't believe in auras, but his seems *pure* somehow. Or maybe it's not him – maybe it's just the fact that being in character means I don't have to deal with all the baggage of being Maisie. I've never worked out how to show men parts of myself while keeping so much closed off, leading to me pushing them away before things can get serious. But here I don't have to be Maisie pretending to be someone I'm not. I can just be Crystal Gladstone.

Will, I decide, gets all of Crystal Gladstone. Because tomorrow, after we go our separate ways, Crystal Gladstone will no longer exist.

'I have a hotel room,' he replies, one-upping my offer of a campervan.

I laugh. 'I can't beat that.'

We go out into the night, the air fresh with possibilities. He leads me a different way than the one I used to get here, away from the animal pens and across an open patch of field. As we go, I look up at the sky above our heads. It almost makes me gasp.

'Does it always look like that outside of London?' I ask. Now that we're away from the floodlights around the marquee, there are *so* many stars. Is this how it always looked back in Carlisle? I ask myself. Have I lived in London for so long I've forgotten such a basic, primal beauty?

Of course, it's completely out of character for Crystal to ask such a question. She might not be a farmer, but what sort of #vanlife enthusiast hasn't slept under the stars?

But Will's smile makes it worth it. 'Incredible, isn't it? It's the sort of thing you never get used to. I know one or two spots in London where you can see them pretty well on a clear night.'

'No way. Where?'

He smiles at me and keeps moving. 'Maybe one day I can show you.'

I almost wish he could.

Will's hotel turns out to be just outside the showground, a cheap Holiday Inn that I can't imagine getting much traffic at any other time of year. Now, though, the lobby is thrumming with people coming and going. I take his hand as he guides me to the lift – which I'm a little disappointed to find already contains an older couple, having come up from the basement car park. In the harsh light of the elevator, Will somehow looks better than ever. He's tall, broad and chiselled, but he doesn't read as pleased with himself about it in the way some guys do. If we had the lift to ourselves, I'd be throwing myself on him here and now.

'This isn't the way I imagined tonight going,' he says as I close the door to his room, kicking off my shoes. 'But I'm definitely not complaining.'

I loop my arms around him and give him a chaste peck on the lips. 'This isn't your regular MO at these things, Mr Contractor?'

He smiles bashfully. 'Not really, no. Like, almost never.'

'I find that hard to believe.'

'Honestly,' he laughs, a bright, happy laugh.

'Well, me neither,' I say, guiding him towards the bed. He sits on the edge and I straddle him, then set to work taking off his shirt, one button at a time.

'Then we're the same.'

From there we go slowly, undressing each other and inching closer to the centre of the bed. The more we touch, the more I feel the pent-up tension leaving my body. In the moment, it doesn't even matter that we don't know each other at all – I feel wanted, wholly and unreservedly. And I want him too. How had it taken me so long to realise I needed this? The frustration I've been feeling at work, the pangs of loneliness when Beth and my breakfast schedules failed to line up, and the existential, career-questioning dread of Sunday nights – what if all that was just a basic hormonal signal that I was misinterpreting? What if I just really, *really* needed to get laid?

Thank God for Crystal Gladstone, and her carefree spirit.

★

'That was exactly what I needed,' I tell him when he finally collapses on top of me. It may sound flippant, but I'm being 100 per cent serious.

He kisses me on the forehead, then pushes himself up. 'Crystal, you are incredibly beautiful.'

I feel a little pang of guilt, hearing my lie come out of his mouth. It's a sudden reminder that the illusion of acceptance I felt in his arms was just that – an illusion. He doesn't understand me. He can't.

He peels the condom off as he stands, then staggers woozily, holding it comically in one hand as if he's unsure what to do with it. 'Head rush,' he gasps, regaining his balance just long enough to lob it into the bin on the far side of the room. 'God, I am going to . . .'

Pass out, he doesn't say, instead collapsing onto the bed like a falling tree. I snuggle backwards into him and his body silently envelops me, one big arm gently swinging down like the harness at the start of a rollercoaster. I feel secure. He traces patterns along my arms with his fingertips, so softly that it makes my hairs stand on end.

It would be so easy just to fall asleep here and forget everything.

Too easy.

I let myself snooze for half an hour. It's hard to leave, but I know what I have to do. Even so, tonight has been surprisingly wonderful. A glorious, necessary reminder that I can still have fun. I get dressed as quietly as possible.

'I'm going to go,' I whisper. 'I've got a big day tomorrow and I'll sleep better in my own bed.'

He smiles and reaches out to gently touch my cheek, and

kisses me once on the lips. Then, as much as I don't want to, I wrench myself away.

It's 2.13 a.m. as I leave the hotel, but I don't go straight back to my campervan. I still have a trap to set for the morning, before I can catch a precious few hours of sleep. I draft a message to Jason, who has been waiting up for me, on our encrypted messaging app:

Still up? I'm omw to the marquee now, get ready to override the cameras

His reply comes in less than a minute:

On it now

*

Six hours later, I'm climbing up the tiered seating ready for Archie Henderson's commencement speech in the Future of Farming Pavilion. Despite the name, the so-called pavilion is just another marquee, this one with plasticky skylights in the white canvas roof that makes me feel a little like a plant in a greenhouse. I take a seat two-thirds of the way back, and after a brief introduction from an emcee who, just like my intel predicted, takes off pronto, Archie strides out to middling applause from the onlooking farmers.

'Good morning, Arpingham!' he shouts, undeterred. He looks younger than he did in our photos – sprightly for forty-six – and his accent has that vague burr middle-class Northerners play up when they want to sound salt of the earth. Behind him, a projector screen lights up with the logo of the company for which he is sales director: ILS Industries, the great last hope for British Agriculture.

'Now!' he announces. 'I hope you're not too disappointed that it's me here today, and not our illustrious CEO. But as I'm sure you know, if you know anything about us, Pascal is as stubborn as the proverbial mule when it comes to not leaving the office. You couldn't get that man to stop working for all the money in the world.'

That makes me laugh. There's something about the way Henderson feels the need to keep bigging up the mythos around his boss that rings a little pathetic in public. Especially when behind closed doors Archie is perfectly happy to besmirch Pascal's name to genocidal terrorists, swearing blind there's no way his boss will find out about their under-the-table deals.

'On! The plus side,' he continues. Overemphasising his first words seems to be something of a tic. 'I've got some cracking offers for you this weekend. Pesticides, herbicides, fungicides, biopesticides, you name it. We'll have displays and samples all weekend for you to get your hands on, and our expert scientists will be at every showing point to answer any questions you might have about our cutting-edge ingredients – all of which will give *you* the peace of mind that you're investing your hard-earned money into something guaranteed to earn you more.'

A murmur goes up from the crowd at this, and I'm not sure if it's appreciative or sceptical. ILS has been notoriously tight-lipped on the exact makeup of their breakthrough pesticide. Beyond reassurances that 'a sustainable future' is at the forefront of their concerns, they have exploited all available loopholes so as not to risk copycats of their 'miracle' product.

Not that it's harmed their sales much. I catch some shaking heads among the old-timers, but a group of younger guys in snapbacks ahead of me are whispering to each other excitedly. As I learned in my research, ILS increasingly have the sales figures to back up Archie's bravado, particularly from the tricky demographic of younger farmers. Emerging from nowhere in the post-Brexit confusion, they have quickly become the second-largest seller of agricultural chemicals in the UK – a staggering achievement in such a risk-averse industry.

It's just a shame that a contingent of their unscrupulous employees are selling said pesticides to terrorists.

On stage, Henderson is telling this story with blokey bombast, leaving out the unsavoury truths and interspersing his narrative with various charts and photos of happy country folk standing in front of their fields.

'We! Are the little team that could!' he shouts over an impressively steep line graph. 'In less than a decade, we've gone from Yeovil Town to Arsenal; from nobodies in the National League to coming within spitting distance of winning the Premier League. We are up against the old titans of BASF United and Syngenta FC, and we intend to win! The results speak for themselves . . .'

I glance towards the part of the stage where I rigged my trap earlier today. It's too far away to see if it's still there, but there's no reason it wouldn't be. I just have to wait for my moment. From the huge hydroponic display I can see peeking out from the wings, that should be any minute now.

The hydroponics are important, because when Henderson's alone on stage, he can move anywhere. He's

71

erratic. Unpredictable. But when they bring the display out, tall and packed as it is with plants and suspended metal bars, there's one precise spot he has to stand in for health and safety reasons – their insurance was *very* specific. So all I have to do is wait for him to get into position and press a little button on the remote in my pocket, indistinguishable from a normal car key, and my trap is sprung. Lights out for Mr Henderson.

'And that brings us up to today,' he's saying, 'and to our first showing. The culmination of years of research, the plants you see here have been bombarded with every microscopic and macroscopic baddie you can imagine, but with the power of our new Verdicure formula—'

—and the display is wheeled in. It scrapes across the stage and it's difficult to hear what Henderson is saying, but the important thing is that he's moving steadily towards his mark, just as intended. I slip my hand into my pocket, thumb itching as I caress the moulded plastic shell of the key fob. I know that the absolute worst thing I can do is press it early, but my moment could come any second now. Just wait, and . . .

Three . . .

Two . . .

One . . .

Something clanks in the rafters. Before anyone can react, a point light detaches itself from the strut above Henderson's head and dives towards him, rotating slightly as it descends. Time stretches out, everything goes slower than it usually does, and he must notice movement above him because he lifts his gaze to look the light right in its glowing red eye as it swoops for him, like some futuristic death robot. His mouth goes slack, his last word trails off, and some elemental part of his brain works overtime to interpret what he's seeing and what he can do about it.

But he's too slow.

The lamp clocks him on the head so hard that his skull splits open like a jacket potato, blood and brain rolling out across the stage like too much Heinz baked beans.

And I'm like: What. The. Fuck.

Because that wasn't what I had planned at all.

7

Three and a half hours later, I'm dashing down Stoke Newington High Street in the East End of London, embarrassingly late to meet my friends for brunch.

The wrap-up after Archie's death went even smoother than I expected. The police showed up in fifteen minutes, and from then it was just another fifteen until they sent me on my way with a leaflet for counselling in case I needed someone to talk to about all the horror I'd witnessed.

The drive, on the other hand, was frustrating. When I got in the campervan, my phone estimated that I'd make it to the street I'd arranged to dump the van on for 11.50, which would leave me ten minutes to do what was supposedly a twenty-five-minute walk to the brunch spot. I'd be a little late, but whatever – Google Maps *always* underestimates my walking speed.

The app's estimations, however, were based on the presumption that I would be driving a normal modern car. Crystal Gladstone's campervan did not quite meet the expected ratio of weight:horsepower, and as such, however far I pushed down the pedal, it struggled to get much over 60 mph. As I drove, I watched my estimated arrival time slowly tick up from 11.50, past 12.00, and beyond.

There was also the fact I had to find somewhere to stop and get changed. Now I ought to be unrecognisable with my trademark denim and my natural hair and eye colours, but I can't shake the nagging anxiety that I've forgotten some stray detail that'll give me away – something I wasn't able to deal with in the cramped darkness of the converted Toyota but which will be immediately obvious to everyone else.

Finally, to make matters worse, Gabby didn't answer any of the calls or texts I left her illegally as I was driving. Not until right now, anyway.

'*Are you in danger, Maisie?*' she asks over the phone, which is already turning clammy from the sweat of my face. '*You seem out of breath.*'

'Not in danger,' I reply as I jump over the lead connecting a woman in a leopard print jumpsuit to her tiny dog. Well, maybe in a little danger, but nothing I can't handle. 'I'm back in London, just running late to meet some friends. But something weird happened on the job; we need to talk.'

Frustratingly, that's about as specific as I can be out in public. Maybe if she'd answered her phone earlier I would've been able to explain myself, but apparently she was in another meeting. On a Saturday? She never used to work Saturdays.

'*Something weird? But you got it done, didn't you? I heard about it on the news. It sounded like everything went as planned.*'

'Yes, *someone* got the job done. But it wasn't how I planned it. It was supposed to be a . . .' Speaker tower, I almost say, but I've just had to slow down behind a group of new mums pushing their prams three abreast on the pavement and I'm getting enough attention as it is. 'A little different,' I conclude, vaguely.

'*That is concerning. Do you mean to suggest there was another agent on the case? Did you see anyone suspicious?*'

This was the main thing I was thinking about as I gunned the campervan back into London – at least when I wasn't thinking about how late I'd be to meet Beth, Liv and Michelle – but nothing stuck out. To be fair, I hadn't been expecting the presence of another agent, and for most of the time I was there my mind was firmly on other things.

'No, nothing suspicious. I don't know. But it's got me a little freaked out.'

'*That's understandable, Maisie,*' Gabby says, ever a reassuring presence. '*Look – it's the weekend, and I can tell you have somewhere to be. I'll call in Jason for some overtime research and hopefully by Monday morning we'll have more of a sense of the situation. All OK?*'

As always, Gabby's calm, sure tone eases my nerves. 'All good,' I gasp, building up speed down a quieter stretch of pavement. 'Thank you. Call me if you need me.'

'*See you on Monday,*' Gabby says firmly. '*Enjoy your weekend.*'

And then she's gone.

★

Different versions of what could have led to Archie Henderson's death are still churning in my head as I push open the café door at 12.36 p.m., sweat beading on my forehead. I spot Liv and Michelle at the back of the room straight away, their respective boyfriends obscured behind an artsy-Polaroid bedecked pillar, and start sheepishly winding my way towards them. Before I can get very far, the door jingles open behind me and a hand lands heavily on my shoulder.

'Ohmygod, Maisie,' pants Beth in my ear, too winded to notice how much she made me jump. She's taking huge gasps of breath between every other word, but I can just about make out her meaning. 'Your cardio . . . Insane . . . Was trying . . . Catch up . . . They'regonnakillus.'

I look in towards Michelle, who has spotted us and is waving frantically from the table, the man who must be Arman leaning around the pillar to smile benignly in our direction. Liv and her boyfriend Sam are looking over, too, with slightly impatient expressions.

'Guys, I am so, so, so, sorry that I'm so late again,' I say as I sit down beside her.

'Me too,' Beth adds, taking the final chair. 'Really sorry.'

'It's just work, and . . .'

'Yeah, work,' Beth concludes. 'Work. Too much work. Sorry again.'

'Also hi, guys,' I add for Liv and Sam's benefit, who nod coolly back in unison. But now Michelle looks like she's on the verge of tears, one hand held up to cover her mouth.

'So sorry,' Beth repeats one more time.

Then Arman speaks up: 'What's the problem? It's only five minutes, right?'

At that Michelle's dam bursts and she erupts into laughter so intense that she has to grab my shirtsleeve to keep herself on her chair. 'Oh my days, both of you! What are you like!' she says between taking great gasps of air. 'I told you, Arman, these two are *literally* the same person sometimes. This is *mental*.'

'Why?' I ask.

'What've we done?' Beth adds, glancing at me in confusion. Arman looks just as baffled as we are.

'Honestly!' Michelle exclaims. 'Don't you remember all the times I've threatened that if you both keep showing up late I'm going to tell you to come half an hour earlier? Well, I tried it! And it worked! But I didn't expect you to both show up at the exact same time!'

Then the laughter hits me and Beth. It really is mad, isn't it? The look on Michelle's face is enough to wring the morning's tension out of me like water from a sponge.

'You know us better than we know ourselves,' says Beth.

'That's ten years of friendship for you,' says Arman.

I look at Michelle and smile. From some people this sort of thing might feel like a passive–aggressive rug pull, but she doesn't have a pass–ag bone in her body. She's one of those people who, when she smiles, she holds nothing back and makes the whole room smile with her. Right now she's *beaming*.

Even Liv and Sam make polite chuckling noises, though they're obviously less impressed by our antics than Michelle is. On the one hand it's fair enough – it is a bit shit that it's got to the point where Mich feels the need to plan around us like that. But on the other Liv and Sam both work in jobs that from the sound of it you can stop doing at 5 p.m. and simply forget about: no overtime, no unpredictable hours, no stress hanging over you when you're out of the office. It's not like Beth and I *want* to be distracted by work all the time.

'OK, this is very funny,' Liv says once the laughter's gone quiet. 'But just to be clear — for my birthday trip to Margate, the time I've given you is the correct one, OK? I want to get there before lunch and the train leaves when it leaves, so if you're late . . .'

'We won't be late,' I say quickly.

Beth agrees. 'Promise we won't.'

It's not quite enough for Liv. 'You've both managed to take the time off work? No last-minute surprises?'

'Promise,' I say, though strictly speaking that isn't how it works. The best I can do is not take any jobs that will have me working that day — and hope nothing *extremely* important comes up that Owen couldn't handle.

'OK, good,' she says, finally relaxing. 'Because I love you girls. I'd hate for you not to be there.'

Then the food arrives, and it's genuinely great — though the beans with my fry-up make me feel a little queasy. Since we're here to meet Arman, Beth and I pepper him with questions as we eat. The more he speaks, the more I get the sense of how perfectly he and Michelle seem to be made for each other. Even their outfits, while not strictly matching, are so complementary that they could be on facing pages of a catalogue — both in textured black tops, punctuated by chunky metal clasps and jewellery.

In the way they look at each other, laugh with each other, I get the sense they're already beginning to understand each other implicitly. For some reason, I can't help but think about last night and smile. It was just a casual fling, and he didn't even know the real me, but am I crazy to think there was a real connection there? Not that I ever expect to see Will again – it's just nice to have some proof that I am still capable of forming that kind of connection, despite, you know, all the killing and stuff.

'So, since you all studied together in Scotland,' Arman asks, turning the conversation away from himself, 'was moving to London a group decision or more like, dribs and drabs?'

'Maisie was first,' Michelle answers. 'Weren't you, Mais? Right out of uni she knocked it out of the park by snapping up an internship with Lady Gabby Hawthorne. She even lived with her for a few months at the start.'

Arman pulls a face at me to show that he is suitably impressed, but for some reason alluding to that period of my life always gives me chills, even given everything that came after. A lot happened in those few months. A lot changed. Maybe it was because I wasn't used to it yet, hadn't hardened to it, but even now it feels raw. I think of a plughole, clotted with blood and bone.

'Wow,' says Arman, oblivious. 'What was that like, working with someone famous? Did she throw any big diva tantrums?'

I chuckle at the thought of Gabby throwing a 'diva tantrum', but inside I still feel cold. 'No, not at all,' I say, more casually than I feel. 'Actually, she looked after me. She still does – even seven years on.'

'Does she still make you do all those self-defence classes?' asks Liv. 'That was a bit intense, wasn't it?'

I cringe a little at how open I was with the three of them, back before I knew what working with Gabby would really involve. 'It's more like she lets me join sessions with her personal trainer,' I say. 'Cheaper than a gym membership, and I can do it while I'm on the clock.'

'Pretty good perk,' Arman agrees.

When I think back on how I ended up killing people for money, it almost feels like it happened by accident. Back when I really was just Gabby's live-in PA — before Jason and Owen and Steph came along, before the idea of Novum had ever crossed our minds — Gabby suggested I start working with a self-defence trainer in her basement gym.

'You don't know what sort of world you're entering,' she said, sensing my initial reluctance. 'The circles I am required to operate in are at the elite levels of British society. The men in this world are dangerous, Maisie. They genuinely believe themselves to be untouchable by the courts, the police, and the media. And do you know what? They're right. A young woman in this society, with no money, with paltry connections, who cannot defend herself, is a target. It's as simple as that.'

I didn't believe her — couldn't bring myself to believe her — and honestly, I'd never thought of myself as someone with much interest in martial arts. But what I said to Arman about the cost of a gym membership was true: Gabby was essentially offering free fitness classes with a personal trainer several times a week during my scheduled work hours, and she'd even reduce my responsibilities as her PA to make time for it. When I thought about how much money I'd save, it seemed crazy not to take her up on it.

And she was right, of course. As it turned out, the self-defence classes *were* necessary. I learned that about six months later, at the studio of one Theodore Dieter, a well-known music producer who Gabby was hoping to tap for a charity single she was putting together. Gabby and I were supposed to meet outside and then go in together, but she was running late.

Dieter appeared from somewhere while I was waiting on the pavement outside.

'Waiting for me?' he asked cheerfully. 'May as well do it inside, eh? No sense standing out here in the cold.'

'I really should wait for my boss,' I said. 'Sorry. You go in and we'll catch you up.'

'You sure about that?' he said, stamping his feet in the January snow. 'You sure you're sure?'

I would've waited outside. Should've waited outside. But it really was cold that winter, and I didn't. He took me to an empty studio – soundproofed, I realised too late.

If you've read a newspaper since #metoo you can imagine where this story goes. He made a move on me. I turned him down. Then he made another move, the sort of move that suggested turning him down again wasn't really an option. He came closer, he grabbed me – but I wasn't some helpless waif. At this point I'd had months of training, priming me on what to do in a situation like this. As soon as I realised I really was in *that sort* of situation, adrenaline flushed through my body. My training kicked in. Before I knew what had happened, Theodore Dieter was lying on the floor with a tuning fork through the jugular.

Then Gabby phoned. Not knowing what else to do, I answered it. Not knowing what else to say, I told her everything.

'Are you safe where you are?' she answered once I'd got it all out. Her tone was level, accent clipped as ever. A safe pair of hands. 'No one else is in the studio? No one's looking for either of you, as far as you know?'

Looking for me? 'No, I . . . there's no one else here. Just me and Mr Dieter.'

'Good,' she said. 'Stay where you are, Maisie. You did nothing wrong. I'm coming to get you. Everything will be OK.'

That charity single never came to anything, but something else did. It was after that that Gabby told me what she knew about corrupt, powerful men, and about the companies like Removals Inc., who largely operated at their beck and call. She showed me how the world really worked, and suggested what we might do to change it. One thing led to another, and Novum was born.

★

'You all right, Maisie?' Beth asks.

What had we been talking about? 'Yeah, fine,' I say, feeling my tiredness catch up with me. 'Sorry, I was away overnight for a work thing and I didn't get much sleep.'

As I talk, the icy chill leaves me. My emotions have been all over the place this morning, but under them all, still, is the afterglow of last night. Is this really what good sex can do to you? I've been missing out.

'Oh?' asks Michelle as if she can read my mind. 'Did something happen?'

I laugh but demur. 'No, nothing like that,' I lie, then regret it slightly. Maybe it would be safe to tell the girls about my encounter with Will – it's not *really* work related, after all, even if it happened on a mission – but not with the boyfriends here.

With my work life exhausted and my romantic life under wraps, we move on to lighter topics: TV shows, gigs, celebrity breakups. One mimosa turns into two. When we leave the café, the sun is high, and even though it's probably only 23°C despite being July already it feels like it's properly warm and dry for the first time in months.

'Should we pick up some cans and sit in the park?' Michelle suggests.

'Sounds lovely,' I agree.

And it is. We lay our unnecessary jackets on the slightly wet grass like picnic blankets and watch London come to life in the way it only does on the rare warm day of a disappointing summer. It feels like the whole world has come out onto Clissold Park: there's barbecues and reggae music, kids on roller skates and dropped ice cream, friends, couples, families, and more languages and accents than you can count.

It's so nice that I forget all about the question of who really killed Archie Henderson, and what next week is going to look like as we attempt to figure it out.

★

We leave as the sun is setting in a pink and orange haze above the terraced roofs. Michelle and Arman go on ahead, arm in arm; Liv and Sam left about an hour ago to feed their dog, so I drop back to talk to Beth alone.

'They're cute together,' she says.

'They are,' I say, looking ahead. Arman is laughing at one of Michelle's jokes, his smile almost as infectious as hers. I'd be lying if I said I didn't feel a twang in my chest: the part of me that wants what they have. That wishes my life could be that simple. 'You ever fancy something like that?' I ask Beth.

She smiles weakly. 'Ugh, I want to say yes, but then I just think, how would it work, you know? I mean, I was late getting here, I've been late to or missed the last three things we all did together. I don't think I could fit anyone else in at the moment.'

'Have you been dating at all?' It's crazy, I realise that I don't know the answer to that question. In all my efforts not to let anything that might point back to Novum slip out about my life, I've stopped knowing the details of hers.

'Just a couple here and there,' Beth sighs. 'Nothing to write home about. What about you, though? I sometimes wonder whether all your work trips are covering up for a scandalous love affair.'

'All work, I'm afraid,' I say, shooting her a curious look. She's joking, but there's a slight edge to her voice and I can't work out why.

We fall silent after that, parting ways at Stoke Newington Overground station – Beth and I heading to our flat in Mile End, Michelle and Arman back to her place in Walthamstow.

'Maisie, it was so, so lovely to meet you,' says Arman after we've hugged goodbye. 'And I was meaning to say – I love those earrings. They're so fun. Are they horses?'

8

I'm less relaxed on Monday morning about the possible presence of another hitman on the Henderson job.

It's crazy, isn't it, how distant your work problems feel when you're not in the work mindset? All through the rest of Saturday and Sunday, it was so easy to write off what happened in Arpingham as a Weekday Maisie problem that Weekend Maisie had nothing to do with. My night with Will had been a much-needed reminder of the importance of having fun, so all weekend that's exactly what I did. After we left the park on Saturday, Beth and I continued our slow marathon through all of Netflix's cheesiest romcoms with a film about an exceptionally tall teenage girl caught between feelings for an even taller Swedish exchange student and her short king best friend. It was pretty good, actually – despite only having 42 per cent on Rotten Tomatoes. On Sunday we went to IKEA to buy lamps. We took it slow, joking as we wandered through the eerie assortment of fake, impossibly on-theme children's bedrooms, and making elaborate plans of how we could redo the living room if we had infinite time and money and actually owned the place. We didn't even set foot in the lamp section until we'd been there for over an hour, and came home laden with a FORSÅ for Beth's bedroom workspace and a lovely big LAUTERS to make the living room a little cosier.

We kept busy, is what I'm saying, and by so doing we successfully staved off the Sunday Scaries for most of the day. But when they came, they came hard. After a simple dinner of microwaved leftovers, we locked ourselves in our rooms to face our fears about the coming week.

Now, as I slump towards Highgate, shoulder to shoulder with the rest of the city's commuters on their painful slog back to their desks, Weekend Maisie's joys feel utterly weightless beneath Weekday Maisie's all-too-tangible concerns.

Because seriously – what the fuck happened in Arpingham?

In all my years as a hitwoman, I've *never* had another agent show up on my case and get in the way like that. Of course, I've always known other hitmen exist: in the UK most of them work for, or more accurately *through* Removals Inc. It's sort of an Uber for hired killers, miles away from Novum's personalised, ethical approach. If someone put a high enough price on Henderson's head and posted it on Removals' infamous dark web message board, *someone* would take it. Henderson had a lot of enemies, so his ending up there isn't too surprising, but someone showing up at exactly the same place and time as I chose, and taking almost exactly the same approach? That's a little eerie.

That's even assuming it was another professional. It could, theoretically, have been a fluke – maybe the light just happened to fall off – or an elaborate suicide. Nothing is impossible, but neither of those options seem particularly likely.

And then there's the question of what we tell Pascal Robinson. For once, I'm glad Steph is here, so that there's absolutely no chance of that decision coming down to me.

★

It's 8.57 according to the LCD clock on the gate when I tap my way into Gabby's driveway. I don't even remember the last time I was here this early on a Monday morning, though to be fair, it's a first for Gabby, too: she usually has two meetings at this time in Central London, with the Hedgehog Project and Girls Code, but she told me by text first thing that she'd cancelled them both. No, there can be no distractions this morning: our discussion of what happened in Arpingham will begin at 9 a.m. *sharp*.

I run into Jason in the hallway.

'Morning,' he nods. 'Best not keep her waiting.'

'Sorry for ruining your weekend,' I say as we go up the stairs. 'I take it you found something, then?'

He pauses, looking a little nervous as he glances back at me over his shoulder. 'Not your fault,' he mumbles, 'but . . .' He nods in the direction of the kitchen – where I can hear Owen and Steph chatting over the rushing noise of the kettle – and puts a finger to his lips. I raise an eyebrow but go quiet. Is this just classic Jason neuroticism, or is there a reason we're keeping this on the downlow around our colleagues?

Jason pauses outside Gabby's office, and tentatively pushes open the door. Gabby's office is absolutely off limits to all of us unless she explicitly calls us in. Going in there always feels like being called to see the headteacher.

'As always, Maisie, your instincts were correct,' says Gabby after we've sat ourselves down in front of her desk. 'There was someone else on the Henderson job. It took us a while, didn't it, Jason, but we have conclusive evidence of someone setting up the trap that killed Archie Henderson.'

In contrast to the rest of the house, this room is austere. The only real decorations are a photo frame on the desk, which I've only ever seen the back of, and two French Poignard daggers with beautifully twisted handles hung on the wall opposite the window. Elegant, but dangerous. Gabby to a T.

'It wasn't *too* bad,' says Jason beside me, squirming in his seat.

Gabby looks at me. 'Jason is being modest. He did excellent work this weekend – as did you, Maisie. I don't want you to feel that just because you ran into unexpected circumstances you are somehow at fault. Given the situation, you handled yourself perfectly.'

'Thank you,' I say. 'So what happened? Do we know who it was?'

'Not yet,' Gabby says, pushing the screen of her computer sideways so that all three of us can see the blurry CCTV image of a man in a black hooded sweatshirt, facing away from the camera. According to the timestamp, the photo was taken at 12.32 on Saturday morning – at which time I would have been, well . . . otherwise engaged. There are some parts of what happened in Arpingham that Gabby and Jason do *not* need to know.

'We were hoping you could help with identification,' Gabby continues. 'Look through these photos. They don't reveal much, but if they remind you of anything you saw in Arpingham, anything at all, it could give Jason something to go off as he continues his search.'

She passes me the mouse and lets me flick back and forward between the images in the folder. Other than a vaguely masculine build under his baggy, shapeless clothing, it's hard to get a sense of – well, anything about the guy. Even the clothes themselves are about as anonymous an assassin outfit as you're likely to come across. The photos don't appear to show anything incriminating, until I reach one where just his leg is visible on the edge of the frame as he climbs the scaffolding up to the support housing the light array. The fact Jason even spotted it is testament to a *lot* of time spent trawling through the camera feed at the weekend. I can't help feeling a little responsible. If we're ever in a situation where I could buy him a drink, I decide I'll buy him a drink.

'He looks like a professional,' I say. 'The route he's taking through that tent isn't intuitive – he's plotted that out carefully to avoid sightlines and identifying angles. Judging by the timestamps, he set up his trap and got away in under five minutes. It's impressive work.'

'Quite,' Gabby agrees. 'His only mistake was in getting caught as he climbed the scaffolding. If it wasn't for that, we might not have suspected this man at all.'

'Except for the fact he was skulking around at night,' I offer, thinking aloud.

Jason audibly winces. 'Ah, sorry,' he says. 'I should've mentioned. The timestamps are all wrong. Whoever set up the system got everything off by twelve hours. Not something you notice in the afternoon, where it just looks like a twelve-hour clock, but yeah – this isn't half midnight, it's half past noon.'

Noon? I take another look through the images, feeling a strange and growing respect for the blurry figure they depict. Doing this work at noon is crazy. It's not that there's no advantage to working at that time: for one, if someone did catch you lurking they'd be less likely to suspect anything. But the risks, though! When anyone could have walked in, when you wouldn't have the cover of night to mask your retreat if you were spotted . . . Even if I hadn't had Jason overriding the cameras for me, I still would have gone in at night. Getting in and out while everyone is on their lunch break is risky as hell. Ballsy, even. And you know what? I respect it.

'I take it he didn't show on any of the cameras to or from the pavilion at around this time?' I ask.

Gabby looks to Jason, who shakes his head. 'No,' he explains. 'There were a couple of candidates with possibly similar clothes, but no one giving us any reason to really point a finger.' He pulls out his phone and flicks through a few pictures of men in black hoodies, many of them bald, most of them apparently members of the crew. 'Ring any bells?'

I shake my head. Nothing – except the realisation that the black hoodie our suspect was wearing looks awfully similar to the stage crew uniform, which will make him even harder to trace. 'No, sorry. Send me what you've got and I'll take a look later, but this could seriously be anyone.'

'That's understandable, Maisie,' says Gabby, with an air of finality, swivelling her monitor back towards her. 'And as I expected, to be honest. Thank you, Jason – you may leave. Please continue to look into this, and if you find anything else share it with me or Maisie in private, OK? Let's keep this one hush-hush.'

So Steph *won't* be being brought in? I wonder if Gabby has finally clocked on to her lax approach to security. Jason pushes his chair back with a clatter and quickly leaves the office.

Gabby watches him go, then checks something on her computer and types a few words. 'How have you been, Maisie?' she asks, in a softer, less professional tone. 'With everything that's been going on lately, we haven't had the chance to really talk. Everything going well? How's your home life?'

I pause before replying. Gabby asking about my home life is a bit like Beth asking me about work, though not quite as nerve-wracking. There isn't the same risk in Gabby knowing what I do with Beth as there is in Beth knowing what I do with Gabby, but I still like to keep those worlds separate.

'Yes, all good,' I reply. 'I went to IKEA yesterday. Bought some lamps.'

Gabby nods. 'That's good. Are you still living with . . . I'm sorry, you'll have to remind me . . . Bridget?'

'Beth,' I say. I've been living with Beth ever since she moved to London and I stopped living here, but Gabby's brain ruthlessly filters information on the basis of how useful it is for her to remember it. She will invariably know the names, occupations, and family situations of every person in attendance at a fundraising banquet, or the details of every person of interest on a mission, but when it comes to people like Beth, she's hopeless.

'Yeah, Beth's doing well,' I say, not sure if it's a lie. 'She's got a new job recently.'

Gabby beams. 'Oh, that's excellent news. Well, pass on my congratulations.'

'Will do,' I say, willing her not to ask what the job involves.

Gabby has hinted in the past that living with a flatmate might not be the most prudent course of action for someone in my position. Actually, she's more than hinted: she once said, 'I don't see why you feel the need to live in a flat-share like a student when we pay you more than enough to live on your own.' But some days it feels like Beth is the only thing keeping me sane. Regardless, I imagine Gabby would not be happy to know my flatmate is also, as of a few months ago, a talented researcher for hard-hitting current affairs documentaries.

'Maisie, about this Arpingham situation,' Gabby says instead, switching to work talk. Even though we're back to discussing murders, I can suddenly breathe a lot easier. 'It's hardly the biggest mess we've got ourselves out of, is it? Compared to when I had rescue you from Corsica along with the British Ambassador, or when that triad got wind of us up in Glasgow, this is almost nothing. With any luck, it was just a fluke: someone else happened to take out a hit on our target at the same time as Robinson did, they lucked into getting a competent assassin from whatever agency they used, and that assassin happened to use the same approach as you did, because why not? It's an obvious choice. Henderson wasn't exactly well loved, was he?'

She pauses, and I can hear a whistling bomb about to land, like in a Looney Tunes cartoon.

'But . . .' I prompt.

'But we do need to be careful,' she says with a tight smile. 'Right now, Novum is in a delicate position. We offer a boutique service, which means our clients can trust that their affairs will be handled with integrity. More and more potential customers are waking up to what we offer, choosing assassins like you, Maisie — with clear morals and the nerve to do what must be done — over unvetted, undiscerning contract killers, like those offered by the competition.

'No other company is doing this — we are flipping the industry on its head. But Novum is still a relatively small fish, and we are somewhat vulnerable to sharks. It is *possible* that this was a fluke, or that someone else is taking out contracts on members of this ILS conspiracy. But equally, it is possible that someone out there is intentionally trying to disrupt our work.'

'Someone from Removals?' I ask.

'They're the obvious suspect,' Gabby says, with a thoughtful glance out the window. 'You know, Maisie, Removals are an odd organisation. At a low level, they are a disparate association of contractors who simply carry out whatever jobs are offered to them as long as the price is right. I have . . . contacts, shall we say, who have access to the Removals job board, and one of them has informed me that every single member of the ILS C-suite and board of directors is currently listed as an acceptable target. Considering that payments for prospective jobs are held by Removals in escrow until the job is completed, that suggests ILS has some enemies with significant resources.'

I whistle. 'Guess that explains Pascal's paranoia. Any idea who is backing them?'

'The options are limitless. Another agrochemical company, most likely. They tend to be somewhat ruthless. Anyway, don't let that scattershot approach mislead you. Removals *do* have a centralised corporate division, too – one that is far more intentional in how it works to carve out Removals' space in the industry. For a while now, I have been concerned that this head office would one day deem Novum an unacceptable threat to their bottom line and start to apply pressure.'

I let that sink in. It's not that the idea is new: when Novum had first started, Gabby had mentioned in abstract the risk that established agencies might feel we were stepping on their toes and lash out. As time went on, we learned more about Removals in particular, coming across evidence of their work and how they operated through our clients' hearsay or while researching our targets. But I didn't know she had been worrying about it to this extent.

'So what should we do about it?'

Gabby smiles and leans back again. 'For now, we don't. At this time, we know nothing for sure. As such, we avoid letting this get back to Pascal – I see no point in worrying him until we know for sure what we're dealing with. ILS is an important client for us, and I don't want to risk that relationship. Plus, there's nothing in the contract to suggest we have to tell him.'

I nod. That makes things simpler.

'We'll keep this from Steph for now to avoid putting her in an awkward position, but I'll bring her in if I deem it necessary. Meanwhile, Maisie, you should be alert to the possibility of our hooded friend showing up again. If this happens, I want you to find out everything you can about who he is and why he's pursuing these targets, while still getting the job done to the standard our clients have come to expect. Pascal has already contacted Steph and me about another prospective assignment – let's use it to remind him that he made the correct decision in choosing Novum.'

I'm not convinced that this man showing up again really is as likely as Gabby makes it sound – one coincidence is hardly a pattern of behaviour. If he did, though? I'm not quite sure how I'd feel about that. On the one hand, it would be a nuisance. On the other . . . I haven't truly been challenged in my job for a while now. Given this guy is the sort of nutter who would scamper up a lighting rig and set up his trap to kill a guy in broad daylight, he could certainly make things more interesting.

'Steph has been sent the full details of the next mission,' Gabby concludes, 'so you and Jason can get them from her. Pascal thinks Saturday might be our best chance, so could you let me know what you think this afternoon?'

'Will do,' I say, picking up on the cue that we're done here.

'Thank you, Maisie,' Gabby says as I stand. 'I'm sure you'll be wonderful.'

I go to leave, but she calls after me before I reach the door. 'Oh, and Maisie – although we're keeping Steph and Owen out of this for now, I don't want you getting the impression that I trust them any less than I do you.'

'I don't—' I stutter, but it's a bit hollow.

Gabby smiles. 'I know you feel some ownership of Novum, given our history, and that's understandable. Positive, in fact. In many ways you *are* Novum. You always have been. But we are a team, now – all five of us. I don't want to see you getting territorial. OK?'

I nod. 'Good,' Gabby says. 'This mission ought to be a fun one – you're going sailing.'

9

'Elizabeth. Elizabeth! Eyes *inside* the boat, please, we have guests waiting, in case you hadn't noticed?'

I tear my eyes away from the porthole to come face to face with the formidable Leila Crawford, Bar Supervisor on the *Atlantis Kiss*, a medium-sized yacht in the possession of one Clint Bushell. Current location: leaving the Essex coast behind in search of somewhere less rainy. So far we have not succeeded. We *have* made it far enough out to leave behind the secure channels we use for voice communication during missions, though, which means I'm flying solo this time.

'Sorry, Leila,' I murmur, shuffling back to the bar. If she'd seen what I've just seen, she'd be looking out of the window too. I'm not sure what exactly caught my eye as I passed the porthole on my way to collect some more glasses, but when I looked out I saw a firmly built man, dressed head to toe in tight black scuba gear, emerge from beneath the waves and clamber onto a deserted lower side deck. He was raising his hands to the zip across his chest as if he was about to start stripping off.

'Do you know if any of the guests are into diving?' I ask, feigning nonchalance.

'What, like driving cars?'

'No, *diving*. Scuba diving.'

Leila rolls her eyes. 'What they're into, Elizabeth, is being served their drinks.'

I get back to work, brooding over how Gabby pitched the mission to me at the start of the week. It'll be fun, she said. You're going sailing! Well, so far sailing has meant a load of rich assholes apparently pissed off to discover that, shocker, the sea isn't any drier than the land. The weather isn't even *that* bad — it's just drizzle, even if it seems to be interminable — but it's bad enough to sour the mood. All the guests are huddled under a plastic awning on the back of the ugly white boat, drinking round after round of drinks from the open bar, loudly wondering why Clint Bushell made a last-minute decision to have his birthday party on a bloody yacht, of all things, instead of at his house like usual, given the horrendous summer we've been having.

That last part I could answer, actually, though so far no one has asked me it directly: they just ask each other in front of me, as if I'm not there. The *real* reason why Clint's birthday party is on his boat this year is that he has suddenly become a lot more security conscious after the man he was conspiring with to sell UK agricultural products as illegal weapons overseas was killed in a bizarre accident involving a light fixture, and he thought that having his birthday party on a boat instead of at his house would make it easier to ensure that such an accident didn't befall him, given that on a boat you can guarantee all your guests and staff are properly vetted and anyone who isn't supposed to be there ought to be dissuaded by all the water.

Unless a member of the bar staff unexpectedly needs someone to cover her shift, that is, leading to a few of the checks being forgotten about when wrangling in a replacement. Or, apparently, if one of your unwanted guests owns scuba gear and knows how to use it. I'm starting to think hosting any kind of party, boat-based or otherwise, might not have been the best course of action where staying alive was concerned.

'All right, all right, all right!' shouts the man in question, appearing out of nowhere in a bucket hat and tracksuit, beaming as he walks – a little unsteadily, I might add – behind the people queuing for the bar. 'How are we all doing? Not bothered by the weather, are we? Forecast says it should clear up any minute.'

Ha! For his sake it better – if not he might end up with a mutiny on his hands.

'Clint! My man!' shouts some guy at the front of the crush, sticking up a hand in a wave. I'd just heard him complaining to the bored-looking woman next to him about what an ordeal it was to be missing some golf competition on TV, but now you'd think he'd been waiting desperately to see him. 'Over here! Want me to get you anything?'

'It's Ronno!' yells Clint, face bursting into a smile and coming over. What exactly they say next I don't catch, because someone orders a gin and tonic and we keep the gin down the far side of the bar. Dammit! There are distinct advantages of sneaking aboard in the guise of bar staff, including easy access to the target's drinks (plan A is to spike Clint with a slow-acting poison as soon as he orders something I can guarantee is going only to him), but I underestimated how much actual work it would involve. This is turning out to be a real nuisance.

When I get back, Clint and Ronno have disappeared, their needs apparently met by one of my more diligent colleagues. Scanning the crowd to see where they went, I see something that almost makes me spill gin and tonic right down the woman who ordered its blouse.

There is a man. He's sitting at a table by himself, trying to act as if he was there all along. But he was not there all along. Believe me, I would have noticed if he was.

One thing about this man is that he's strangely wet-looking. Like he's just come out of the shower or, say, the sea — not just his sandy blond hair but his legs and forearms too. And the clothes he's wearing — a loud Hawaiian shirt and some tan shorts — appear to be made of exactly the sort of lightweight, quick-drying artificial fabric you would choose if you were picking clothes you thought might get wet and wanted them to dry quickly; for example, to wear under a wetsuit, in the sea, and you didn't want them to look too suspicious when you crawled onto dry land. But, despite this, they are wet. Not too wet, not so wet you would notice unless you were looking out for it, but wet nonetheless. There is a slight puddle on the floor beneath his plastic chair. Again, it's not so much that anyone who assumed he was there all along would think anything was amiss, especially since his trainers are somehow bone dry. But *I* noticed. Because I *know* he wasn't there all along.

He hasn't looked towards the bar since I spotted him, which is good, but he does keep glancing in the direction of, ah yes, Clint, red-faced and slumping slightly in his chair.

He's with Ronno, and a few faces I recognise from our intel including Clint's girlfriend Anka, all sitting around a raised table on the next tier of the deck, loudly sharing a bottle of Champagne.

Of course there are many reasons why a man at a party like this might look in the direction of the birthday boy. He could be a true friend who for some reason hasn't been included at the high table but is concerned about his apparently intensive drinking, or a sycophant waiting for the right moment to make some grand gesture of loyalty. Or he could be intending to catch Clint alone with a business proposition – as ILS Industries' finance director and chief book-cooker for Archie Henderson's little scheme, Clint has the sort of CV that would make all sorts of people want to do business with him.

There is no reason to *assume* that this man wants to kill Clint Bushell.

At least, there wouldn't be if he was just any man. But this isn't just any man. He just pulled himself out of the sea, for a start. From his build he certainly *could* be the man on Jason's CCTV photo, though I have no evidence of that yet. But that's not my biggest concern. My biggest concern is that I spent the night with this man in Arpingham.

'Excuse me, miss,' says a customer, looking unimpressed with what ought to have been a vodka Coke. 'There's no Coke in this. It's just vodka.'

I take a look at the tumbler I've just set out for him. It's filled to the brim, but it does look awfully clear for a vodka Coke. I grab a pint glass from the rack and pour the vodka from the tumbler into it, then top it up with a squiz of Coke to a ratio of about 1:1. 'We'll call it a double,' I say with a forced smile.

I keep my head down and get on with my annoying pretend job as I think about my next options. What did Gabby say? *Find out everything you can about who he is and why he's doing it, while still getting the mission done properly.* The subtext being, actually kill the target yourself this time. But finding out more about him aside, at this point I still can't prove that this man is who I think he is. I could be wrong and he wasn't the guy in the scuba suit, or maybe he's a legitimate guest with innocent reasons for going scuba diving alone in the middle of a party. The best way to prove this guy's a hitman would be to wait for him to make his move and catch him in the act – but at that point I'd have forfeited the opportunity to kill the target myself.

All of which is made more complicated by the fact that I've slept with him.

I glance around to check Leila isn't lurking somewhere, then intercept another colleague, Rachael, on her way back from the toilet. 'Leila said you have to take my station,' I tell her.

'And where are you going?' she asks.

I pick up a tray and load it up with a bottle of white wine and a few glasses so it looks like I'm doing something. 'To the top table,' I say. 'Special delivery.'

'You're forgetting the ice bucket,' Rachael says. She doesn't look happy about it, but she is at least taking my spot without argument.

I shoot her a withering stare. 'Rachael, you should know that Clint *hates* ice.'

But I'm not going to Clint's table – not yet, anyway. First, I want to make sure Will sees me and gauge his reaction. Because the big question is, if he really is the assassin of Arpingham, did he know who I was when he slept with me? I think of Gabby's suggestion that Removals could have sent an agent out with the specific intention of messing with Novum. Is it possible that our night of passion was all part of his plan? If so, there might be two men on this boat having unhappy accidents.

*

'Crystal?' asks the man who called himself Will as he sees me approach. The procession of emotions across his face is convincing enough: surprise and hesitancy, followed by a subtle flush of embarrassment. In other words, they're exactly the sort of emotions you'd show if you weren't expecting to run into someone you'd hooked up with at a different event when your mind was somewhere else. They're not necessarily the sort you'd show if you'd previously seduced that person for some ulterior motive related to the fact you are both assassins, but I can't rule it out. 'What are you doing here?'

'Will!' I shout, setting my tray on the table and leaning in close for a hug, which he awkwardly stands to accept. It makes me cringe a little to be acting like this – ignoring the complications of my job, if I really had just happened to run into him again, I'd want to play it much cooler. As it is, though, I want to provoke a reaction, which means I'm going to have to be a little more proactive, even if it means embarrassing myself in front of the best one-night stand I've had in my life.

'Oh, what a surprise, Will!' I continue, repeating his name loudly to see if he reacts awkwardly to being called it in public. 'Fancy seeing you here. I am *so* sorry for running out on you like that back in Arpingham. How have you been?'

'I'm good,' he says, sitting back down and relaxing slightly. He doesn't seem fazed by the name thing, which suggests it's either his real name, a pseudonym he's used more than once, or more likely, no one here knows his name to begin with. 'And don't worry about that. I was sad to see you go, but you've got to do what you've got to do, haven't you?' Then he notices my uniform. 'Are you working here?'

I shrug casually. 'Ugh, yeah. I'm still waiting for my socials to really start earning, you know, so I have to take a few things like this in the meantime.'

He gives me a quizzical look, but there's some affection there, too. 'I'm sure they'll get there soon,' he says sympathetically. 'Fancy a drink?'

'I'm on the clock,' I say apologetically. 'Should be taking this wine up to the big table.' I nod in the direction of Clint's group, again fishing for a reaction. This time there is one: a nervous flick of his eyes in Bushell's direction. This makes me more convinced that his other responses were authentic. Though, now I look myself, it could just be that Clint has got up on the table and is gesticulating wildly with the bottle of wine while his girlfriend Anka tugs at his trouser leg, apparently imploring him to get down before he hurts himself.

'Watch out for them,' Will says quietly. I can almost feel

my ears perk up. I want to play dumb and ask what there is to worry about, but before I can answer:

'Elizabeth!' Leila's voice booms across the deck. 'What on earth are you playing at now?' I spin around to see her marching directly towards me. Oh crap. I give one last glance towards Will before I'm escorted away, and even an Oscar-winning actor couldn't fake the genuine look of confusion on his face.

'Elizabeth?' he mouths.

I smile apologetically as I'm dragged back to my post, Leila haranguing me the whole time about how I'm the sloppiest employee she has ever had the displeasure of working with, and who provided my reference, anyway?

Before we can get back to the opposite side of the deck, there's a crash from the upper level. Clint Bushell has fallen off the table and is now lying in a crumpled heap on the floor.

★

From there a few things happen at the same time. Anka helps Clint up and leads him through a doorway towards the cabins, firmly refusing any assistance from the rich, drunken louts Clint seems to surround himself with. Everyone on the lower deck notices what has happened, which sets off a flurry of hopeful whisperings that we will soon be giving up on this whole yacht party nonsense and returning to drier land. As yet this remains unconfirmed, and the boat's course remains steadfastly seaward. Meanwhile, Leila gives me my final warning: one more fuckup and I can say goodbye to my chances of being hired again. I'm not really listening, and as warnings go, I've heard worse. I'm more concerned with the fact that Will – that's the name I'm sticking with even if I don't quite believe it – has taken advantage of the confusion to slip away, apparently unnoticed by anyone other than me. And I have a pretty solid hunch where he's off to.

'I'm getting seasick,' I tell Leila.

She stops polishing the glass she's holding to stare at me. 'What?'

'The boat is rocky. I'm getting seasick. I need to go to the toilet.'

She throws up her hands as if to say, *whatever, do whatever you want, I don't care anymore.* Which, as far as I'm concerned, is perfect.

There are three staircases between the lower open deck and the upper deck with Clint's high table (towards the stern) and the nicer cabins (towards the bow). The first staircase simply joins the open spaces together, allowing revellers to come and go between the two tiers. It is highly visible, congested, and altogether not suitable for a woman in my position. The other two staircases are further forward, and go straight from the lower deck to the corridor that leads to the cabins. There's one on each side of the ship, one almost behind the bar, the other not far from where Will was seated, but they join at the top, behind the door Clint and Anka just passed through.

I'm hoping they'll be quieter. After locking one of the toilet doors from the outside to give myself an alibi later, I'm glad to find that the staircase behind the bar is so quiet, in fact, that by the time I'm halfway up I can hear voices from the corridor above.

'Stay there, OK?' says a woman. From her accent I can be pretty sure this is Anka. 'You can go back to your friends in a few minutes, but you've had a bump to the head. I'll find Dr Michael to take a look at you. And no more alcohol! You've had enough already.'

Sensible woman. Though I have to say, I recognised Dr Michael from our files, down on the lower deck, and I'm not sure how easy it'll be convincing him to do his job given the state he was in.

Clint's reply is less sensible: 'But it's my birthday!'

'And if you want to see your next one, you'll do as I say,' Anka snaps, slamming the door to shut Clint in his cabin. Her heels clip-clop in my direction up the corridor, but as expected she passes the stairs to go on through the double doors.

As I wait for her to be *gone* gone, I quickly go over my priorities to make sure I've got them in the right order.

1. Clint Bushell needs to die. We have more than enough evidence of his involvement in Henderson's scheme that I'm certain his death would make the world a better place. Also, it's what Pascal wants, and Gabby would not be impressed if I messed up such an important contract.

2. My *hunch* is that Will was the killer at Arpingham and is here to kill Clint, but as yet it's only a hunch. I need to prove that, and then find out who sent him and why.

3. If possible, I should kill Clint before Will gets the
   chance. Maybe this is more my pride speaking than
   anything practical, but it rankles having some man
   swoop in and try to do my job for me.

But the best way to prove Will is a killer would be to
catch him in the act, meaning priorities 2 and 3 might end
up being mutually exclusive. If it comes to that, I decide, I'll
just have to swallow my pride.

There's movement on the opposite staircase. I creep up to
see who's coming into the corridor and get a flash of damp,
muscular calf and Will's trainers as he heads quickly towards
Clint's cabin. It's funny to think he was probably lurking in
the opposite staircase, waiting for Anka to leave, just like I
was.

I follow him up, staying quiet as I stick to the edge of the
stairway, and peek around the corner to see Will delicately
testing the doorhandle. It's locked. I lean back into hiding,
then slip just the very tip of my phone past the corner and
into the corridor to snap a quick creep shot, making full
use of my phone's zoom lens. When I check it, my heart
jumps. It has captured Will looking not at the door but
up the corridor, directly towards where I'm hiding. I half
expect to hear footsteps moving towards me, but instead,
half a second later, I hear the unmistakable scratching of a
lockpick – which isn't something I do when I feel like I'm
being watched, personally speaking.

I take another look at the photo. *Damn* he looks good.
The low angle brings out his physique without it looking
too forced, and the front of the boat through the glass

door behind him lends a sense of adventure to the scene. The funny thing is, if you saw the photo you wouldn't even think he was up to anything dodgy – he could make it his profile picture and no one would bat an eye. He's completely casual. That's exactly how you want to look when you're checking no one's watching you before you start picking a lock, but I'm impressed by how well he's pulling it off.

I fire the picture off to Gabby on our encrypted messaging service – to be picked up once I have signal again – while I wait for him to finish unlocking the door.

Saw this guy in Arpingham, too. Coincidence?

Then I hear him open and close the door to Clint's cabin and I slip the phone back in my pocket. Moving quietly, I speedwalk down the corridor and stop outside the closed door. There are sounds inside, but nothing anyone else would notice – just a muffled thump that could be almost anything.

I pause, thinking about my best approach. Not for the first time on a mission like this, I wish I was carrying a gun. The UK's restrictive gun laws are a mixed bag for a hitwoman: good for not getting shot, since even the toughest security guards aren't supposed to have them (though they occasionally do regardless), but bad for when you yourself want to shoot people. Of course, we *have* guns at Novum: Gabby's basement firing range boasts a selection that would make a Texan doomsday prepper jealous, from dainty little pistols you can slip in a handbag to belt-fed machine guns like something out of a Schwarzenegger movie, but we decided that attempting to sneak even a teeny tiny weapon onto Bushell's boat was too risky, given how paranoid he is and all the mandatory bag checks.

Will, however, will not have had that concern, coming up from beneath the waves with his waterproof bag. Best to assume he's armed, then.

More sounds from inside the room. A window opening. Something big being dragged. A splash, almost imperceptible – from outside the boat.

Ah. Clever. An erratic, drunk, paranoid target, out on the open water. Where else would you hide the body? Even if he eventually washes ashore, everyone would assume accident or suicide.

Again, though, it's a ballsy play. It would only take one person leaning out past the railing of the party decks to see where we're going, and the body falling from the top-deck window would be more than a little conspicuous. By the lack of uproar from that direction, though, I'd say he's gotten away with it. Impressive. Impressive, impressive, impressive.

I press myself against the wall behind the door for him to re-emerge. He does so in short order, glances both ways to check he hasn't been spotted, then closes the door – without properly checking behind it. I wait, breath still held, until he's started walking away, then take the tiniest, quietest peek into Clint's room to ensure I've not horribly misunderstood the situation and Will was just popping in for a quiet chat. But the window is still open, some of the dumbbells from the weight set seem to be missing and there's no sign of Clint. By my reckoning, there's only one place he could have gone.

I pad silently after Will. He's heading for the front of the boat, which makes sense: from near the bow he can loop

111

around to the side deck he first clambered onto, where he presumably stashed his scuba gear. He's got something under one arm – a laptop, no doubt snatched from Clint's room – and a telltale shadow under the bright polyester of his shirt confirms, as expected, a pistol tucked into the back waistband of his shorts.

We emerge onto the foredeck, which is mercifully empty – Clint apparently wanted to keep it as a private space for only his closest companions. Glancing up to make sure we can't be seen by whoever's at the helm, I rush Will from behind, in one swift movement grabbing the pistol from under his shirt and raising it to his chest.

He spins to face me, hands instinctively rising in surrender. He already looks shocked when he sees me, but he does a second double take when he realises who's accosting him. 'What? Crystal? What are you doing?'

'You know it's Elizabeth today,' I tell him with a smile. I step forward, pressing the end of the gun against his chest and manoeuvring him into the shade of an overhanging gantry. We're standing close, which means anyone who happened to see us would assume we were a couple who'd snuck away somewhere off limits for a bit of privacy. As long as they didn't glimpse the gun in my hand, at least. I take a punt. 'How's business at Removals?'

An unmistakable flash of recognition crosses his features, and I know I've pinned him correctly. Gabby was right – this man is a Removals agent through and through.

'Business is good,' he says, confirming it outright. I don't know whether to be excited about running into someone else in my line of work for the first time ever outside of

Novum, or disgusted. Killing people for money *without* a proper ethical framework is gross. In fact, it's the sort of thing that might find you winding up on the wrong side of a Novum contract.

'How about you?' he asks, unflappable under pressure. 'You're obviously trained, or I would have heard you. I know you're *not* with Removals, or you wouldn't be asking. And you can't be working for Clint, or you would have stopped me. So, from the sense of moral superiority you're radiating, I'd have to guess you're with Novum – the *ethical* hitman alternative.'

He sneers that last part, so loaded with venom that I can't help but grit my teeth. The fact he would go straight to Novum is suspicious. If nothing else, it proves Removals agents *do* know who we are, and his tone suggests he's harbouring a grievance. Was it just a lucky guess? Or did he already know who I'm working for?

My lack of response makes him laugh. 'Knew it,' he says. 'It's a good marketing strategy, I have to admit. You must get a lot of clients who'd feel too iffy about the whole contract killer thing to go with the usual options. You can delude them into thinking they don't need to feel bad about having someone killed.'

'It's not my fault some of us have principles,' I snap, digging the gun further into his chest.

He looks surprised, but by my words, not my actions. 'You actually believe it, don't you? All that ethical hitman stuff, only killing targets who deserve it. Well, I'm sure you can find a way to rationalise me into an acceptable target as easily as anyone. Shoot me, if you're going to.'

The itchy feeling in my trigger finger fades: he's called my bluff and he knows it. Yes, this guy is a hitman and in all likelihood he's killed innocent people – who knows how many. But I don't have any proof of that, and the only people I *know* that he's killed are people I was planning to kill myself, which doesn't exactly give me much of a moral high horse.

'Why are you doing this?' he asks, his tone level and gravelly. It reminds me of just how easily I fell into his bed, back in Arpingham. It's a conflicted feeling – what could have been a good, positive, innocent memory that has in retrospect become so much more confusing.

'Because I want to make something clear,' I say. 'Two things, actually. First, that you'll stay out of my way from here on in. If I run into you again, I won't hesitate to take you out. And second . . .' I press the gun into his chest so that he knows I'm really not joking with this one '. . . you better not have known who I was back in Arpingham.'

He moves his mouth to speak, but we're interrupted before he can say anything.

'Clint!?' Anka shouts from the corridor. 'Where did you go?'

Crap. Will and I spend another second with our eyes locked as the realisation of our situation sinks in. Then, simultaneously, we start running. For a few paces we're going the same way, then we reach the railing at the edge of the foredeck. He vaults over it and drops, landing with a roll onto the side deck where I saw him emerge from the ocean. Meanwhile, I climb it like a ladder, pushing off from the top rung without breaking my stride to leap along the side of the boat, arms outstretched, reaching for a handhold. My fingers connect with the edge of a window frame and I pull myself in, slamming against the hull so hard that it almost winds me. I glance down to see Will stepping into the wetsuit he's grabbed from behind a storage container, ready to return to the waves, but I don't have time to think about him now. I jump to the next window and pull myself inside – into the toilet I locked earlier.

Someone is banging on the door. 'Elizabeth!' Leila is shouting. 'Are you still in there? If you don't come out of there right now you are going to pray you never do – do you understand me?'

Still breathing heavily from my narrow escape, I push my hair back to stop my sweat from pooling in my eyes and tentatively open the door to find Leila standing there, arms crossed, not a drop of sympathy in her expression. 'Got it all out yet?' she asks.

'I think so,' I say uncertainly.

'Well, you better. I can't trust you on the bar, but you're not the only one who's been chucking up their lunch. Dustpan, brush, mop, bucket, I want this place gleaming – OK?'

Christ. Why does Will get to make a stylish escape in his scuba gear, while I have to spend the next however many hours until we return to shore cleaning up puke?

10

'Ooh, who's that?'

Shit. I lock my phone screen, and flip it over in my lap, but it's too late – Beth's already seen it. Now her expression is intense, like Maple waiting for me to throw her a ball, hyper-fixated with no chance of distraction. I get the sense Beth won't let go until I provide an explanation.

'It's just a picture,' I try, already knowing it'll be futile. 'It's no one.'

'It didn't look like no one,' she says, her sly smile widening. 'It looked to me like a very attractive man in a very bright shirt.'

Shit shit shit shit shit. All I was doing was taking one moment away from the film we're watching to check if Gabby had sent me anything else following on from yesterday's mission. I wasn't worried about Beth seeing the conversation – even though our messaging app is secure, we try to keep incriminating details out of it. But I had glimpsed the photo of Will (if that is his real name) looking chiselled and sun-kissed, hair still wet, the open sea visible behind him, and paused. It was right there above her reply and, OK, *maybe* it distracted me a little, and *maybe* I spent a little longer looking at his face and the visible sliver of lightly haired chest than was strictly necessary, but—

'I knew it!' Beth yells, making a sudden lunge to grab my phone. 'You had a look about you at Michelle's brunch last weekend: you kept zoning out, and you looked like you hadn't slept – no offence – but you were also weirdly glowing and I *knew* it. You're seeing someone, aren't you? Who is he?'

'I'm not seeing anyone,' I tell her, pulling my phone away. 'It's nobody.'

'You can't fool me that easily,' Beth says. 'Tell me, tell me, tell me!'

I can tell she's readying to make another lunge for my phone, having totally lost interest in the film we've been watching. This one is about an American father and daughter falling in love with attractive locals while they renovate an old villa in the Italian countryside.

'Did something happen on your work trip?' she guesses.

My traitor cheeks start to burn in response, prompting Beth's grin to spread even wider. 'It did, didn't it?' she asks, leaning back, apparently satisfied with her victory. 'Maisie Baxter, I can read you like a book.'

'OK, fine, yes, something happened,' I admit, putting my phone back into my lap. 'But it wasn't anything major. I just hooked up with a guy I met at the evening event. That's all.' I sigh involuntarily as a fraction of my secret life slips out past my lips. It feels good. Dangerously good. As risky as it is to tell Beth anything that even touches on my work life, now that I've started, the urge to share more is difficult to resist.

'And now you can't stop thinking about him?' she asks. 'Must have been a pretty good night.'

'It was,' I admit. If only it had stayed that way! I still don't know how relaxed, easy-going Will from the farm show had turned into condescending, combative Will on the yacht, but it's retroactively soured our night together, which I'm pissed about. Why can nothing ever be simple?

'Can I see the photo?'

That makes me pause. Would there really be so much harm in showing Beth what he looks like? I *want* to be able to let her in on things like this, desperately want it, but . . . Before I can decide, Beth launches a surprise attack. She grabs my phone, pulls away from me, and in one swift movement enters the passcode, which she doesn't know, shouldn't know — except she does, apparently, because it unlocks.

'What the hell, Beth?!' I exclaim. 'How long have you known that?'

She laughs and dodges me, pushing herself up onto the arm of the sofa. 'You are so much more predictable than you think you are. *Obviously* it would be Maple's birthday.'

'How do you remember that?' I groan. I never should have underestimated Beth's ability to remember details about her friends' lives. I make a play to wrench the phone back, but her relative elevation on the arm of the chair gives her too much advantage. Before I know it, Beth's in my camera roll.

'OK, Maisie,' she says appreciatively, zooming in on Will's face. 'I can see why you're still thinking about him!' Her brow furrows as she talks. 'Wait, is this a creep shot? Where are you, a boat? What the hell?'

'Yes, we're on a boat,' I admit flatly. 'It was a work thing. Can I have my phone back now?'

'The plot thickens,' Beth says, beaming as she pans over to his bicep. 'OK, you can have your phone back – *if* you promise to tell me everything.'

Everything? No, that would not be OK. Far from it. In fact, telling her even a fraction of everything would be really, really, *really* bad. I start to panic, and some of it must cross my face because Beth softens instantly.

'Oh Maisie, I'm sorry,' she says, handing my phone back to me without a fight. 'I shouldn't have done that.'

I want to downplay it, act casual, but for some reason I can't. Why not? On a mission, with people I don't really know, disguised as someone else, this would be easy. But with Beth . . .

I silently slip my phone into my pocket.

Beth pauses the film and turns to face me, crossing her legs on top of the couch.

'Look, I'm sorry for grabbing your phone,' she says. 'I just – I got so excited when I realised there was something new with you that I got carried away. We used to joke like that all the time, didn't we? Remember when we got drunk and you messaged Simon from my Facebook account that I was through with him? And how the next day I realised how right you were to do that for me and cooked you a big thank-you pie?'

I do remember. It was raspberry and apple and she'd burned the crust a little bit. It was delicious.

'It's OK,' I say quietly. 'Can we put the film back on?'

I'm aware my reaction is about as far from 'OK' as it's possible to get, but for some reason changing my attitude is like trying to turn a container ship at max velocity before it crashes into an iceberg – and believe me, those things are *hard* to turn.

'Maisie . . .' Beth sighs. Then she goes quiet, and I can see she's thinking about how to say something. She almost starts out with a few different versions before changing her mind and pulling it back. 'Don't you sometimes feel like for all the time we spend together, we don't really know what's going on in each other's lives? We see each other every day, we literally live together, but when was the last time we *really* talked?'

'We talk a lot.'

She pulls a face. 'Come on. We don't talk about anything real. I know work has been a lot for both of us, and I know I've been part of the problem, too. But a few years ago, if you met a guy you'd have told me straight away. It's OK if you don't want to anymore, but . . . sometimes I feel like I get so few chances to really see you, you know? You're always holding something back.'

I don't know how to respond to that.

'I don't understand what's changed,' Beth says. 'Is it me?'

My heart sinks. 'Of course it's not you.'

'Then what is it?'

'It's . . .'

However much I want to tell Beth everything, she doesn't understand what she's asking. It would be the end of our friendship, my career, and probably my life this side of prison. Also, given Beth's connections, I imagine the story would inevitably get made into some documentary that would launch her into the stratosphere while also letting everyone I've ever loved know that I'm an evil, scheming murderer. I can see it now: *I Lived With A Hitman: The Beth and Maisie Story.* Or maybe they'd emphasise the Gabby Hawthorne angle and go with *The* Springwatch *Kingpin: One National Treasure's Empire of Death.*

But Beth's right. I have been holding back. It's shoddy subterfuge, if nothing else, leaving holes like that which pique her curiosity and allow her to imagine whatever she wants to. I should have lied to her more, fabricated a whole other life to mask what I've really been doing. It's horrible, but it's the only way to be safe.

'Maisie?' she prompts.

'I'm sorry,' I say. 'Actually, I've been thinking a lot lately. It *was* just a hookup, but it made me think about what I've been missing, about how my life could be different. I've stagnated, I think, not necessarily with work but with everything else. I think I'm going to start dating again.'

Beth smiles, glad she's apparently getting somewhere. But her smile hurts, when I know how much more I have to lie to her.

'So,' she says. 'Will you tell me how you've been feeling?'

It's not exactly a question about what happened with 'the guy I met', but he seems like a good place to start. So I tell her everything. Or the safe version of everything, at least. I tell her how we met at a conference I was attending, and how we slept together thinking we'd never see each other again. Then I tell her how I *did* see him again, to my surprise, just one week later, at another work event – which, yes, took place on a yacht. I tell her how by that time, the tone had shifted – how it became clear he was working for a rival organisation and that he wasn't against playing dirty when it came to business. I don't tell her that he disappeared beneath the waves after killing a tech bro turned arms dealer.

'Do you think you'll see him again?' Beth asks once I've said my piece.

I laugh. 'At this point it seems like he'll keep showing up, so I don't know if I have a choice.'

'Do you *want* to see him again?'

Good question. 'I'm not sure. I think, on balance, yes – partly just because I have no idea what his deal is. Plus he ended up beating me to this . . . uh . . . sponsor, and I want the chance to get him back – professionally speaking. After that . . . Well, we'll see.'

'Does Gabby know?'

I wince, which gets a laugh from Beth. 'About his existence, yes. That we slept together, no. And let's hope it stays that way.'

'What's his name?'

And by this point I'm so used to telling most of the truth that it just comes out. 'Will.'

Oops.

I probably shouldn't have said that.

But then, if call-me-Will is half as good a hitman as he appears to be, the name is almost certainly fake. Besides, it's not as if Beth can do any internet stalking even if she wanted to, without so much as a fake last name to go on. It will be fine.

★

'Excellent work, Maisie,' says Gabby the next morning. We're back in her office – just me and her this time. 'That photo was everything we needed. Jason plugged it into a little facial and body recognition programme I've had him working on, and it seems to have worked a charm. We found this . . .'

She spins her monitor sideways again to reveal a picture of Will dressed in tight-fitting tactical gear with body-armour over his chest and a bandolier of utility pouches. He's standing on a shooting range holding a modified FAMAS assault rifle: that stubby gun with the weird-looking handle, commonly used by French gendarmes. On the wall behind him, emblazoned in blocky red letters, are the words REMOVALS INC.

'Pretty unambiguous,' I say.

'Indeed,' says Gabby. 'But it goes beyond that.'

'Oh?'

She steeples her fingers, a mirror image of the tomb I can see poking its peak over the hedge, out of Gabby's window. 'This man isn't just *any* Removals agent, Maisie. After we found this, I pulled some strings at MI5. Based on what my contact told me, this is none other than Agent Perseus – the only Removals agent with a hundred per cent success rate. If Removals' head office wanted to squash us, this is the man they would send.'

I take a deep breath as she clicks through some more photos. All are of Will – or I guess I should start thinking of him as Agent Perseus? In one he's driving a speedboat, aviator glasses gleaming with a reflected sunset, sniper rifle slung over his shoulder. In another, he's sitting at a poker table wearing the smirk of someone who wants everyone around them to think they're onto a winning hand – or bluffing. He looks different, in the photos, dangerous, even compared to how he came across on Clint's yacht. It's almost impossible to believe this is the same man who whirled me around to 'Cotton-Eye Joe' without a care in the world, and kissed me so tenderly.

I push the memory away. *Stay professional, Maisie.* 'What else do we know?' I ask. 'What's his standard MO? Any strengths or weaknesses?'

'Very proficient in firearms, evidently,' Gabby says, as the monitor shows a blurry drone video of a sniper taking up position on a flat-roofed building. There would be no way of knowing it was him, but the text overlay from Jason's software informs us that a 'gait analysis' it has performed shows a '97.5 per cent chance of positive identification'. In the video he pauses, pulls his rifle forward from its shoulder strap, fires a single bullet into the distance, and casually strolls away.

'That, we believe, was the killing of Adriano Costa,' Gabby says.

I whistle, impressed again despite myself. The murder of the mafioso was mainstream news, in part because the bullet that killed him passed through a wing of his luxury villa, smashing two windows along the way, then through a third window into another wing entirely, where it caught him in the bathtub.

'How? That looks more like central Naples than his villa in the suburbs.'

Gabby smiles. 'Correct. Costa's villa was about two kilometres due east.'

Wow. If true, that would put him just outside the top ten of the longest-range-ever confirmed kills with a sniper rifle, at least according to Wikipedia. Though as with many things, Wikipedia doesn't know the half of it.

Gabby continues: 'Through a combination of Jason's evidence and my own connections, I have pinpointed a number of cold cases or suspicious deaths that I believe to be his handiwork. Based on these, we can get some sense of his operating patterns.'

Gabby is still clicking through images: some in the grainy black and white of CCTV, others apparently taken on phone cameras.

'Oh, bloody hell,' I say. 'Where did Jason find all these?' Subtext: *if there are this many photos of Agent Perseus out there, how many are there of me?*

'Spooky, isn't it?' Gabby says, sensing my concern. 'But don't worry – you know Jason is an uncommon genius. These photos are not available online: most of them are from private cloud services or corporate intranets.'

'Well *that* has me resting easy,' I joke. 'Let's hope Removals never try to poach him.'

Gabby doesn't seem to find me funny. 'You are considerably more careful than this Agent Perseus character. Or at least you should be.'

I swallow, not liking the sound of where this is going.

'You said you recognised him from Arpingham. Where exactly did you see him?'

'Well . . .' I begin, picking my words carefully, like a soldier advancing through a minefield. 'I was performing some reconnaissance . . .'

Fuck this. I've managed seven years with Gabby Hawthorne as my manager without her knowing a single detail about my sex life – not that there was much to speak of – and I don't intend for that to change now. Just like Beth, Gabby can get the sanitised version.

'I was at an event called the Young Farmers' Night,' I continue. 'You know, to get a sense of the mood on the ground, familiarise myself with the environment. He was there. He was in the crowd and we chatted a bit. I'm *confident* he had no idea who I was.'

Gabby interlaces her steepled fingers and clasps her hands together. 'Are you sure?'

Am I? I run back through our interactions in my head. He seemed surprised to see Crystal again, even more so on hearing her get called Elizabeth. The fact he was careless enough to let me sneak up on him and steal his gun suggests he had no sense that another professional was operating on the boat. But he'd obviously heard of Novum – and seemed to have it in for us. Is it possible this is all a coincidence?

'You're very quiet, Maisie,' Gabby says. 'Is there anything you're not telling me?'

I have to give her something. 'Our interactions were . . . somewhat flirty, I admit.'

Gabby looks concerned – too concerned, given how little I actually said. 'Now that *is* worrying. Did you get the sense his behaviour was intended to catch you off guard?'

Did I? Well, if it was, it certainly worked. God, have I just been letting him fuck with me this whole time?

Gabby lays her palms flat on the table. 'It would be absolutely typical for a man in his position, Maisie, sent after an organisation like ours, to attempt to use sexual or romantic deceit as a weapon. If you encounter him again you absolutely must not fall for it. It would be a ploy, a way to get you to trust him. You must not allow him to sway you – at all costs.'

I swallow and nod. There's no point arguing with her now. 'Understood.'

'And Maisie – I doubt he'll let you hold him at gunpoint again as easily as he did this time, but if he does . . .'

'Take the shot,' I say.

She holds my gaze. 'Agents with Removals are not like us. They do what they are hired to, however they are hired to do it. They kill indiscriminately, using whatever methods come to hand, no matter how cruel. Expecting higher principles from a man like this is like asking the driver of the 94 bus why he believes it's important to pass Piccadilly Circus. It is his job – nothing more.'

I sit in silence, processing what she's just said. It hurts, because I wanted – still want – Will to be something more than this. Not that I've got much to compare it to, at least recently, but our night together had felt so genuine. Could he be manipulating me?

Gabby breaks the silence. 'Thank you, Maisie. That is all.'

★

It's Thursday lunchtime when Steph pulls Jason and me into a last-minute planning session around her laptop.

'Does he realise we're not on a retainer?' I complain when she explains that Pascal would like us to take out the next link in the conspiracy chain this coming Saturday. 'Can you remind him we need to actually accept the job before discussing dates and locations?'

Steph is unsympathetic. 'If you're not up for it I can give it to Owen.'

As if. Owen might not care who he's killing, but Gabby does. If I've already said no, there's no way she'd sign off. We have the same standards for taking on a job. But Gabby's concerned look when we discussed Agent Perseus, and her insistence that Pascal Robertson is a priority client, have me second-guessing myself.

'Don't be ridiculous,' I mutter. 'Of course I'll have a look.'

Steph purses her lips as she brings up a picture of a man with thinning white hair and dressed in tweed, probably in his late seventies. 'This is a big one. Pascal is sure that Edmund Gainsbury financed the initial distribution costs of the pesticide overseas and has been profiting off that investment ever since.'

'How come he didn't show up in our research?' Jason asks.

It's a good question, but Steph doesn't bat an eyelid. 'It looks like he was spooked by Cyril Hargreaves' death. He stepped down from the ILS board and hired a load of personal security the day after you killed him. Since then, Gainsbury's been practically a recluse out in his spooky Sussex manor. Saturday is our only option.'

'That suggests knowledge of the conspiracy, at least,' I admit.

'Right,' Steph agrees. 'As do the bank statements showing substantial deposits from one Clint Bushell, paid in incremental sums every two weeks for the last few months, right up until his death. Gainsbury has been making a pretty penny off his initial investment.'

'Can I . . .?' asks Jason.

'Already sent you them, babe,' she says with a smile. I knew Steph was taking on more of the client-centred stuff, but when did she become so competent? It's impressive – and a little intimidating.

'Maisie,' she says to me, 'I know this is short notice for you to make up your mind, but I really can't imagine you of all people having any moral objections. Gainsbury's name has been *known*, let's say, in certain whisper networks for some time. Nothing was ever officially proven – with men like that it rarely is, is it? – but Pascal's investigation has turned up extensive evidence of abuses, in some cases dating back decades.'

Steph shows me the files and the evidence makes me sick to my stomach. Arms trading aside, this is the sort of man I'd happily execute any day of the week. The sort of man Novum was founded to eradicate. A genuine monster.

'What's so special about Saturday?' I ask.

Steph smiles. 'It's his son's birthday party. But don't get sentimental – they're not close. Pascal thinks we can get you in as entertainment.'

11

'Never a dull day at work, eh?' says Jasmine: wisecracker, 'exotic dancer', and my colleague for the night.

Usually I'd roll my eyes at a statement like that, but even I can admit we've reached a new level of surreal. Because right now, Jasmine, Emerald and I are sat in a cardboard cake in bikinis, about to burst out in a party full of pervy rich guys, one of whom is receiving the cake as a birthday present from his even pervier dad. Who I have been hired to kill. Not that Jasmine knows that last part.

'Remember, girls,' she continues, growing serious as the trolley we're perched on starts to move, 'whatever happens in there, we stick together.' From what she told us as our taxi barrelled down winding country roads, Jasmine seems almost as clued up as me on Edmund Gainsbury's past behaviour – which does make me wonder why she'd agree to take a job at his country manor.

The trolley lurches forward, and I shoot a worried glance at Emerald, who's been looking a little queasy since the car ride. 'Oh no,' she whispers. I wince, picturing the wiggly route from the kitchen to the party room on the floorplan I'd spent yesterday studying.

The heat and the lack of space or light are bad enough but the combination of different motions is enough to send even my iron-clad stomach swinging. And Emerald . . .

'Not in here, hun,' says Jasmine soothingly. 'Hold it in. Think of something nice.'

'I can do it,' Emerald whispers, like an affirmation she doesn't really believe. 'It's under control. It's under control.'

Finally, mercifully, the trolley comes to a halt. From outside we hear the sound of treble-heavy pop music – Lady Gaga, maybe? – and a room full of men counting down from ten.

'Here we go,' says Jasmine as they reach five. 'You OK, Em?'

Emerald doesn't reply. I feel myself tense involuntarily as they count down to two, then they're at one, and with that the three of us are jumping up and out of the cake like meerkats emerging from a hole in the ground, blinking in the sudden daylight out at a crowd that . . . doesn't look quite as pleased to see us as you might've expected.

'Awwwwwww,' say the men in the room in unison as the music cuts out, leaving the three of us standing awkwardly in silence on a tabletop, glancing at each other. True to her name, Emerald is still a little green.

'OK, *very* funny,' says a man in quite nice glittery makeup. 'Whose big idea was this, then?'

I take a look around and quickly realise the issue. I don't want to stereotype, and I can't speak for everyone in the room, but the vibe I'm getting is that these men are not exactly the most interested in *female* strippers. This is probably the highest concentration of posh gay men I've ever seen in my life.

'I'm *terribly* sorry, girls,' says the man who I recognise from our intel as Steven Gainsbury, though he looks a little different wearing nothing but a leather jockstrap and a pink feather boa, face glittering under a tasteful array of sparkly makeup. He gestures towards his getup: 'My dear father thinks all this is just a fashion statement.'

'He thinks we're *artists*,' says the man on Steven's elbow. He's a little more dressed, with baggy black combat trousers and hefty boots, topped off with a fishnet vest. 'He's living in denial.'

'But you're here now, and the more the merrier!' says Steven. 'Any of you girls fancy a drink? Or a cardigan?'

'Don't mind if I do,' Jasmine says with a grin, stepping out of the cake and swiping a glass of champagne in one fluid movement. She raises it in a toast. 'Good on you, babe. Here's to not following in your dad's footsteps.'

Meanwhile, Emerald is swaying alarmingly. 'I need the bathroom,' she mutters to no one in particular, ripping through the cardboard icing as she makes a beeline for the door.

Jasmine and I exchange worried looks, and I take my chance, signing that I can follow after her. Jasmine nods, so I smile apologetically to our host. 'Sorry, she's a little motion sick. I'll go with her.'

'Poor dear,' says Steven Gainsbury, with a courteous wave. 'First door on the left.'

I stay a few minutes with Emerald as she retches over the toilet, then tell her I want to go check up on Jasmine.

She flaps a hand, sinking onto the bathroom floor. 'I'll be fine,' she says, 'Just need a minute.'

It looks like she'll be a while, which is good for me, since I have no actual intention of doing what I said. Instead, I pad across the hall and into what was marked on our intel as an unused bedroom. I'm a little worried as I open the door that it might have been claimed by one or more of Steven's guests, but it's empty – just an untouched bed and a chunky wardrobe, both made from the same expensive-looking wood as the doors and panelling.

I sit on the bed. 'Infiltration complete.'

'*Well, that was easier than expected.*' Jason's voice is loud through my usual earring-disguised speaker.

I chuckle uneasily. When we were planning this mission, my biggest worry was how to escape from a room full of leery men. As it turns out, I needn't have been concerned. Still, this doesn't bode well for the quality of our intelligence. With the short turnaround and everything else going on, we didn't have time to check through it as rigorously as we usually would, let alone spend much of it prepping. Apparently, one consequence of that is thinking that infiltrating a man's house via a group of unwanted female dancers for his gay son's birthday is a good idea. We're lucky Gainsbury's such an asshole that nobody on his team blinked twice.

I get up and check the wardrobe in case someone's left a set of clothing. A servant's uniform would be ideal, since it would let me blend in at least a little. Plus, I think with a shiver, there's the cold to worry about: the Gainsbury manor is old and draughty, and the heat in the party room seemed to be coming entirely from the revellers in various states of undress. No such luck – instead, I pull out a long, fluffy dressing gown, which I wrap around me.

Pressing my face against the cold, warped glass of the window, I peer out across the courtyard garden, double-checking the layout of the house against the map I've memorised. I pick out Gainsbury Senior's window in the opposite wing and mentally chart my intended route. I just need to get downstairs, then from a little door in the kitchen I can stick to the shadows of a hedge, a low wall, a fountain, and another hedge to get to a drainpipe that should take me exactly where I need to go. Easy.

The stairs aren't an issue, and the kitchen is mercifully empty — but just as I'm about to make my beeline into the night, someone grabs me from behind and pulls me back into the shadows of the porch.

'No you don't,' I hiss, jabbing an elbow backwards into something solid.

My blow should have winded an untrained man, but it hardly even elicits an *oof*. I twist around, already half-knowing who it is. His grip is firm but not too firm. It loosens almost immediately when I resist, and sure enough, I find myself face to face and chest to chest with sharp cheekbones, chiselled jaw, and bashful, smiling, enchanting, *familiar* eyes.

'Will,' I say matter-of-factly, as if this was as vaguely distasteful as bumping into an ex-fling on a night out. 'Or should I say Agent Perseus?'

'Good to see you again,' he replies, lips quirking — probably at the dressing gown I'm wearing, I realise in horror. In contrast, he's wearing black suit trousers and a bomber jacket with GAINSBURY MANOR SECURITY stitched on the chest. Once again I realise he's found a means of entry that would allow for carrying a gun, and doesn't mean hiding inside a cake.

He loosens his grip entirely. 'You know, after everything we've been through, it'd be nice to know your actual name. You know mine.'

'Do I, though?' I ask. I'm trying to give the impression of a cat nonchalantly walking away from a fall, which means not pushing away from him too quickly, despite the fact our bodies are pressed together in a way I'd usually be uncomfortable with. But he hasn't moved away, either. 'Unless you're telling me you're really called Agent Perseus.'

'Professionally speaking, I am,' he says. 'But we weren't exactly introduced in a professional capacity. So . . .'

'I don't think so,' I say, attempting to intimidate him by stepping in even further. I want him to feel my breath on his cheek when I speak again: 'We're not that close yet.'

'"Yet", is it? So you're telling me there's a chance?' I know he's joking from the way his eyes twinkle as he says it, but *fuck*! Even after all my confusion this past week, I can feel myself falling for his charms, just like in Arpingham. *Shut your ears, Jason*, I attempt to project telepathically, glad he's had the good sense to stay quiet. I need to salvage things, *fast*: remind him that just because we've slept together, that doesn't give him the upper hand.

'Yet or ever,' I snap, backing away slightly. 'We're professionals. But you're becoming predictable. I let you go back on Clint's yacht, but you remember my warning, don't you? I won't let you distract me again.'

'I'm trying to distract you, am I?' He laughs. 'And have I been successful?'

If he only knew the conversations I've had over the past few days . . . 'You've barely registered,' I lie. I need to focus, and that's clearly not going to happen when I'm around him. 'Now, if you'll excuse me . . .'

I take a step backwards into the courtyard. As I move away, an unexpected emotion, somewhere between awkwardness and fear, flashes across his face and he pulls me back into the shadows. I pretend to resist and spin 180 degrees, using the motion to disguise my slipping a small blade from under my hair. 'You better have a good reason for this,' I say, coming to a standstill with my back pressed against him, and the blade to his stomach. His body is radiating heat and I fight the urge to lean any further into it. Something animalistic is waking inside me – roused by the potent cocktail of his scent and the nearness of his body and, I have to admit it, the exciting sense of peril that surrounds him. I don't usually get turned on on missions – not consciously, at least – but no one can get this far into a career like mine without being at least a little excited by danger.

'Is saving your life a good enough reason?' he asks.

'What?'

He laughs. 'Don't you do recon at Novum? One more step and you would have woken up the whole village.' As he speaks, his breath tickles the side of my neck. It's distracting – and not unpleasant. Heat pools beneath my stomach. 'There,' he says, reaching past me to point into the courtyard, the bulk of him enveloping me. 'Don't you see them?'

I look where he's pointing. At first, I don't see what he could possibly mean. There's the gravel path that leads to the far wing, the windows I checked earlier, and, closest to where he's pointing, the low, angular hedgerow I was intending to hide behind. Then, I see a crosshatch of red lasers around the perimeter of the building, low enough to the ground that you couldn't crawl beneath them.

'Tripwires? That wasn't on our . . .' I blurt, stopping myself when I realise what I'm about to say.

'Intel,' he finishes for me. 'Yes, I've gathered.'

'*Fuck, sorry, Maisie, I don't know how we missed that,*' says Jason. '*I'm on it – bear with . . .*'

'There are a lot of things you're not aware of,' Will continues, oblivious to Jason babbling in my ear. 'The new security system is just the start. Maybe you should sit this one out.'

His words seem calculated to make me even more pissed off than I already am. 'You'd like that, wouldn't you?' I say, using the tip of my blade to remind him how little protection even rock-hard abs provide against stab wounds. 'Getting to run back to your boss and tell him you've scared off the pesky Novum upstarts?'

'Is that what you think this is?'

'What else am I supposed to think?'

'*Almost there, Maisie,*' says Jason in my ear. '*These amateurs have the entire alarm system connected to the Wi-Fi; it'll just be a few seconds now.*'

'I don't know – that you don't understand what you're doing here?' Will's easy façade is cracking now, his voice laced with frustration. 'That maybe there is more going on in this house that you aren't aware of. Tell Gabriella that you can't complete the mission due to unforeseen complications that take it beyond the remit of your contracted responsibilities. Go home.'

As he talks, I think back to Gabby's warnings: he'll almost certainly try to get my attention, cast doubt on my work. That he's *fiercely* loyal to Removals and will stop at nothing to take out the competition. But why does he still intrigue me?

'*Got it,*' Jason barks through my earpiece. '*Tripwires are disabled. Go-time, Maisie.*'

As I glance towards Gainsbury's wing to confirm that the laser grid has indeed vanished, Will pushes me away from him, face suddenly unreadable. He must have sensed that I was on the radio, I realise, but it's too late – I've already let the thought distract me enough for him to grab me by the wrist so hard that I drop the knife, and drag me roughly into a rack of coats. I think of Gabby saying that if I had him at gunpoint again, I should take the shot. It was knifepoint this time – but whether I wanted to kill him or not, I've missed my chance.

'Sorry about this,' he says, reaching inside his jacket to pull out a pair of handcuffs. Before he can do anything with them, I lower my shoulder and ram myself between his bottom few ribs with a force guaranteed to knock the wind out of anyone. He staggers backwards and I slip past him, dashing across the dark courtyard.

'Turn them back on,' I shout to Jason, as I shimmy up the drainpipe I spotted earlier, then kick in a first-floor window leading to the central staircase. 'I'm in.'

'*Security system reactivated,*' Jason confirms. Then: '*What the fuck was that was all that about?*'

'Removals have it in for us,' I say, taking the stairs three at a time. 'Ask Gabby.'

Jason's scoff suggests he picked up on more of the vibe between Will and me than I'd have liked him to, but there's no time to worry about that now. As I approach the landing on Gainsbury's floor, I hear the short, irregular snuffle of crying. I flatten myself against the wall and inch up the final few steps, making sure to keep my footfall as light as possible. Slowly, carefully, I peek down the corridor. There's a woman slumped against the wall less than a metre from me, legs splayed, the too-white light of her phone's torch casting dark, gothic shadows onto the ceiling.

'Jasmine?' I whisper. *What the hell?*

'What are you doing here?' she asks. Lit from beneath she looks like a kid telling a ghost story at a sleepover. 'You weren't supposed to leave the party.'

You're telling me, I want to say. But even beyond why, how the fuck did she get past all the security? Are you telling me I could have just come through the house without being noticed?

'I was looking for you,' I lie. 'We stick together, remember?' When her face crumples, I assume the worst. 'Is it Gainsbury?' I ask, kneeling down to check her over. 'Did he hurt you?'

'No – I just – I wanted to confront him.' Jasmine's sniffles have become heaving sobs. 'When I said I'd heard stories about him, they weren't just rumours . . . My friend . . . I told the security team he'd asked to see me, but I didn't – it wasn't . . .'

I stare at her. 'You didn't what?'

Maybe I'm more paranoid about this sort of stuff than your average person, but from what she's saying it sounds like Jasmine and I might have been heading for Edmund Gainsbury's bedroom for the same reason. I notice a kitchen knife on the floor beside her: its clean, unused blade.

'Oh, Jasmine,' I breathe, feeling anger and sympathy rising inside me. Because whatever Gainsbury did to Jasmine's friend, I know only too well how she's feeling.

'Don't go in there,' she whispers when she sees me glance down the corridor. There's still another corner before the bedroom, but she seems to know what I'm thinking. 'I wish I hadn't. Poor Steven—'

She stares at me in pure panic as she's cut off by the screech of an alarm. Will must not have been able to override Jason's tampering, though why he decided the best course of action would be to set it off himself I have no idea.

'*That alarm is bad news, Maisie,*' says Jason in my ear. '*I've looped the cameras so it should take a minute for security to figure out exactly where you are, but they'll know something's wrong.*'

'Stay there,' I yell at Jasmine above the din. 'I'll be right back.'

I grab Jasmine's knife, hide it under my dressing gown, and then I'm on my feet again. But before I can reach the door of Gainsbury's room, the glass window at the end of the corridor swings open and a man in the uniform of the security guards steps through – the rope of a grappling hook held in one hand, a sleek black pistol in the other, pointed right at me.

'Don't!' Will shouts, pacing towards me.

It's always a bit scary having a gun pulled on you, but I keep it together. 'Still obsessed with being first on the job, are you?' I say, hoping the distance is enough that Jasmine can't clearly hear me. 'What, do you only get paid if you bring back proof it was you?'

But the flirty, competitive spirit that marked our previous interactions has vanished. This time, Will is completely serious. 'I'm telling you, you don't understand what's going on here. I won't let you do it.'

'You won't let me?' I repeat. 'Wait, are you *protecting* him? God, you Removals agents are shameless. Is the money you get protecting a monster like Gainsbury really worth the stain it leaves on your conscience?'

Will scoffs. 'You really are a true believer, aren't you? How can you claim Novum's work is ethical when you're so happy to go around doing dirty work for Pascal Robertson?'

That almost makes me laugh. 'In case you hadn't figured it out yet, the last two times I met you, you *stole* my targets. These men are selling pesticides overseas to be used in horrific war crimes. They *deserve* to die.'

'Gainsbury is different,' Will says.

'Different!?' I snap in disbelief. 'How? Because he's also a rapist?'

I think of everything I've learned about Edmund Gainsbury during our rushed planning phase: the decades of hushed-up sexual assaults, the large amounts of money he'd received from Clint Bushell. Then there was what Jasmine suggested had happened to her friend . . .

Jasmine's words come back to me, their meaning finally

registering through the confusion. *Don't go in there. Poor Steven.* A calm comes over me.

'He's not a part of that plot,' Will continues, oblivious to what I've just figured out. 'He's been working against them. That's why it's vital he stay alive, at least until . . .' He trails off, perhaps reading my expression – my sudden lack of tension.

'Sorry,' I say. 'It's a bit late for that now.'

Already pale, Will's face turns white.

The alarm finally shuts off. At the same moment, there's a flurry of movement back down the corridor and two older men in uniforms identical to Will's round the corner. Jasmine is awkwardly trotting behind them, looking a little sheepish.

'All right, mate,' the first one says to Will. 'What've you found for us? Bit of excitement for your first week, eh!'

I'm curious how they're going to respond to Will's gun, but he slips it out of sight before they see it. 'All right, Baz,' he says, affecting a blokey, jocular tone at odds with anything I've heard him use before. 'You know, I'm not sure myself.' He turns to me, and I see just how thin his mask of nonchalance is. 'What *have* I found here?'

'I'm just a dancer from Steven's party,' I say, raising my voice an octave or so. If he can play innocent, so can I. 'I was looking for my friend. She came up here; I'm not sure why.'

The guard apparently called Baz tilts his head towards Jasmine. '*Her* we know about already. But *you* left her crying to come this way . . . And why's that?'

'I heard a noise. I thought someone was hurt.'

The other guard replies this time, apparently not wanting Baz to get all the glory. 'A noise? What kind of noise are we talking?'

'Good question,' affirms Baz.

'I – I'm not sure,' I stammer. 'I think it came from in there.' I point towards Gainsbury's doorway, which prompts Baz and Not-Baz to exchange apprehensive looks.

'Bit weird he hasn't come out, isn't it?' says Not-Baz. 'He usually hates it when there's any kind of commotion.'

The corridor is silent as his words settle – no commotion at all. But it's nothing compared to the silence that seems to emanate from Edmund Gainsbury's bedroom door.

Baz slowly goes to open it. I hang back, but even past his shoulder I can make out the figure sat in the desk chair, back to the rest of us, the room lights still on. At first it looks like he's just sitting there, like he's somehow managed to keep working through all the noise. But once you notice it, it's unmistakable. The slump of his shoulders. The way his neck is tilted. The brown glass bottle, unlabelled and unstoppered, on the desk beside a handwritten note. He's already dead.

Will steps past the body and reads the note aloud. 'Personal and professional, I'm sorry for it all. Dearest Steven, I hope you can forgive me, for this and my past failings. Where I am going, only Our Lord can say. I don't expect Him to save me, but I only hope that what I have done tonight represents one small step towards absolution.'

As he finishes the last line, his eyes raise to meet mine. *Do you believe me yet?* His expression seems to say.

'Bloody hell,' Baz offers. 'He spends all this money on us

and his new setup cos he's worried about folks killing him, and then he bleeding goes and does it himself.'

I glance at Jasmine, who seems to be in a daze. I find myself strangely relieved to be sure that it wasn't her doing, even if that's what she thought she wanted. Not everyone should know what it's like to kill somebody.

12

The police come and go. Jasmine and my proximity to Gainsbury at the time of his death earns us a few suspicious looks, but the officers seem satisfied that our stories corroborate their examination of the crime scene, so it's not too long before they move on to someone else. Jasmine performs admirably under pressure, and for once I don't have to worry about some detail I missed giving me away – this time, I genuinely didn't do it.

The whole time, I'm holding out for a moment where I can slip away and talk to Will in private. *Gainsbury is different*, he'd said. But if Gainsbury truly wasn't involved in the conspiracy, why did Pascal send us here? And why the urgency?

I don't like any of this. Given the rush we were in to accept the job, Gainsbury's history of sexual violence alone was enough to condemn him, and the regular payments from Clint Bushell into his account did nothing for his case. But those payments were the only evidence we'd been able to find of his involvement – and that evidence is feeling pretty shaky now.

I don't get a chance to speak to Will, though. We both

have our covers to maintain, and neither of us have a reason to talk in private that anyone else would understand. Instead, when the police are done with Jasmine and me, the two of us leave to find Emerald, who immediately sweet-talks one of Steven's guests into lending us his driver so we can get home. We're almost back to London when Gabby texts me. **Jason filled me in. Let's chat. OK to come in for 7 a.m. tomorrow?**

I typed a reply on instinct, before I even have time to register tomorrow is a Sunday. **No worries. See you then!**

★

'You'll have to come up, Maisie,' Gabby shouts down as I close her front door behind me. 'We don't have long, so sit with me while I get ready.'

It's 6.58 a.m. and sunlight is streaming through the back window of the kitchen at the far end of the hallway, causing the row of hanging cast-iron skillets above the cooker to gleam a dull gold. I pause for a second, wondering why that makes me feel strangely nostalgic. Something about the light. With all my late mornings, I probably haven't seen the sun at this angle since I was living here.

I pause outside the slightly ajar door to her bedroom. 'Are you decent?' I call through the crack.

When I enter, Gabby is sitting at a dressing table in a silk dressing gown, her face almost ghostlike from the thin layer of foundation she has just applied. She holds a brush in one hand and a cigarette in the other, its acrid smell filling the room.

'I didn't realise you smoked,' I say. But then I've never

been in her bedroom. It's always been off-limits – Gabby's inner sanctum.

'There are things we all try to keep hidden, even from those closest to us. I find it helps me clear my mind before starting the day.'

There are things we all try to keep hidden . . . Where is she going with this?

She stubs the cigarette out in a crystal ashtray. 'When we first learned Agent Perseus was involved, I asked about your interaction with him in Arpingham.'

My stomach sinks but I don't say anything.

'You told me that there had been some harmless flirting, didn't you?' she prompts.

'I did,' I say. Oh, God. Are we really doing this?

'I was curious when Jason mentioned Perseus was quite, shall we say, emotional when speaking to you last night. So curious that I personally looked through the CCTV images from the farm show, on the off chance that I might stumble across something Jason missed. And I have to say, it didn't take all too long to find images of the two of you walking out of the grounds together, hand in hand. Does that sound familiar?'

Well, there's not much point denying it now, is there?

'Gabby, I—'

Gabby holds up a hand to silence me. 'Maisie,' she says, 'you should know that by now I can read you like a book. I knew you were holding something back. Believe me, I've heard it all before and I won't hold it against you. But it's only if you're fully honest with me that we can start to move past it.'

This is the exact tone of voice that I always fear when I'm talking with Gabby. The 'not angry, just disappointed' tone. It has a way of worming inside me.

'Yes, we slept together,' I admit, mouth dry. 'I didn't think it was . . .'

'Relevant?' she suggests with a sigh. She applies her powder, lays the brush on the dresser, and turns to face me. 'Maisie. This is quite relevant indeed. The fact he had this sort of handle on you, if left unaccounted for, could have got you killed.'

I think of how I've been acting since I met Will. I've been less focused on the job. Sloppy. Reckless.

'I didn't know who he was at the time,' I say, justifying myself. 'And he didn't recognise me. He doesn't even know my name.'

Gabby laughs at that, a scorning, staccato *ha!* 'Names are meaningless, dear,' she says coldly. 'At least to people like him. He's a master manipulator. The fact he has made you feel like this – that you need to hide things from me – is his job, and I'm afraid he's rather good at it.'

Is that what's happened here? I think back to his insistence that there was more to the situation than I was aware of, his frustration when I didn't believe him. The only thing that I hid from Gabby was the fact that Will and I slept together; Gabby was the one pressuring me to take on a rushed job with shoddy intel.

'What do you make of his hatred of Pascal Robertson?' I hedge, trying to move the subject away from my sex life and back to what I came here to talk about.

'Predictable,' she scoffs. 'Pascal is worth millions to us – of course Perseus is trying to undermine our relationship with him. He knows that Novum holds our clients to the highest of standards; if he casts doubt on Pascal's motives and we stop working with him, he thinks he'll go scurrying over to Removals.'

But why? There are so many ways to destabilise Novum – including killing me, which he's had the opportunity to do – that we have to be missing something. Why is Gabby so sure that's what's happening here?

'What does Jason think?' I ask tentatively. 'How was he when you spoke to him last night?'

Gabby sighs now. 'He was rattled, to be honest with you, Maisie. The man keeps to himself, but he's still invested in Novum, in the work we're doing here. He feels you jeopardised the mission by holding back so much.'

Her implication hangs in the air. I've let them all down: not just Gabby, but also Jason, probably even Steph and Owen somehow. I've been swept up in this and now it's time to let it go.

But I can't help myself. 'Why go to the trouble of trying to save Gainsbury, though? Why change his MO all of a sudden, go from killing our targets to suddenly trying to save them? Gabby, why wouldn't he just kill me if he is really as ruthless as you say—'

Gabby's eyes flash. 'That is enough, Maisie. Everyone on the team is working with Pascal, yet you are the only one to have any problems. It's the same with Steph. I understand you're upset about some of the changes we've had recently, but you need to trust that I know what I'm doing.'

This is the closest we've ever come to fighting, and I

don't quite know where to go from here. Gabby must realise, because her face softens. She pulls open her dresser drawer and hands me a picture frame.

'I've never shown you this, have I?' she asks. The photo shows a small wedding party arranged in front of a stately home. Judging by the hairstyles, I'd guess it was taken in the late 1980s. It takes me a moment to realise the woman at the centre is Gabby. She's looking away from the camera, right at the beaming, balding young man her arm is linked with – her face the unmistakable expression of a woman in love. It's enough of a shock to pull me out of my thoughts.

'I never knew you were married,' I say.

'There are things I haven't told you,' she says wistfully, looking down at the photo with the same unreadable expression as ever. 'This man,' she says, pointing to the groom, 'was Duncan Hawthorne. At least, that's who he was to me. God, it really does feel like a lifetime ago, these days. Before the Wall fell.'

I catch her drift. 'He was a Russian agent.'

A bitter laugh. 'East German, actually. Which added to the sting a little, when I found out. A real Soviet would have been somehow more dignified. At least, that's how I felt at the time.'

'Why did he go after you?'

'For my father,' she says, indicating the older man standing beside her. He's in a suit, but the black eyepatch and upright bearing make him instantly recognisable as someone with combat experience. 'MI6, in case you can't tell. Daddy wanted me to follow him into the family business, though it wasn't right for me – I was never so "Queen and country" unless it was on my own terms. But as it happened, his business came to me. Daddy was livid when he found out what I'd done, of course. There were signs, and I should have noticed them, but when you're young and in love . . .'

'I'm not in love, Gabby.'

She looks at me. 'No, of course not. In a sense I'm grateful to Duncan for showing me how the world really worked. And Father forgave me, eventually, in his fashion. Though it took a lot of work to make amends.'

She gives me a significant look.

'Yes, you made a mistake,' she continues. 'A whole series of mistakes. But you are also going to learn from them, and more than that, you're going to set things right.'

Am I? I wouldn't even know where to start. But Gabby has none of my uncertainty.

'We are going to lay a trap,' Gabby says, definitively. 'And you, Maisie Baxter, will be the bait.'

I feel dazed, wrung out. Despite everything, I'm almost flattered by how certain she is that Will's sole purpose is to come after me. And it could be an opportunity to find out what he was trying to tell me at Gainsbury's.

'So,' asks Gabby. 'What do you think?'

'I'm in,' I say. Because what other options do I have?

★

'Maisie?' Beth calls from upstairs as she hears me come in. 'That you?'

Our flat makes up half of a London subdivided terrace house that seems to be 80 per cent stairway: we've got two bedrooms, a bathroom, and a combined living room and kitchen, all of which are on different levels. A narrow vertical slice of real estate, sandwiched between a chicken shop and a Ladbrokes.

'Yes?' I shout back as I start up the first flight of stairs. 'Who else would it be?'

Beth's sat at the living room table in her pyjamas, eyes bright and cheeks flushed. 'Everything OK?' I ask.

'Yes, great,' she replies. 'Woke up to an email from a source that has blown my story wide open. There's no way in hell Dom can shut it down now. I just have to make sure I'm prepared for the pitch meeting tomorrow . . .' she trails off as we lock eyes '. . . have you just got home?'

'I had a meeting with Gabby.'

'This early on a Sunday?' she says. 'Is everything OK?'

'Honestly? I don't even know anymore. But I can't talk about it right now.'

She looks at me for a moment, as if making a decision, and then gets up out of her seat. 'OK, this'll distract you then. Wanna see what I found?'

She flops down onto the sofa and hands me her phone, open on an Instagram post. I feel my heart flip and then fall into my stomach. It's Will.

He's dressed in a sharp black suit, with his arm around the shoulders of another man in an even sharper suit – sharp enough to be a groom. The way they're smiling with their arms casually draped around each other suggests theirs wasn't the sort of bond you could fake when infiltrating a wedding, or even spending a few weeks in deep cover, getting close to your target for a job. It's most likely a real photo – Will in his civilian guise, photographed alongside someone with whom he shares a genuine relationship. Except, and here's the real clincher, that man isn't just any man. The groom is none other than Sean Davies, the ILS employee Pascal Robertson claimed had been killed after raising concerns about discrepancies in their inventory.

'Oh no, did something happen with you two?' Beth is looking at me concerned. 'Shit, I didn't mean to upset you. I thought you'd want to see!'

'No, I do,' I mutter as I scroll through the comments, ignoring her apologies. There's a wave of tributes to Sean posted in the days following his death, and below those one from when the photo was first posted: *Omg Will Thomas!! Thought you'd disappeared off the face of the earth.* 'It's just—' I stutter, trying to cover my shock at realising that Will's been telling the truth about his name all along. 'It looks like his friend died.'

Beth's face is unreadable, but I don't pay much attention to what she says next. There's a ringing in my ear. Because if Jason was able to find every single picture of Agent Perseus in existence, from CCTV images to clips from private iClouds, how could a public Instagram post that Beth is able to find not be among the absolute first things to show up for him? It must have, right? But it wasn't included in the photos Gabby showed me. Whether that was because Jason hadn't passed it on to her, or she hadn't passed it on to me – someone at Novum is keeping secrets.

13

I smile to the men at my elbows and their companions as I take my seat at the table behind the Isobel Lautner place card towards the back of the Avalon Rooms dining hall. The action is made only a little more uncomfortable by the pistol taped under my dress. My tablemates nod politely but make no attempt to involve me in their conversations. This is as planned: Gabby and I decided that sitting me between an oil baron and a media executive, each of whom had just married their distinctly younger second and third (respectively) wives was a good way to avoid unwelcome chatter.

To be honest, tonight, I wouldn't mind the distraction. The week has slipped by in an uncomfortable blur since Gabby asked me to go undercover as a honey trap for a man I don't even want to kill. Every day I made my usual commute to North London, where Gabby and I worked closely together on our plan to murder Will Thomas at her charity ball. Neither of us have mentioned the fight we nearly had on Sunday morning, and Gabby has been acting as if nothing is wrong. We even went to Bond Street together to pick out some clothes. She made a show of acting astonished by how beautiful I was when I tried on the dress we'd eventually buy – how certain she was that the 'man in question' would fall irresistibly for my charms, giving me the chance to 'do what I needed to do'. A month ago I would have been flattered by the attention. Now it was all I could do to keep up the pretence that it still mattered.

I glance around the room as if looking for people I know to take stock of the situation. The theme for tonight is *A Midsummer Night's Dream*, and the 'enchanted forest' decor is ever-present without being overdone. Spotlights glimmer through layers of drapery like starlight through a forest canopy; every table has a flask of dark, gnarled branches as centrepiece; and even the knives and forks have twisted metal handles that evoke tangled briars.

Owen is sat at the large table closest to the stage, right at home between the owner of a gym franchise and a famous fitness influencer. He's in character as Geordie Byrne, a supposed ILS pesticide-racket conspirator upon whom Gabby has taken out a hit via the Removals job board. That's not the full extent of his involvement in the mission, though. Jason had a family emergency earlier in the week and hasn't returned since, and Gabby insisted I need backup. Apparently, the best replacement for a hacker in my earpiece is a bodybuilder with a gun: if anything goes sideways in my plan, he has authorisation to shoot to kill. Considering I need a private chat with Will, this could turn into an issue.

Gabby and Steph are chatting up a storm by the edge of the stage as they wait for the event to properly begin. I feel a slight twinge of jealousy, seeing them together like that. That used to be me at Gabby's side, let in on all the gossip she had on the other attendees. I hadn't objected when Steph started taking that place, confident that Gabby would always be there if I needed her. Now I'm not so sure.

All this week, I'd spent any moment I could get away from her trying to make sense of what Will had said to me, why he'd been so insistent that Gainsbury was different to the other jobs. Answering that seems like the first step towards figuring out this whole mess, but my research got me nowhere, and Jason was no help either. I'd been hoping I could at least probe him a little about the Instagram post, but even before he called out of work he'd spent the whole week avoiding me — eyes glued to his laptop with noise-cancelling headphones on.

Still, I might not know what's going on at Novum or ILS, or who I can trust, but I do know that Will's going to be here tonight. Somehow I can sense it. Call it hitwoman's intuition.

I distract myself by studying the waiters as they buzz between the tables, refilling carafes of water and taking drink orders. None of them are Will, but then there are countless other ways he could make his entrance. He could be a bartender; he could be working the cloakroom. He could be across the street with a sniper rifle. I hope he won't do that.

I've almost given up looking when movement at the doorway catches my eye. *And there he is.* He's in a white tux and bow tie with black leather shoes, the jacket accentuating his broad shoulders and tight hips, the trousers hanging *just so* around his well-defined legs. His outfit is not, in a sea of black tuxes, the sort of a thing a man would wear if he wanted to avoid being noticed. It's almost like he's calling our bluff. It is, I have to admit, incredibly hot.

I track him through the hall, weaving between chairs

and tables until he reaches an empty seat – directly opposite Owen. I could almost laugh.

They're staring each other down: Owen angrily – despite the fact he's supposed to be in character; Will with an ice-cold expression that I've never seen before, even when he was pointing that gun at me. I try to visualise the seating plan we drew up in the hopes of figuring out who he's impersonating, but it's all a blur. Out of habit, I half expect Jason to pipe up with an answer, but I'm not even wearing my radio earpiece. What is Will playing at?

Gabby ascends the stage to rapturous applause.

'Welcome, everyone, to my absolute favourite event of the year,' she begins. 'Why is tonight so great? Because tonight I get to spend time with the people who have done more than anyone else for the projects dearest to my heart.'

Despite everything, I relax as Gabby's voice fills the room. It's easy to forget, when you work with her every day, the Gabby Hawthorne that the rest of the world sees. Events like this remind me. She might not be saying all that much, but her voice and her stage presence are magnetic. Call it star power, call it an X factor – there's just something about Gabby that can't help but compel the ear and the eye.

I'm only now realising how dangerous that is.

'Do you know her well?' the oil baron's wife asks her husband beside me.

'Oh, *absolutely*. You know, when one of her charities fell on hard times, back in the early 2000s . . .'

I sneak a glance in their direction. *Could* Gabby know him? She made no particular reaction to seeing his name when we went over the seating arrangements, but to hear him tell it, their relationship was 'more than a business partnership, a genuine friendship'. Most likely he's just bloviating to impress his wife, but then . . .

There are things I haven't told you, she'd said, before revealing she was once married.

'She's a typical bleeding-heart type, mind,' the oil baron continues. 'She started out with everything in the world, but she squanders it all on silly projects like this – saving the hedgehogs and what have you. Back then, I told her that if she invested her money *sensibly* she could keep these things going a hell of a lot longer. Now I get the sense that she's started to come around to my way of thinking, but it could be too little too late . . .'

Now *that's* interesting. Gabby has been distracted lately, but I thought that was because of Will and ILS. If one of her charities has run into financial trouble, that would be an easy explanation. Looking at her on stage, you wouldn't guess it. But that's her job, isn't it?

Once Gabby is finished speaking dinner is served, but I can't taste it. During the speech, I could mask watching Will but now it's more difficult. I risk one glance only to find he's staring right back at me. Our eyes lock, and my stomach flips. How can his gaze feel so charged from such a distance? I break away, not wanting to get swept up like this in a public space. Sure enough, as I wrench my eyes off him Owen nods to me then returns to Will with his best killer stare – an attempt at macho intimidation that's entirely out of character for the ILS board-member persona he's supposed to be wearing. He's going to be trouble tonight – I can feel it.

'Are you all right over there?' says the media executive's

wife as our plates are cleared away. Her husband is nowhere to be seen and I realise with a start that she's talking to me. 'You know, I think it was quite unfair of whoever arranged the seating to sandwich you between these two old farts like that. Especially when there are such handsome younger men in attendance.'

She nods over at the far table, where Will and Owen now appear to be in deep conversation with their respective neighbours.

'I'm fine, thank you,' I say, with what should be an effortless smile. 'Really, it's no trouble at all.'

She smiles knowingly. 'I'm sure you'll get a chance to talk to him later.'

That's the plan, I think. I can only hope it's that simple.

Not long after, Gabby reappears onstage to invite us to the adjoining ballroom for tonight's entertainment. I jump to my feet, expecting to be one of the first through the door, but it looks like everyone else is itching to dance, Will included. I try to keep my eyes pinned on his bright white jacket but it's only a few moments before my view is obstructed, and by the time I'm in the ballroom I've lost him completely.

The ballroom is a breathtaking space to enter. It's vast, for a start, with its original Victorian hardwood floor and a painted vaulted ceiling that has only seen minor modernisation over the years. It's been decked out with twinkling candelabras and free-floating stained-glass windows hanging overhead, which cast swaying, multicoloured patterns of shadow and light onto the dancers below. There are benches and small tables around the edge of the room, leaving most of the space open. At the far end of the dance floor an octet mounted

159

on a diamond-shaped stage is tuning up and as couples join the floor in dribs and drabs, waiters flit around with trays of drinks and canapés.

The first two dances come and go. Then I feel a presence behind me.

'You got a plan yet?' Owen whispers in my ear. 'Believe me, I am *this* fucking close . . .'

I spin to face him. 'Excuse me, do I know you?' I ask loudly, drawing the attention of a few nearby guests.

Owen rolls his eyes and cracks his fingers. 'Do you *know* me?' he repeats, matching my volume. 'Yeah, good one. *All* I was saying was—'

I don't think he's stupid enough to blurt out everything now people are listening, but I *do* think he's stupid enough for whatever he's about to say to risk our mission regardless.

I cut him off. 'If you're asking for a dance then I'm afraid I must decline.'

'Perhaps I may . . .' comes another, more polite voice. I look around to see the media executive from before, looking a little sheepish. 'I'm sorry, Isobel, I couldn't help wondering if you were looking for a partner for the next number?'

'Why of course,' I say, allowing him to walk me towards the dance floor. Taking one look back, I'm glad to see Owen has slunk away. Honestly! I thought I knew what he was like, but I still can't believe how close he came to blowing my cover. I'll be raising this with Gabby the next time we have a meeting – assuming we ever have one, that is. Let's see how tonight goes, first.

'Actually, I was more concerned about the way that man was looking at you,' the media executive says quietly once

Owen is out of earshot. 'Quite a scary chap, isn't he? And you looked positively mortified. Of course, if you *do* fancy a turn . . .'

I consider his offer. My plan is to get close to Will, but maybe I'd have a better chance of seeing him from the centre of the floor, instead of lingering on the edge. My only concern is whether he and Owen are so impatient for a fight that they make a move before the song ends . . .

Then something catches my eye on the far side of the room. It's Will. Of course, it's Will. He's talking to a couple of other people from his table, a man with red hair and a woman in a silver dress. He turns towards me and our eyes lock for the second time tonight. I get the sense that he's going to break off his conversation and cut across the floor to me there and then, but the woman taps him on the arm and he gives me an apologetic smile – and walks with her out into the centre of the floor.

I smile at the media executive. 'Actually, that would be delightful,' I tell him. As I consent, I notice his young wife over his shoulder looking on with a strangely maternal air, like she's proud to see her little boy plucking up the courage to make friends.

I allow him to lead me into the centre of the room, getting a glimpse as we go of Will taking up his own position with the silver-dressed woman. Something twinges inside me. What is his game? Why is he being so provocative but not acting on anything? And why is he dancing with another woman's hand around his waist when I'm right here?

Not that it bothers me, of course.

The music starts, and with it the whole room starts

moving in ¾ time. Ballroom dancing is an essential part of any assassin's toolkit, but I'm glad to see my partner knows what he's doing too. While other couples are mistiming their steps or tripping over each other's feet, we box step, spin turn, and chassé with a practised ease. The whole time I'm keeping track of Will in my peripheral vision, trying not to be bothered by the way she looks at him.

What I *should* be doing is keeping track of Gabby, and especially Owen. If it weren't for them, I could take my time and pick the perfect moment to corner Will. Sadly, neither of them is in my eyeline. All I can do is hope that as long as it still looks like I'm trying to get close enough to Will to take him out, they'll leave me to it.

'You're rather good,' my partner tells me as I step in close after a spin. 'You know, dancing has always been a passion of mine, but so many women today just don't take it seriously. My wife, for example . . .'

We take a sudden lunging chassé, which interrupts his thought process.

'The first two dances were enough for her, then?' I ask.

'I'm afraid so. But no great harm, I'll find other partners. Couples who get funny about their significant others dancing with other people quite miss the point. It's a *social* dance, isn't it?'

Over his shoulder, I catch Will taking an unsubtle look in my direction – so unsubtle that I catch the woman in the silver dress, having seen where he's looking, rolling her eyes.

'That was splendid,' my partner tells me before he goes back to his wife. Will has left the dance floor too – and he's alone. This is my chance. I make my way towards him, but he sees me coming and meets me halfway. I stop and hold out a hand.

He takes it. 'I believe we have already been introduced,' he says. 'But I'm having a little trouble remembering your name. Crystal comes to mind, for some reason. Or was it Elizabeth?'

Up close, I realise that his jacket is just slightly off-white – a slightly warmer shade that sets off the cold blue of his eyes.

It's Isobel, tonight. That's what I should be saying, but for some reason I can't say it. I know both of his names and he still doesn't know mine – and for whatever reason, he was honest with me from the start. If I want him to tell me what's really going on, I'm going to have to start giving up a little in return.

'It's Maisie,' I tell him as we walk to the middle of the room. 'It's always been Maisie.'

'Maisie,' he says, solemnly, almost testing it out. 'It's good to see you.'

★

On the stage, the leader of the octet gets up to announce that they're going to mix things up for the next number. A couple of the instrumentalists have got up to swap their strings for small bandoneons.

'Can you tango?' I ask him.

He grins, and he's back to the man who got loose to 'Cotton-Eye Joe' in a marquee full of farmers. 'I've been known to. Can you?'

I don't answer. Something is tugging at my heartstrings. It wasn't real then either, but I desperately wish we were back to the uncomplicated, simple, no-strings-attached dance at the farm show.

We face each other, a pace or so apart, eye to eye, as the first strains of the music rise. It's haunting and uncertain to begin with, a stark contrast with the chirpy pomp of the waltz. I step towards him and raise my left arm over my head, allowing him to hold me by the small of my back. His touch is gentle, but when my left hand clasps his right, palm to palm, the contact sends a wave of goosebumps up my forearm.

The concertinas squeeze and we begin moving together, my body responding naturally to his signals as I let him lead me. He walks into me for four, his presence almost domineering as he pushes me backwards – and I draw him in. Then he softens. I walk towards him and he backs away, our legs moving together in perfect rhythm. Everything about it feels so in sync that I can't help but kick my leg around him when we stop, and by the time we follow it up with a promenade, I have no idea if it was my signal or his that led us there, or if the idea occurred to both of us simultaneously.

I catch sight of Gabby over his shoulder as we step sideways, slow-slow-quick-quick-slow, down the length of the hall. She's at the centre of the far, long edge of the room, cradling a glass of sherry. I flash her a professional smile – everything is under control. She nods back approvingly, then whispers something to Steph, who looks at me, too. Then Will and I turn, and they disappear from my eyeline.

Now that my colleagues aren't watching, the professional mask drops from my face without my willing it. Our hold becomes closer as we turn, so close that I can feel the creases of his shirt brush ever so slightly against the front of my dress.

I breathe deeply, my face almost buried in the crook of Will's neck, inhaling the scent of pressed linen and pine aftershave and just a hint of his sweat.

'Will,' I begin. 'What's going on?'

But the next bar comes and suddenly we're walking together in the direction of Owen, who glowers back at us from the far, shadowed end of the room like a gargoyle with a martini glass. I feel Will tense as he sees him. 'That man. Your colleague.'

'Who – Geordie Byrne?' I ask, trying the fake name Will should have seen from the Removals job listing and our leaked intelligence – along with Owen's picture.

'No. The man *claiming* to be Geordie Byrne.'

So Will knew it was a trap and came anyway. But was it for me, like Gabby seemed to think, or . . .

Our eyes meet and he pulls me into an audacious whisk that almost has us colliding with another couple.

'How do you know he's not Geordie?'

'Because I know he's a hitman,' Will says, voice low and dangerous.

'What makes you say that?' I ask, not sure if I'm ready for his answer.

'I know that he killed Sean Davies for Pascal Robertson.'

Distracted, I fail to read his cue and misstep into an ocho, our feet colliding.

'Your friend,' I breathe as I right myself.

I think about Steph's remark that if I wouldn't kill Gainsbury, she could ask Owen to do it – and how confident I was that if I turned down a job, Gabby would nix it altogether. But is that really how it works? Or were there jobs which I *thought* Novum had turned down for ethical reasons, that he was doing on the sly? What about jobs that didn't even come to me because Gabby knew what I'd think about them?

'Yes,' he says. 'That's why I'm doing this.'

'Then why are you dancing with me?' I whisper, my lips almost to his ear.

If Will has been after Owen all this time, then Gabby was right about him. Everything until now – how much of that was just him trying to use me to get to Owen? I look up at him. His face is deadly serious, glancing again in Owen's direction.

'Honestly?' Despite everything, his face softens. 'Because I can't keep away from you. Even when I really shouldn't. And, because, Maisie . . .' he trails off and his face becomes serious '. . . someone has been lying to you.'

'I know,' I say. 'It better not be you.'

Then without missing a beat, I cup his face in my hands and I kiss him.

14

'As beautiful as you are, it should be no trouble at all getting Agent Perseus alone for you to do what you need to do.'

Gabby's words echo in my mind as I kiss Will Thomas, long and hard, in the centre of the dance floor at the Avalon Rooms ballroom with what feels like half of the London Who's Who watching. It was the only option, I tell myself. There was nothing else I could do to make Gabby believe that I was still sticking to the plan, that Agent Perseus and I going off together in a minute or so is all part of a calculated plot to knife him in the back when I get the opportunity.

I have to admit, though, he's a really good kisser. So much so that long after we've kissed enough to give the illusion of my seducing him, I keep going, moving my hands from his face up into his hair, tugging on it gently. After all, I never thought I'd get another chance. Around us, the music comes to an end and I can hear the other couples laughing and talking as they return to their seats or get ready for the next number, but we don't stop.

Eventually, I pull away. Over his shoulder, I can see Gabby again on the far edge of the room, watching me with a characteristically unreadable expression. Steph stands smirking beside her. I wink at them and the edges of Gabby's lips turn up in a smile. Owen, worryingly, is nowhere to be seen.

The thought of him makes me sick: that Pascal – and Gabby – would use Sean's death as a way to curry sympathy and explain the extreme security measures, all the while knowing full well that Sean was dead because Owen had killed him. It would explain why Owen wasn't at that client meeting – there's no way you could rely on him to keep a poker face during a conversation like that.

I interlace my fingers through Will's and guide him to one of the many doorways along the edge of the room. With a distinctive swish on the thick carpet, the door swings open to reveal a thankfully empty stairway.

'Maybe Owen was acting on his own,' I suggest, once we're alone. 'Without Gabby. Without the backing of Novum.'

It sounds like I'm grasping at straws, because I am. In the early days, Gabby and I *were* Novum. I had full control over every kill Novum carried out, because I was the one doing them. It's not impossible I made some mistakes along the way, but we took the ethics of it all seriously. We talked long and hard about what it meant to take a life, what we were trying to achieve, the impact we wanted to have on the world. We saved women like Skyla Dawn from scumbag record producers. We took out evil drug lords and corrupt cops and all kinds of monsters from the upper levels of society who thought they could abuse their power with impunity. We took money for it, yes, but that money allowed us to continue our operations, to continue to do good.

Will gives me a look. 'It's possible,' he replies diplomatically. 'But I saw him, Maisie. The night before Sean was killed, I'd been round for dinner at his and my sister's flat — they were married, you know. Owen was lurking outside, looking like he was ready to fight someone. I remember thinking he seemed dangerous, but what are you going to do? You can't jump someone for looking at you funny. Sean and Sarah were going to bed; I thought he'd be gone by the time they went to work in the morning. I almost forgot about him until I saw his face on the Removals job page.'

There might be a world where Owen goes out and kills people without Gabby telling him to. But I know for an absolute fact there isn't a world where Gabby doesn't find out about it. And Sean was killed seven months ago.

I wonder if Owen recognised Will too — not just as Agent Perseus, but as someone connected to Sean. Or had he recognised him during prep, and told Gabby? Is that why she put him on this job? Or had he asked for the job, scared that his secret was going to come out?

'Let's get out of here,' I say. There's a side-room that Gabby and I had identified as one of the suitable places to take him out. It has a window which, with the help of a stepladder I made sure was in the room earlier, can connect to an adjoining rooftop — ideal for what was meant to be my speedy exit, but will now be for both of us.

Or at least, that's the plan, but as I explain this to Will I think I hear something. Will seems to as well.

'The Thornton Inn, Holborn, 611,' he whispers quickly.

Then he trips me.

What should have been a simple case of shifting my

footwork to maintain my balance turns into my legs literally disappearing from underneath me. There's an ugly, vertigo-inducing moment of weightlessness as my upper body hangs, unsupported, in the air – then, when I expect to fall hard onto the wooden shiny floor, he catches me by the shoulders and he pulls me into a surprisingly gentle headlock. Then, he puts his free hand in his jacket pocket, pulls out his gun, and points it at my temple.

'Any sudden moves and she's a goner,' he says to Owen, who has burst through the door at the bottom of the stairs. Owen's gun is raised, too, but I have to hope that Will using me as a human shield is enough of a reason not to try and shoot him. For a second, it looks like he doesn't give a shit. Then his brain must catch up and he stops moving, gun still trained on Will.

'OK,' says Owen. 'Let's not do anything drastic now.'

'You killed Sean Davies,' Will spits out. 'You did, didn't you?'

Owen's eyes flit to mine in a telltale sign that he's lying. 'Who?' he asks a split second later, playing dumb.

Does he know I can tell?

'Sean Davies,' Will repeats firmly. 'You were outside his house the night before he died.'

'I'm sorry, mate,' Owen says in a drawl so arrogant I'm surprised Will doesn't pull the trigger right here, right now. 'I don't know who you're talking about.'

Owen is only a couple of steps away now. I make eye contact with him, and exaggeratedly mouth the word *three*. I'm a little worried he won't get what I'm going for, but a flicker of recognition suggests he does.

'I told you,' Will repeats unconvincingly. 'No sudden moves.'

It's strangely affirming to realise Will's read of the situation aligns with my own. He's giving Owen time to 'rescue' me, and giving himself the chance to escape without blowing my pretence. It's a lot of trust to place in me, given almost all he knows about me is that I'm a hitwoman at the same company as the man who killed his friend. But I also don't understand *why* he's doing this. If he's here to kill Owen, why not take the chance to do it?

No time to worry about that now. I mouth *two* to Owen — then on *one* I slam my elbows back into Will's belly, hard enough to look convincing but not hard enough to wind him — he'll need his breath, where he's going. At the same moment Owen lunges for Will, intending to grapple him onto the floor, but Will dodges back, breaking his hold on me. Owen tries to grab him again, this time managing to snatch his pistol. Will lets go of it and turns, making a mad dash for the window. Meanwhile, I rip the gun out from under my dress and fire wildly after him, once, twice, three times, none of them going anywhere close.

Owen fumbles with Will's gun for a second before realising the safety is still on, but figures it out before Will can reach the mezzanine doorway. I make a show of going after him, continuing to fire but just-so-happening to block Owen's sightline. My fourth and fifth bullets go a fair way wide, chewing up the wood of the stair door and shattering one of its glass panes respectively, but I need to make it seem believable. My sixth shot, fired just as Will pushes through the doorway, goes so close to his head that it makes him blink as it whistles past his ear. OK, that one was maybe a *little* too close.

'After him!' I shout as I start dashing for the doorway Will's just vanished through, Owen right behind me. But, oh no, what was that, did I just trip? I guess even a highly trained hitwoman like me can have bad days because I stumble, kicking my leg out to the side as I stagger forwards. Owen reacts too late and falls up the stairs in a manner that would be comical if it didn't involve one of his shoes landing with such weight on the back of my calf.

'Get off me!' I shout as if it was all his fault, and keep running up the stairs.

By the time we make it to the mezzanine, Will is a blurred shape vanishing through a doorway on the far side of the balcony. We run after him, and I'm relieved to realise Will has made it to the room with the ladder on the roof exit. Before we can catch up, he's already dashing across the far roof, having used the ladder to bridge the three-metre gap over the alley. He sees us coming and fires a couple of warning shots behind him, smashing the windows and giving him time to pull the ladder away. Owen and I retaliate with a hail of bullets. I send my shots wide again, but this time there's nothing I can do about Owen. I hear a yelp of pain as one of the bullets connects, and for a second I think it's all over – but wherever it hit him, he's obviously still able to move. He crests the peak of the roof and disappears.

'Jesus Christ, how bad a shot are you?' Owen yells at me over the din of our ringing ears.

I round on him, jabbing my finger in the direction of his chest. 'Oh, you're one to talk, after you blew my cover,'

I retort. 'I *had* him. I would have had him, but you couldn't leave well enough alone, could you? You couldn't just trust me to do my fucking job, could you?'

I don't need to fake my anger. Every frustration that I have about Novum, everything that has been building this past week is burning behind my words. My rage is white hot, and he can feel it. He might be twice my weight and a cold-hearted psycho, but Owen shrinks back at the intensity of emotion I'm managing to project with every jab of my index finger in his direction.

'Come on, Maisie,' he attempts. 'I was protecting you.'

'Oh, give it a rest,' I snap back at him. 'All you did was spook him into a surprise attack.'

Actually, I've realised by now, I should be happy with Owen – he gave me the perfect opportunity to get Will out of here without looking too suspicious.

'Whatever,' I say finally, when he doesn't reply. 'It's done. You can explain it to Gabby. I'm going home.'

15

'Hello?' I call quietly as I push open the door of the hotel room Will told me to go to, unsure of what I should be expecting to find inside. Will was literally just shot, so he could be dead in a ditch somewhere, or someone else could have set a trap. Then there's still the slight chance – though I'm *pretty* sure by now he doesn't want to kill me – that this is all just some elaborate ploy to get me alone.

'You made it,' Will says as he hears me come in. I can't see him yet, though his voice sounds a little strained. 'I'm glad you're OK, but to be honest, I had hoped you'd have the decency to be fashionably late.'

Then I see him. Will Thomas is lying across the bed on his side, trousers strewn on the floor, holding a hotel towel firmly to the side of his left buttock, evidently to staunch the bleeding from the bullet Owen put in him.

'Bad day to wear a white suit,' I say, noticing how soaked the legs of his trousers are in blood. 'How did you even get in here?'

'Very carefully,' he replies. Well, at least getting shot hasn't affected his love of a bad joke. 'But look, do you mind sitting in the bathroom or something while I . . .?'

'While you what, wait for it to get better?' I take a seat on the end of the bed and look down at him. His back is firm and wide through the thin fabric of his shirt. 'This isn't a pulled muscle, Will. Have you even cleaned it out yet?'

He winces as my weight dips the mattress slightly. 'Not yet, no,' he admits. 'I'm trying to get the bleeding to stop.'

'Look,' I reason, 'I appreciate your gentlemanly stoicism or whatever this is, but if you don't take this seriously you could get an infection and wind up in hospital having to explain why you've got a gunshot wound.' I feel him tense up in preparation for a counterargument, so I cut him off before he can say anything. 'It's not like it's anything I haven't seen before. And you seem to be having trouble with getting a proper look at it, so can I . . .?'

Will relents. 'There's a medical kit inside my jacket,' he says, nodding to where he's thrown it on the back of an armchair. 'Be careful, though. Don't want to stain that beautiful dress of yours.'

I am careful, gingerly peeling the towel back. By the looks of things he's been extremely lucky – the bullet has torn along his skin rather than planting itself in his body. But the towel is alarmingly sodden and it's definitely a wound that wants to be taken care of.

'OK, you're going to need stitches,' I tell him, applying pressure with one hand while rummaging through the medical kit with the other.

He groans. 'I don't suppose you can help with that too?'

'Will Thomas, it's your lucky day.' I pull out the forceps and needle and hold them up to the light, then find the other bits I need. I don't tell him that I've never stitched up a real person before; only suture pads in Gabby's living room. 'Talk to me while I do it; it'll distract you.'

'OK, then, Maisie.' He slows down almost imperceptibly when he gets to my name, as if he's enjoying finally being able to say it. 'What do you want to know?'

'Anything. Everything. What sort of mess have we found ourselves in, do you think?'

'Right. Well, before we get into—' He breaks off with a hiss as I begin to flush the wound with saline solution. 'Before we get into all that, I want to make it crystal clear that I didn't know who you were at the Young Farmers' Night.'

'I should hope not,' I say, though I feel the tug of a smile. It feels good to finally have it confirmed. 'But you did know about Novum?' It's half to distract him as I finish cleaning out the graze, half to be absolutely sure he's telling the truth.

'Well – yes, I'd heard about Novum, but I didn't know any of you would be on the Archie Henderson case.' He flinches as I begin the first stitch. 'I took that job on a whim, really: I'd never bought the police investigation into Sean's death so when ILS C-suite started popping up on the Removals job board a couple of months ago it felt like too much of a coincidence to ignore. Same with Clint Bushell.'

'But not Gainsbury?' I must pull on a stitch a little too hard because Will lets out a yelp before answering.

'Gainsbury was . . . an odd one. After I got a hold of Bushell's laptop on that job, I found out he was terrified of Gainsbury – who seemed to be one of those characters who finds out about everything, one way or another. He was never actually involved in the nerve agent scheme, but he knew what they were up to, and Bushell was trying to keep his mouth shut by paying him. Bushell also didn't seem to know anything about Sean's death, so I got curious, started working as temporary security at Gainsbury's mansion a few weeks before he died, tried to snoop about a bit.'

He pauses, as if figuring out how best to word the next part of his story. I continue stitching in silence.

'You saw in Gainsbury's suicide note that he had this fixation on redemption. I think that was genuine. I never managed to access his laptop, but I heard snapshots of conversations and phone calls. It sounded like he was compiling some sort of document that, if it got out, would be incredibly harmful to ILS. Proof of the nerve agent conspiracy, but also something else — most likely whatever it was that Sean discovered. The man was old, he was ill, he'd spent his whole life being a monster. I guess this was his way of finally doing something right.'

'And that's why you didn't want me to kill him? Because after all of these years he'd had a change of heart?'

'No. Because for as long as Pascal stays hidden in his office, getting him will be almost impossible. I need a way in — or a way to flush him out. Whatever Gainsbury was putting together, there was a chance it could be used as a weapon. To get justice for Sean.'

I thought I'd managed to keep level-headed back at the Avalon Rooms when that particular bombshell was dropped. But now that we're sat in the quiet, and I no longer need to worry about Will dying, it's all catching up to me. Owen was the one to kill Sean. Pascal paid for it, and Gabby signed it off.

Could it really all just have been a lie? All those late nights with Gabby building the company from nothing, all the heartache as I convinced myself that it wasn't wrong to have blood on my hands, that Novum was the ethical choice, all the lies I told to my friends, all the times I kept things from them because they wouldn't understand – all of that was in service of what, a marketing strategy? A gimmick that Gabby managed to sell me on, just as she did our clients?

Or did Gabby really start out with good intentions, and something got lost along the way?

Because as much as Novum's killed some awful people for Pascal, it seems like we've killed some innocent ones too. I fight to keep my hands steady, but once I've tied the knot on my last stitch and downed tools, Will nudges me and pats the pillow next to him. 'It'll be OK. Come sit up here.'

I prop myself up with the standard-issue pillows and settle down beside him, sitting up while he stays facing me on his side.

'Seriously, how did you get in here?' I ask.

'Removals have a network of saferooms across all major cities,' he says. 'There are concealed entrances in and out of them to make sure you go unnoticed. It's how to make sure you're OK once you're in here – that's the problem.' He gestures at his wound, then looks at me, curious. 'Doesn't Novum have anything like that?'

'Novum . . .' I trail off. Novum *doesn't* have anything like this, but that's because Gabby is always there, clearing up after us. She's just one of those people who can take care of things; who finds a way of charming people into giving her exactly what she needs. What she wants. Why is it only now I'm realising she's been turning all that shine on me too?

After a minute or so, Will breaks the silence.

'I can't believe we met in a dance tent at a farm show.'

'The power of bad cider,' I agree solemnly, and he chuckles.

'Do you think some part of us knew we were the same, and that's why we sought each other out in a crowded tent?' he asks. 'Do you think we saw that in each other?'

I play with the duvet cover instead of meeting his eye. 'How many other hitmen do you know? Could you pick us out of a lineup?' I'm being facetious but I am curious – and maybe a little bit scared of his answer. Despite everything that's happened tonight, every horrific revelation, I'm starting to want whatever this thing is between the two of us to mean something beyond our work.

Will rubs his thumb in little circles on my ankle. 'You know, I meant what I said at the ball – that I can't keep away from you. It was *fun* going toe to toe with you on the yacht, and even at Gainsbury's, for a while. I'd forgotten what fun felt like for a bit there.'

Well, just go and crack my heart wide open, Will Thomas. I remember how he'd seemed almost surprised at himself when we started talking at the farm show, the way he'd thrown back his head and laughed as we careened about. How naive, how self-absorbed, to assume that I was the only one trying to escape something that night.

'That night was the most "myself" I've felt in a long time,' I say quietly, not quite knowing how to convey how much that means to me.

He pulls himself up towards me with a wince, resting up on his forearms so that his face is inches from mine.

'You made me feel like a complete person,' he says. 'I forgot that I had anything to hide.'

And that's exactly it. That's the feeling I've been wanting ever since I got a taste of it the last time we were in a hotel together – not too dissimilar from this one, now that I think about it. Will must be thinking the same because something shifts, and his earnest look turns heated.

'I haven't been able to stop thinking about that night,' he whispers. 'About you.'

Then he's leaning in slowly – so slowly – and when I don't move away he brushes his lips against mine. I deepen the kiss and sink down into the pillows, letting out a breathy sigh as he moves on to kissing my jaw, my neck.

'This dress,' he gasps, hands dancing across the silk when he comes up for air. 'It's insane.'

I allow a moment to imagine what Gabby would say if she knew this was happening, how her plan for me to dazzle him may have worked after all, just not quite how she intended. And then Will's hand slips up my dress and he's kissing my neck again, and all thoughts of Gabby are gone from my mind.

It gives me a thrill that he remembers where I like to be touched, that he must have replayed those few hours we spent together over and over since our night together. I arch up, showing him my appreciation, showing him that it feels good, showing him that I want more.

At one point he gets onto his knees to adjust his angle and I'm met with a face full of his white shirt. I unbutton it steadily and splay my hands across his chest, dragging them down to where the V-line disappears into his boxer.

'You're a tease,' he groans and I smirk. With no trousers on, I can tell exactly how much of a tease I'm being.

I take my time, indulging in the noises he makes, the way his breath stutters. Only when we're both wound up so tightly that we're on the edge, do I sink back down on the mattress, pulling him on top of me. He pushes down into me and I let everything go, let my body take over, until I'm wrenched back into reality by the sound of a phone ringing.

It takes a second to realise it's mine. My first instinct — driven by guilt, perhaps — is that it's Gabby, suspicious that I left Owen to explain the situation. I reach over to silence it, ready to text her to say I'm somewhere public and can't slip away, but the caller ID says Beth.

'I should get this,' I say and stand.

'*Maisie?*' Beth says, and just from that one word I can tell something's wrong.

'What is it?' I ask. 'Are you OK?'

'*I'm fine,*' she answers. Liar — she's speaking too fast and her voice is too pitchy for her to be remotely fine. '*It's just — something's happened through work and things have gotten a bit weird. You might want to . . .*'

I hear something crash in the background.

'Beth? What's happening?'

She speaks again and now she sounds genuinely terrified. '*Maisie, stay away from the house until I phone you back. It's not safe. Phone Michelle or Liv and stay with one of them and if you don't hear from me by tomorrow phone my work, OK?*'

Another crash. Beth screams. And the line goes dead.

'I have to go,' I tell Will. 'You going to be OK?'

'What happened?' he asks.

181

For a split second I think about how much to tell him. There's still so much I don't know about this guy; and even though I am one, a hitman isn't really someone you want around your friends. On the other hand, if the flat really is as dangerous as Beth claims, strength in numbers wouldn't hurt. Especially when I'm starting to get the sense he's the only person in the hitman world I can remotely trust.

'It's my flatmate,' I tell him. 'I don't know what's happening but she's in trouble. I need to go home.'

Will nods and pushes himself out of the bed, onto his feet. He winces but seems satisfied enough that the stitching will hold. 'I'll come with you.'

16

'Above the Ladbrokes,' I whisper to Will as we approach mine and Beth's flat. 'You see it?'

We're not exactly inconspicuous, I realise, as we walk down Mile End Road. I'd snatched some sweatpants to replace Will's bloody trousers from the hotel laundry room, along with a hoodie to make my ballgown a little less conspicuous (not to mention cold), leaving us both wearing a bizarre combination of formalwear and slacker attire. I got the taxi to drop us off at the petrol station down the street, with the idea that we could scope out the problem before heading in, but assuming whoever's been hassling Beth had the sense to post a lookout – and that they're still there, of course – they'd have to be complete idiots not to have seen us coming.

'The one with the light on?' asks Will. There's a bus stop across the street so we pause there as if we're waiting for something, only risking furtive glances in the direction of the flat.

'Yep,' I reply. 'That's Beth's bedroom and the living room. Lights on in both.'

A shadow moves on the wall of Beth's bedroom, which makes my stomach do a sickening lurch. The whole taxi back from Central London I was bombarding Beth with calls, texts, WhatsApps and Facebook messages in the hope that somehow the next app would be different and this time she'd be able to answer. She never did. Now someone's moving about in her room. Who are they? And more importantly – how *dare* they?

'Look away,' Will murmurs beside me. He's leaning against the bus shelter, looking through a wrought-iron fence and into the black depths of an unlit park, in an attempt to look casual, and I know he's right. I wrench my eyes away, catching a glimpse of a shape moving towards the window as I turn.

'It's harder when it's someone you know, isn't it?' he says, gently touching my arm.

I allow myself a deep breath in and out as I steel my nerves. I'm used to high-stress situations, but having people in my own home, with Beth in danger, makes everything feel way more real – like everything suddenly has stakes.

'You've still got that pistol, right?' I ask. I'd given him it before we left the hotel, a little worried about the fact that I was bringing an already injured man into a potentially very dangerous situation.

'Yes.'

'All right. Don't shoot it unless absolutely necessary. My neighbours are sick enough of us as it is.'

After making a show of checking our phones and the bus stop display in case we have an audience, we cut diagonally across the street as if we've given up on waiting and decided to try another way home. We stick close to the wall as we double back — counting on the fact that looking directly down feels unnatural, and is therefore a common blind spot for a poorly trained lookout. We reach the door without hearing anything to suggest the people inside have noticed us, and while it looked fine from a distance, I can see up close that the lock has been forced — and not subtly, either.

I push the door gently and it swings open without resistance. Then I step into the hallway, Will covering me from behind. Before he can close the door behind him, a male voice shouts from upstairs, Beth's room by the sound of it: 'Any luck?'

I startle, thinking for a second that he heard us come in. Does he think we're colleagues of his, having returned from doing something outside? Tracking Beth down after she successfully ran away? The hope that she might still be out there and safe is sweet — dangerously sweet. I can't let it distract me.

'Nothing yet,' replies another voice, directly above Will and me. He's in the living room, I realise. There's a strange man in *my* living room. 'God, they have so much *crap*! It's going to be a bitch sorting through all this. You sure the guys back at the office didn't get anything more specific out of her?'

'Women!' laughs the man in Beth's room. 'Apparently, all she said was she's made one copy, it's on a silver USB stick, and she's hidden it somewhere good.'

There's a crashing sound from above our heads, like an entire bookshelf being unceremoniously dumped on the floor. Or more than 'like' a bookshelf – by the sound of objects raining down, most likely it was the bookshelf to the left of the TV, stacked with accumulated knick-knacks – photos of me, Beth and our other friends, little objects we brought back from different holidays, and a big chunk of Beth's non-fiction book collection: politics, history, memoir, you name it, she's probably read it. Now all of that has been knocked over by some idiot who can't even ransack a flat properly.

'Careful, mate!' says the man in Beth's room, way up on the second floor. 'How are you gonna find what we need under all that rubbish?'

Both of them laugh at that, one low and gravelly, the other wheezy, and I want to kill them. I want to kill them like I've never wanted to kill anyone. I want to rip them limb from limb, make them watch as I stick my hand into their ribs and pull their hearts out like a human sacrifice.

Will must see me tense, because he lays a hand on my shoulder. 'Easy,' he whispers, so close I can feel his breath in my hair.

I force myself to relax. They've taken Beth, but she's alive. She's at their office, wherever it is. That's good news. And they're looking for something. That means they'll probably keep her alive until they find it, and it sounds like she has no intention of helping them. I feel a weird surge of pride at that. Smart, Beth. All she needs to do is keep her mouth shut until I can get to her. Not that she knows I'm coming.

'Holy shit,' says the other one, now in my room by the sound of it. 'Oi, come look at this. This is a bit weird, no? What kind of girls are we dealing with, anyway?'

'What do you mean?' laughs the one in the living room. He sounds louder – he must have opened the door. 'They got kinky sex toys or something?'

'Nah, mate, weirder than that,' says the first man. I grit my teeth. I guess he's found the secret box I keep under my bed, full of bits and pieces from missions that I should've taken back to Gabby's but never got around to. Which could be a problem, considering some of what's in there. 'Fucking hell,' he goes on. 'As if this job couldn't get any stranger.'

I run through our limited options as I hear the man in the living room make for my bedroom, mentally ordering them from 'death-wish' to 'dangerous-but-doable'. We could probably get the jump on one of them, but even then we'd only get one shot before the other heard what was going on. A two-on-two brawl could get unpredictable fast, even if they have no other friends in here who've been playing the strong, silent type, and that none of them have *real* weapons and know how to use them.

'Hide before the landing,' I hiss to Will and start climbing the stairs, making no effort to muffle my footsteps. 'Hello?' I call in a faux-normal voice when I'm halfway up. 'Beth, are you in?'

The movement upstairs stills, replaced by hurried whispers – presumably deciding how to respond to my clueless flatmate routine. I signal Will to wait, then loudly open the door to the kitchen and pass inside. 'Beth?' I call again, voice quavering. 'What happened? The door was unlocked. Is everything OK?'

My plan is that they'll hear I've gone into the kitchen and think they can cut off my exit from the first-floor landing, not realising that Will is waiting to ambush them. If I'm *really* lucky they'll underestimate my fighting ability and come down one at a time. In that case I'm confident I can handle at least the first one myself, which would allow Will to get the jump on the second one, as long as he trusts me enough to stay hidden. Depending on what they've uncovered in my box of goodies, that ship might have sailed already.

Footsteps on the stairs again – but only one set. Jackpot. Let's see how this goes.

I press myself against the wall behind the kitchen door and wait as he comes down the stairs. 'Don't panic, missy,' he coos in my direction. From his voice, it's the one who was in the living room – the one who trashed our lovely bookshelf. 'Wouldn't want to make a scene, now, would we?'

I stand behind the door and watch him enter the room, feeling a sense of satisfaction that Will hasn't blown his shot. He's *tall*, as it turns out – practically a giant – which is a problem, since I'd been hoping I could get him in a sleeper hold. No chance of that now. Instead I let him enter, whip a rolling pin from the rack, and clock him on the side of his head – hard. My plan is to follow it up by using the hunk of wood to pin him across the throat, but instead of staggering forward like I'd hoped, he hardly reacts. 'Wuh?' he asks, lumbering around to face me.

I give him another whack across the face, then a hard kick to the gut. That takes him down, dragging the wicker and wireframe drawers we use to store preserves and spices with him. A few jars smash as they fall to create a sticky mess on the floor, stinking of cumin and studded with broken glass. I step over it to kick the intruder one last time in the head. He won't be getting up soon.

I exchange a nod with Will, still lurking in the shadows at the top of the staircase. There's no time to chat, though – our friend upstairs is already moving, crashing down the stairs like a stampede of elephants. 'Ed?' he shouts, rushing into the kitchen. 'You all right down there?'

He quickly realises Ed is not all right down here. He takes an uncertain look at me standing over Ed's spreadeagled body, still wielding the rolling pin by one end like a policeman's beat-stick. That's when I notice he's holding a pair of my nunchuks. He brandishes them as he steps into the room.

'Know how to use them, do you?' I ask, smirking.

He takes a swing at me – which makes me feel distinctly less smug, because apparently he *does* know how to use them. The first thing you learn when training with nunchuks is how to avoid hurting yourself with them, and while his form hasn't advanced far beyond that, he's at least mastered the essentials. Holding one stick with both hands, he brings the loose end down in a powerful overhead arc that would have connected if I hadn't reacted just quickly enough to step aside. Instead, it cracks into one of our countertops so hard that splinters go flying, leaving an ugly gouge that's sure to send our landlord apoplectic. I try to return the favour with a strike of my own, but he reels his weapon back in, blocking quickly enough that my rolling pin gets tangled in the chain. He yanks it towards him and I stagger forward, losing my footing and opening myself up for a retaliatory strike.

Which could become a problem, except at exactly that

moment Will appears behind him and gets him in a sleeper hold of his own. He struggles for a couple of seconds, then joins his friend on the floor.

'Sorry for the delay,' Will says, dusting himself off.

'Who are these people?' I ask, stretching my arms to stop them cramping after my exertion with the rolling pin. 'They don't strike me as professionals, but he knew how to swing that around, at least.'

'Maybe this one's been taking karate classes in his spare time,' says Will as he crouches to start rifling through the downed man's pockets. 'But what could they be after? Do you know anyone who would hurt your friend? Anyone at all?'

It strikes me then how impressive Will's composure is, given the situation. At the ball he came face to face with the man who killed his best friend, but put aside the revenge he'd been desperately seeking to make sure I knew I was being lied to. And now, instead of crawling home to be alone, or risking everything to get Owen out from under Gabby's nose, he's helping me save my friend – a woman with no connection to him or his mission – all to stop the same tragedy from happening to me.

'It must be something to do with her work,' I say. 'She's a journalist. She's been working on a big story lately with a potential for legal trouble – it sounds like she might have found something she shouldn't have.'

Giving up on the first unconscious man, Will starts on the pockets of the one I took out. 'Ha,' he says, pulling out a white plastic card. 'Not *that* well trained, then. At least this one wasn't.'

It's an employee ID card. On it is the man's name, photo, date of birth, and the uncomfortably familiar logo of the company he works for.

ILS Industries.

17

It doesn't take long to find what the ILS goons were looking for. All I had to do was think, *where would Beth hide something if she really didn't want anyone to find it?* and it comes to me. Of course: it's in the memory hole.

'What's a memory hole?' Will asks in response to my thinking aloud.

'It's under the fridge,' I say, gesturing for him to pull it out from the wall. He struggles at first, and I feel a bit bad remembering the guy has a literal gunshot wound, but eventually he manages to get the fridge out far enough that I can reach my arm into the hole, and I forget all about him. The USB is sitting like a shiny trinket in a magpie's nest, on top of the locket Beth got from Simon and a picture of the two of us, Beth laughing elegantly while I look close to throwing up. From the outside, there's nothing special about the USB. It's one Beth has had for a while – one I'm pretty sure I've borrowed, once or twice. But whatever's on here, apparently, is enough to get her kidnapped.

'All right, then,' I say, slipping the USB and the Polaroid into my pocket. 'We should keep moving.'

We take a minute so I can change into something more

practical, then we fill a backpack with anything else that might be important – Beth and my laptops, which our would-be burglars have helpfully piled together in the middle of the hallway alongside anything else that looks like it might contain digital memory, mostly old phones and e-readers, plus appropriate chargers, another change of clothes, and my toothbrush. Then we wake our two friends from the kitchen, gag them, and tie them to the heaviest chairs we own.

The sensible course of action, naturally, would be to kill them and dump them in the canal – preferably after interrogating them for everything they know. But I don't roll that way. Being a peripheral accessory to a single kidnapping and attempted burglary is not enough to warrant summary execution, even when it was my flat being burgled and my friend being kidnapped. Given everything I've been learning recently about the consequences of my actions, sticking to my moral code feels more important than ever. If I don't have that, I have nothing.

It's unfortunate – but unavoidable – that when they're found within a couple of hours, they'll describe being attacked by a woman in a hoodie and a ballgown, who wasn't working alone. If Will is right about Novum's involvement in the conspiracy, we may as well assume that that'll eventually get back to Gabby. And if my pathetic excuse for running off at one of the most crucial moments in my career didn't burn every bridge that connected me and her already, then the knowledge I've been palling around with the competition and beating up ILS toughs surely will.

Still, I'm relieved to find Will on board with my approach. I guess that's one more piece of evidence that he really is one of the good ones, at least by the standards of a professional murderer.

The whole time I'm running through options of who sent the men here, because as far as I know, everyone in the ILS conspiracy is dead. Accepting that Pascal Robertson ordered Sean Davies' death is bad enough, but if he's behind this as well then I've killed people on behalf of a man who has now kidnapped my best friend. But why? What could Beth have found for Pascal to send goons after her?

'Give me the gun,' I say. 'I have some questions.'

Will looks at me, and I think he's going to agree to it, but before he can reply there's a sound from downstairs. 'You know your door is open, right?' a woman shouts up the stairs. 'Anyone could just walk in.'

Well, there goes that idea.

'Nice of her to warn us,' Will says.

Then we climb out the window.

★

'We can go to my place,' he says once we've dropped back down to street level. 'It's a little unconventional, but it's safe – and it's not too far from here, actually.'

He's right: by London standards, the journey from our flat to Will's place is far easier than it could have been. All we have to do is cut through Mile End Park, then walk along Regent's Canal in the direction of Central London. It's dark on the canal – some stretches of the towpath have no lights at all, except for the vague reflected amber of the city's streetlights in the overcast sky. Sometimes there are lights on the canal boats, either through portholes or decorating the outside, which flicker gently as the boats rock in their moorings.

It's peaceful, but eerie – not somewhere most women would be comfortable walking this late at night with a man they don't really know, but that's one of the advantages of the path I've chosen in life. If anyone tries something, it won't be my body getting dumped in the water.

My thoughts are a bigger concern, and the eerie quiet does nothing to help them. The thought that Beth has been taken somewhere against her will, the fear about what she might be going through, might be feeling, is ever-present and all consuming.

'Here it is,' Will says finally, as we pass the unearthly skeleton of a decommissioned gas holder, which according to the hoarding on the outside is supposedly getting converted into flats. I had expected Will to say his place was some sort of underground base, Batcave style, or at least a derelict old warehouse that he doesn't technically own but has filled with high-tech gadgets and security systems. I have to admit I'm beginning to understand why hitmen tend to live alone in weird places like that, but somehow this is even more unexpected.

Well, he did say unconventional, I think when I look at the canal boat he's pointing to.

'You named it *The Narrow Escape*?' I ask as he steps onto the deck by the tiller.

'Fitting, isn't it?' He looks so pleased with himself that I realise this is probably the first time anyone else has been able to appreciate the joke.

'Is it?' I ask. 'How often do you find yourself disappearing off into the horizon at what, three miles per hour?'

'Don't knock it until you try it,' he says. 'I'm constantly on the move, have no fixed address. It's arguably the perfect accommodation for someone in our line of work. And you'd be surprised by where this baby can go. I can get places unnoticed that you'd never stand a chance with in a car.'

We stoop through a recessed door and into what could be the kitchen of a small country cottage, with dark wooden countertops and cupboards and a full gas stove. The boat feels larger and more homely than I expected: it's decorated colourfully, with postcards from different parts of France stuck up on the units, knick-knacks on the shelves, photos all over the fridge.

It's nice. It feels like the home of someone who has a full life; not a full-time assassin. But I guess that's the picture I'm starting to build of Will – not just a hitman, not just a civilian.

'You have Wi-Fi, right?' I ask, placing the laptops on the kitchen table. Will points to the code as he bustles around making us tea. I manage to refrain from shouting *Priorities!* at him – after all, the man has just helped me take care of two intruders and invited me back to his. Instead, I mentally run through a plan of action.

First thing's first: the USB. If what's on it is so important that it's keeping Beth alive, then it should help us figure out a way to get her back.

The folder opens to display dozens of PDFs and I click on the first one. The ILS Industries logo is plastered at the top of it, as it is in the next PDF, and the next. Well – that double, triple confirms who she's been researching, then.

For a second I want to laugh at this sick joke from the universe. For weeks we've been under the same roof, desperately keeping our involvement with ILS Industries secret from each other. We've been moaning about work, complaining about our bosses, and the whole time we've been dealing with the same company, albeit from different angles. It's like two friends who realise their Hinge dates are actually the same guy. Which did actually happen to us once. Beth and I have always lived strangely parallel lives.

Concentrate, Maisie. Focus on the USB.

I scroll through page after page of the documents. They're hard to make sense of at first; a collation of a whole load of forms, dense with chemical formulas and scientific jargon reporting on the biological impact of long-term exposure to Verdicure. Skimming through them though, I start to build a picture – and it's not pretty.

'Fucking hell,' says Will, reading over my shoulder as he places a steaming mug in front of me. 'And this stuff is the biggest-selling pesticide in the country?'

Because the harmful biological impact isn't in relation to Verdicure being used as nerve agent. It's when it's being used full stop.

'This is a two-man job,' I say to Will, copying the files onto my desktop and unplugging the USB. He settles down at his laptop opposite and we spend the next thirty minutes or so going through everything. By the time we finish, we've learned that:

1. Verdicure has been proven – beyond a doubt – to greatly harm the fertility rates of people who

are eating crops grown in soil treated with the pesticide.

2. Pascal Robertson has done absolutely nothing to stop the rollout of his 'miracle' pesticide since learning of this. In fact, he has done everything he can to bury the findings, while at the same time increasing production and promotion of Verdicure: in particular, aggressively marketing to countries with high levels of food insecurity.

Sean and his manager Helen's names had cropped up a few times as signatories on the earlier reports, but it isn't until I find the smattering of downloaded emails under all the PDFs that I get a sense of how this all connects to their deaths. In an email to Pascal dated a few weeks before Sean was killed, Helen expresses 'concerns' about what they've found and Sean's reaction to it: he's a good employee and she's worried he'll leave. Pascal's replies are cryptic, but when Sean shows up dead, it's not hard to read between the lines. The same day, Helen emails Pascal to request indefinite leave 'owing to the intense stress caused by recent events'.

There's another email, dated just before Helen was killed – this time between Pascal and Tommy Mitchell, his head of security. 'It's about time we tied up a loose end,' Pascal suggests.

No wonder this USB has got him running scared. Whoever the source is, they have unprecedented access to ILS information and informants, things that even Jason hadn't been able to dig up.

And now Beth has stepped into the line of fire. I think

back to the last proper conversation we'd had on Sunday morning after I'd come back from Gabby's. What was it she'd said? *I got an unexpected email from a source last night that's blown my story wide open.*

Another piece falls into place.

'You said Edmund Gainsbury was working on something that could take ILS down,' I say. 'What are the chances that this is it?'

'I think you're right,' says Will slowly. 'It would explain why Pascal took out the hit on him. I never got a clear sense of what exactly he was working on, only that Clint and Archie were scared of it. I think that's part of why they did what they did – they knew a storm was coming for ILS that would knock the wheels off the Verdicure gravy train, so they wanted to make as much money as they could before that happened. And Gainsbury's suicide note seemed weirdly triumphant, didn't it? It would make sense if that was because he'd finished putting this together and had got it into the hands of a researcher he could trust to make it public.'

It's painful to have it confirmed that, all the time Beth was doing this important work to uncover the rot within ILS, Gabby has been pressuring me to take out hits on behalf of Pascal Robertson – who has now kidnapped my best friend. And for all the horrors we've seen, we're still not any closer to how we get Beth back. It's making me itchy.

'I'll check her computer,' I say, pushing my laptop to the side and switching on Beth's. 'See if there's anything useful on there.'

★

I'm stymied almost immediately by her passcode screen. It shouldn't be too difficult – it's a four-digit PIN, and she guessed the six-digit PIN on my phone in a whole zero seconds flat just a couple of weeks ago. But what would be as important to her as Maple's birthday is to me? My birthday? No, Maisie, don't be arrogant. What about her mum's birthday? They were always close – way closer than I ever was with my mum, even before she ran off on me. But do I even know it? Actually, I realise, I do. We celebrated it with her once, when she came through to visit Beth at uni. I had a horrific hangover because it was the day after St Patrick's Day: we got brunch together and I had to disappear midway through to throw up behind a bush. She was sweet, though, and thinking of her now makes me feel worse about everything that's happened already – how long until I have to explain to her something has happened to her daughter?

My heart is beating as I type the date into the Windows login screen and press enter. *Good evening, Beth!* it tells me, the white dots flying in the happy little circle that means it's booting. And you know what, I'm right there with them.

My jubilance dips when I realise that even then I still can't get into any of her work files – bloody two-factor authentication – but bounces back up again when I realise her personal email has been left logged in. It's only when I see her inbox full of mailing lists and spam that I'm struck by how bizarre a feeling it is, researching Beth in this way, like she's just another target. It would be a horrific invasion of privacy, if I wasn't doing it to save her life. Maybe it still is – sooner or later I'll have to think about how Beth is going to react when I show up to rescue her, gun in hand – but I don't have time to worry about that now.

I spot an unread email from earlier today, between a celebrity newsletter and some spam from her bank.

Concerning ILS, says the subject line. *Please read.*

I click into it.

Beth,

You are not safe. I can't say much else, but I wouldn't forgive myself if I didn't try to warn you somehow.

Pascal Robertson knows what you are doing. Please look after yourself and don't take unnecessary risks. Don't go anywhere alone and stay with friends or family if you can.

You should know that others have tried to do what you're doing and have paid with their lives. You cannot trust your boss.

If you need help, please be in touch. I'm not sure how much use I'll be, but I can try.

The mystery sender has attached two email chains to their message. After a second's hesitation, I click it open to see an email dated three days ago, written by Dominic Waters: Beth's new boss.

Pascal,

I'm afraid one of my employees has been poking around where she shouldn't have been.

I've been dissuading her inquiries, but she has been persistent. She appears to believe she's found *some dirt on Verdicure and I have to say, from what she has mentioned to the team it's the sort of thing that we might have picked up if it weren't for our history – particularly some details concerning your employees Helen Michaels and Sean Davies. But us St Chad's boys stick together, don't we?*

Rest assured that we will not be taking this material forward ourselves, but depending on what she's found, you may want to prepare yourself in case it resurfaces elsewhere.
Yours,
Dom

'Will . . .' I hand him my laptop.

Dom, what a bastard! I think back over everything Beth said about him being horrible to work for, but a so-called journalist grassing out one of his own employees to a potential killer? That's fucked. But that's the problem with rich people in the UK – not only are half of them clinically evil, they're clinically evil bastards who all went to school together and still haven't grown up.

'It's a trap,' Will says, scanning through the emails.

'And when has that ever stopped you?' I ask, taking my laptop back. Then I write a reply: *I'm in danger. Please, I need your help. Can we meet tomorrow?*

I glance at Will, who nods in agreement, and I hit send.

It's a shot in the dark and I don't expect to hear anything back, but it's not like we're swimming in options. If it is a trap, sent as a backup if their kidnapping had failed, it'll presumably involve someone from ILS, and maybe we can pry some sort of information out of them. Either that, or it's another whistleblower. And they would be *very* helpful.

★

'OK, take a look at this.'

Will has spent most of the evening planning ways to get into the ILS offices, while I continue to poke about Beth's laptop. It's something he'd looked at a few weeks ago when he accepted a hit on Pascal Robertson, and quickly discarded after realising just how heavily secured the building is, but now that it's become a necessity to get Beth back he's persevering.

Right now he's turned his screen round to show me a satellite photograph. Except, there's a scrabbling sound, and the screen is now obscured by a dark shape.

'Hey, Kipper,' Will says affectionately, scratching the black and white cat's forehead.

Read the room, Kipper, I think for a second. But the sight of his scrunched-up little face can soothe even my stressed-out heart – at least for a moment. Must be nice being a cat. They don't have to worry about evil corporations or tyrannical businessmen, or their friends being kidnapped, and he probably doesn't have any nightmares at all about all the mice he kills. A simpler life.

Kipper settles in Will's lap and I refocus. 'What am I looking at?'

'The roof of the ILS offices. That building is a minefield: swarming with security, fingerprint sensors on the internal doors, cameras everywhere, yadda yadda. But look at this!'

203

He jabs his finger triumphantly at the right-hand side of the building.

'Wait – there's a fire escape on the roof?' I ask. 'You're telling me we're going to get into Robertson's flat through a fire escape?' Given how insanely paranoid Robertson is about security, it seems unbelievable that he'd have left such an obvious hole in his armour.

Will, though, is undeterred. 'A fire exit like this would suggest that despite all the security measures, they *do* still follow fire code. Which I get – if you want to run a dubious operation like ILS, then anything you can do to dissuade clipboard-armed government investigators from going through your business is a good idea. If we can find a way to get in through that door, then we can get into the office building, find a way to the central staircase and make our way to Robertson's flat. This gives us a pretty good chance of getting in,' he finishes, with more confidence than I feel.

'It gives us a *chance* of getting in,' I say. 'I'm not sure it's a good one. Your confidence is going to get you killed one day.'

He flashes me a grin. 'It hasn't yet.'

As I take in his beaming face, I realise what I'm asking him to do. What I've assumed he'll do, actually, because I don't think I've even asked. Although Pascal is Will's target, there's no way any hitman worth their salt would choose to take him out in his own headquarters. As Will said, the place is a minefield. Getting in there to rescue Beth is going to be one of the most dangerous missions I've done: the only reason I'm doing it is because I literally could not live with myself if anything else happens to her.

But Will . . .

'Thank you for doing this,' I say. 'But are you sure you want to? You've already done so much. You didn't have to come back to the flat, you didn't have to give up where you live, and you didn't have to help with all this research. If I'd come back from the ball without you to find Beth gone . . . I don't know what I'd do.'

He reaches for my hand across the table. 'I'm happy to. I want to. The idea that Robertson is doing this to someone else, that he could hurt your friend the way he hurt Sean – of course I'm going to help.' Then he lets go with a quick squeeze of my hand and winks. 'Plus, with the size of the bounty on Pascal's head, neither of us would have to worry too much about new contracts for a while.'

★

I'm lying in Will's bed when the panic comes. I know I should be sleeping – we'll both need all the strength we can get for the morning – but instead I'm going over all of the bombshells that were dropped today, one by one, and falling into a quiet desperation.

'I can hear your thoughts from here,' Will says into the dark.

'Do you think she's going to hate me?' I ask.

I hear him shift to face me. 'Do you hate her for hiding what she was working on from you?'

Even though I can't see anything, I turn to face him too. 'It's not the same, though, is it? Beth is out there fighting the good fight, and I'm just . . .'

I trail off, unsure. *I stop bad people from doing bad things.*

That's how I've always pictured myself confessing to Beth, should it ever come to it. *Powerful people, who have ruined the lives of so many. Who have done it over and over and will do it again, unless we make sure they can't.* But now that I know I was lied to about Gainsbury, about Owen and Sean, all of it rings hollow.

'I never had a chance to tell Sean what I do,' Will says. 'And I've still not told Sarah; don't know how I ever could when someone like me killed Sean.' He's quiet for a moment. 'But I also know that I would never kill someone else's Sean. And I think the two of them would believe that, if I *could* tell them.'

Somehow as we've been talking, we've got closer and closer. The hairs on my arm stand on end, hyper aware of how close he is to me even in the black.

'How did you start doing this job?' I ask. It's something that I've been not quite asking myself for a couple of weeks now, I realise. It's cowardly, but it's easier to ask him.

He breathes out, considering.

'For a long time it was just me and my sister. Sarah did her best, but I had to learn to survive, and I learned to survive in ways other people would find objectionable. I realised I was good at it, so it became a career.'

'Killing people for money.'

'Doesn't sound great when you put it like that, does it?'

'No,' I agree. 'But I can't talk.'

Any idea I once had that working for Novum – the so-called ethical alternative – necessarily put me above others who'd made similar choices is out the window by now. Good riddance – it's time to face what I do honestly, straight on.

'What's going to happen?' I whisper.

It's a question to myself as much as to him. What'll happen after this, when we get Beth back – because we are going to get her back. How will she see me?

And what about Will? What's going to happen between us after all this is over?

'You can't control it,' he breathes. 'Just do what you can, then let what happens happen.'

I feel his words hot on my face, and then we're reaching for each other. For one – two – three seconds, we're wrapped in each other's arms, kissing hungrily, his hand snaking round my hip, my fingers raking through his hair. But then I'm pushing him away and we're rolling back to our own sides of the bed, breathing heavily.

'I'm sorry, Will. I can't. Not when—' I trail off, not sure what else to say.

'You're right,' he says. 'We should sleep.'

18

When I check my phone early the next morning I find a message from Liv. It reads:

Can't wait to see you for the birthday bonanza! Aiming for the 10 a.m. train. Can you remind Beth of the times? She seems really busy atm and I don't want to nag . . .

And fuck. Because that's tomorrow, isn't it? Liv's birthday trip, which she's been looking forward to for weeks. Setting aside all the awful things that could come from Beth's disappearance, if I don't rescue her soon, Liv and Michelle will undoubtedly start asking questions about where she's got to. When did I last see her? Did she say she was going anywhere? Did she say anything weird? Was she worried about anything?

And I'll know the answers. That's the thing: I'll know the answers and I'll have to lie to their faces, and however much I lie it still won't bring Beth back, because someone at ILS was too worried about what she'd found poking around so the bastard kidnapped her. Kidnapped, and possibly killed her.

Will do, I message back. Then I add: Can't wait xx. Because I, for one, am not going to put that kind of negative energy out into the universe on today of all days.

Before Liv can reply, a text comes in from Gabby:

Hello Maisie. Owen mentioned you were upset about last night. I'm out for meetings all day today, but let's find time to talk soon. Is tomorrow morning at my house acceptable?

Well, first of all, no, because tomorrow I'm going to Margate for my friend's birthday – assuming I've rescued Beth on time and, consequently, Liv hasn't killed us both for being late.

And secondly, because I have no idea what I want to say to Gabby right now.

But I have to act normal with her, too, so I reply: **Sure, I'll be there.**

Because that's what she'd expect me to do, isn't it? Just drop everything to be at her beck and call.

Then I check Beth's email account, not really expecting to see anything. My heart jumps when I see she has three new messages – two are just from mailing lists, but the third is from the anonymous account who warned her to stay safe. Whoever they are, they replied at around 3 a.m. with the address of a café in central London.

I'll be here in the morning. 10 a.m. You'll know me by the blue hoodie and the red baseball cap. Stay safe.

Evidently they didn't plan on sleeping much.

'OK, this is *definitely* a trap,' says Will, reading it over my shoulder. He's not said anything about our aborted kiss last night, which I'm grateful for.

'But it's a lead,' I reply. 'And aside from rocking up to the ILS office, guns blazing in the hope that she's in there, it's the best lead we've got.'

★

I freshen up in *The Narrow Escape's* cramped-but-warm shower, and we leave Victoria Park to catch an eye-wateringly expensive Uber into Central. I've started noticing the price now that Gabby doesn't pay for them all. Thirty-five minutes later, we are unceremoniously dumped a three-minute walk from the Caffe Nero on Bedford Street, not far from Leicester Square. The driver waves us off with a cheery 'Have a nice day!', blissfully unaware of the minor role he has played in a story that has so far involved the violent death of several people, and will likely involve at least a few more.

'Sensible place for this sort of thing,' Will says approvingly as we approach the café. He's right: it's busy, bougie, and well-connected by public transport, all of which either reduces the chances of things going awry or allows for an easy getaway if they do, while still being anonymous enough that no one would blink at two strangers meeting for a hush-hush conversation.

'Still happy waiting outside?' I ask. We'd agreed before we left that we'd do it this way. If it is a trap, Will can lie in wait as the ace up our sleeve. Beyond that, though, we don't have much of a plan – not to mention resources, tech support, or oversight. Suffice it to say, this isn't how I usually go about doing missions.

But I do have Will, and even after our awkward interaction last night, that means a lot.

'I'll be right here,' he replies, slipping a packet of cigarettes from a jacket pocket.

'You smoke?' I sound a little more accusatory than I'd meant to, but Josh the Dickhead had been a smoker, and Will hasn't had the same bitter tang when we've kissed. Somehow the idea clashed with the picture I was building up of him in my mind.

'Only on missions,' he says, whispering it since we're now just a few steps from the door. 'What – would you rather I just lurked outside for no reason? Half the time this is all you need to go unnoticed.'

OK, but if you want to kiss me again when this is all over . . .

I'm hoping he will, but we've still got a long way to go.

★

I leave him behind to light up and go inside, making a beeline for the sandwich counter. That counter's back casing is reflective, which means I can use it to scan the room while hopefully hiding my face. It doesn't take long to spot the man in the blue hoodie with the red cap. From my perspective he's sitting between a tuna sub and a chicken and bacon toastie, but the latter is obscuring his face until I move my head and adjust the angles to find that . . .

It's Jason.

What.

How the fuck is it Jason?

OK, first question: has he seen me? For some reason, despite knowing that they would somehow be connected to Pascal Robertson, I hadn't entertained the trap being someone I know personally. After watching him for a few seconds I decide he hasn't noticed me. That's one big disadvantage of this place as a meeting spot – the vast majority of the tables have no good view of the windows.

I raise my hand as if rubbing sleep from my eyes and

crouch down, trying to look like I've found something fascinating on the label of a ploughman's baguette. I'm doing everything I can to make myself invisible while I figure out what in the ever-living fuck he's doing here. Is he here on Gabby's behalf? Or has he started working against Gabby too?

I take one last scan of the room to make sure Owen isn't lurking in the shadows somewhere obvious, and then inhale deeply. There's only one way to find out.

'Fucking Christ,' says Jason, scrambling to his feet as he sees me approach. It's my first time getting a clear look at his face since I came in, and I've got to be honest, he's not looking good: unshaved, his clothes seeming not so much rumpled as slept in, eyes red with dark circles beneath them. Plus, he looks absolutely terrified to see me. I guess he really was expecting Beth after all, then.

'Jason, sit down,' I say. I intend my voice to be calming but it comes out more like something you'd say to a dog. His eyes dart wildly around the café, starting to tremble as he weighs up his avenues of escape.

'Please, Jason. I just want to talk to you.'

I reach out a reassuring hand to touch his shoulder, but he takes one terrified look at it and dodges back. Then, without saying a single word, he picks up his coffee mug and throws the liquid in my face, prompting an audible gasp from the table next to me.

When I see it coming towards me I expect the worst: the worst being third-degree burns, ruining my face and jeopardising my chances of rescuing Beth in a timely manner (or at all). I duck in time for most of the coffee to go sailing overhead, but a lukewarm splatter dusts my forehead and gets in my hair.

Lukewarm. Not boiling, then. By now, it must have mostly cooled.

'You can't do that!' someone yells on my behalf.

Well, apparently he just did, and it's so unexpected that for a moment I don't know what to do. I'm not startled for long, but it gives Jason a chance to slip by me. I reach out to grab him by the hood of his jacket but for how wiry he is, he's surprisingly fast – and if the other customers weren't staring already, they certainly are now.

Running to catch up with him would only make things worse, so I let him go.

'Are you all right?' asks the woman who shouted in my support, getting out of her chair. 'Let me get you some napkins.'

'It's OK,' I tell her. 'Seriously. I probably deserved it.'

I still take the napkins, though.

Outside, Jason is squirming in Will's grip, arms pinned behind his back.

'Ease off him, Will,' I say. 'It's only Jason.'

Jason and Will take a look at each other, Jason straining his neck to look behind him. They both speak simultaneously:

'You know this guy?' says Will.

'You're working with him?' says Jason.

'Yes,' I say. 'And Jason – I'm not working with Gabby right now, so if you're worried that she sent me after you, then believe me when I say she didn't. A lot's happened since we last spoke. The woman you were supposed to be meeting,

Beth Walsh, she's my flatmate, and now she's disappeared. I need to find her.'

He stops struggling, seeming to consider that for a second.

'Promise you won't run away?' I ask.

He nods.

'Can you help us?' I ask.

He looks even less sure, but nods again.

'Will, let him go.'

★

The three of us find a quiet bench beneath a tree in gloomy Embankment Gardens: as good a place as any in the centre of town to hash out what's been going on. I'm desperate to hear what Jason knows about Beth, but he seems a little frisky still and I decide to let him do the talking to start off with. We don't have time for him to attempt another runner.

'I'm sorry, Maisie,' Jason says once we've sat down, speaking quietly so no one can hear us. 'When I saw you come in, I just thought . . . I thought you were really coming for me.'

It hurts to hear him say it out loud, even if it's not exactly news. 'As if I would kill you,' I say. 'What have you ever done?'

'I went against Gabby—' he shrugs '—I found out how deep this stuff with ILS runs and I didn't want to risk her realising what I knew – or how I felt about it – so I ran away. Ever since then I've been living out of hotels, paranoid that you or Owen are coming after me.'

'So arranging to meet Beth . . .?' I ask.

'Was a necessary risk,' he says stubbornly. 'I know I'm not trained like you are, but I thought I'd know more about this stuff than she did, and I had to help her if I could. When I saw you coming I honestly thought I'd signed my death sentence.'

That hurts even more. Is that really how Jason sees me — just Gabby's attack dog, ready to bite whoever she sets me on?

'I never just did it for Gabby,' I say softly. 'You know that, don't you? Every job I did, I made sure I was doing it for my own reasons. I always knew who I was dealing with, and the consequences my actions would have. I really believed in what we were doing.'

'I know you did,' he says. 'That's what made you scary.'

He lets me sit with that thought for a minute. It's raining slightly, because of course it is, and the park is empty except for a lone coffee kiosk, a groundskeeper in green overalls poking about in one of the flower beds and a young family walking along an opposite lane, the parents under an umbrella and their little boy jumping from puddle to puddle.

Will seems to sense that we're having a moment, because he nudges his leg against mine, then gets to his feet. 'I'll be right over there,' he says awkwardly, pointing in the direction of the kiosk. 'Shout if you need anything, OK.'

I watch him go, thinking about how the moment he figured out I'd worked for Novum, he'd tried to tell me I was being lied to. I turn to Jason. 'Didn't you believe in it, too, though? The ethical stuff? Why work for Novum if you didn't?'

'I did,' he says. 'I might not have talked about it as much as you, but I did. But . . .' He starts to say something, then checks himself and goes silent. 'We really fucked up on that Gainsbury mission, didn't we?' he says eventually.

I let out a humourless laugh. 'We should never have let Steph rush us.'

'Or Gabby,' Jason says. He nods over at Will. 'You know he was friends with Sean Davies, that guy Robertson told us about when we first met him?' He sees my expression and laughs. 'Of course you know. And you know it was Owen who killed him?' We're quiet for a moment, then Jason speaks again. 'I found a picture of Perseus and Sean after you told us he was on the Bushell job. That's when I realised something weird was going on, that it's been going on for months.'

'You should have told me about that picture,' I say, trying to keep the annoyance out of my voice. We won't get any closer to finding Beth if I'm starting fights, either. 'It was important information. We could have used it.'

But Jason's shaking his head. 'I couldn't risk telling you. You would have told Gabby. You weren't ready to believe him, and when I heard your conversation at Gainsbury's, it made me glad I hadn't told you. Then with how that job ended – well, I didn't know what to think or who to trust. I tried to hack it for a couple of days, see what else I could find, but . . .'

'I didn't have all the information, Jason,' I say. 'And that led to me – us – accepting dodgy jobs from an even dodgier client. Maybe we could have brought Gabby round. Maybe Robertson's lying to her and we could—'

I break off, unsure of what we could have done, unsure if I even believe what I'm saying, but desperate for it to be true. From the way Jason's looking at me, I realise I'm even more wrong than I thought.

19

'It's not just about taking on a dodgy client,' he says, voice serious. 'Pascal Robertson *bought* Novum two months ago.'

After Beth's kidnapping, after finding out that Owen was the one to kill Sean Davies, after every horrific Verdicure side effect that Will and I read about last night, I really thought I was done with being shocked. But it still feels like someone has got a hold of the bench we're sat on and pulled it out from under me.

'*Two months!?*' I repeat. I'm trying to whisper, but it's coming out as a strangled hiss. 'You're saying all the time Gabby was getting us to decide whether or not we actually wanted to take cases for ILS, all the time Pascal Robertson was trying to win us over with flowers and sob stories, none of that mattered because Gabby had already made up her mind and sold him the fucking company?'

The idea that Gabby trusts Pascal Robertson – the man who has kidnapped Beth – to such an extent that she has willingly sold him her company is repulsive. But what's even worse is that I believe it.

I catch Jason double-checking to make sure no one is within earshot after my outburst. We're safe – the only living creatures that might hear us are four pigeons, huddled around a discarded croissant – but he leans in regardless.

'Think about it. You know her charities have been struggling, right? Maybe the more financial pressure they were under, the more she saw Novum as a way of bringing in money, not just for Novum, but for everything else she wanted to achieve – even if that meant going against the principles Novum was founded on.

'Because she was never shy about the money stuff, was she? I mean, she employed a "Client Relations Specialist", for God's sake. Even Owen – didn't you find it strange that *the* Gabby Hawthorne would have someone like him on her payroll? Staunch feminist like her, employing a misogynist twat like him. And that was long before she sold to Pascal. Nobody forced her into it.'

It's at this moment that Will chooses to come back, balancing three takeaway coffee cups. For a moment we all blink at one another, unsure where to go from here.

'You can trust Will,' I tell Jason. 'He's been saying the same all along. And you said it yourself – Novum killed his best friend, on Pascal Robertson's orders. He's not going to go running to any of them.'

Will nods and hands us our drinks. I take a sip – what's with this man and his cups of tea? Though, I have to admit, it's taking the edge off my stomach.

'So, what's the plan?' Will asks. 'How are we getting to Beth?'

His question makes me feel sick all over again. Jason and I have been wasting time we don't have, consoling ourselves about Gabby's betrayal, when we should have been focused

219

on saving Beth. Which is only going to be more difficult now that her kidnappers own a bloody hitman agency.

'We've not got much further on the plan,' Jason says, wincing. 'But I was just telling Maisie that ILS have bought Novum – actually, I read a bunch of stuff about their new security measures when I was poking about their servers, so maybe that could help us.'

'You can access their servers?' Will asks slowly.

'Only from Gabby's house. Her network has a direct VPN connection, or at least it did a couple of days ago.'

'And what else can you do if you have access to the servers?' Will probes.

I'm less patient. 'Can you access their cameras? Door controls? Alarms?'

Jason hasn't cottoned on yet, though. 'I could, yeah, but like I say, I'd have to be at Gabby's house and I'm almost certain she wants to kill me.' He laughs nervously. 'Why?'

Will and I grin at each other. We've been looking for a way into the ILS office – this is it.

20

'Movement,' Will says, from where we're lurking behind a Waitrose van parked down Gabby's street.

The three of us have been impersonating old friends who've stopped to chat for upwards of twenty minutes now, hovering behind the van as we watch Gabby's house. We're pretty sure that Gabby is at the ILS offices – while her text that she's out in meetings could well have been a trap, her car isn't by her house and, according to Jason's black magic facial recognition software, she, Steph and Owen have been there almost every weekend since the sale.

Owen's motorbike *is* here, though, parked obnoxiously in the middle of the driveway.

We look now to see him coming out through Gabby's front door, twirling his keys around one finger.

'Where do you think he's going?' I whisper to Jason.

'No idea,' he replies, as Owen climbs on the back of his bike and starts edging it out of the driveway. 'Late lunch?'

That could be a pretty short trip – but once he comes back, he might not leave again until Gabby returns.

'Our best bet is to go for it now,' I tell Jason, 'but it's a big risk. You up for it?'

He looks uncertain, which is fair enough. This is hardly a guarantee of his safety.

'I'll wait out here,' says Will reassuringly. 'I can distract him if he comes back. We have unfinished business.'

★

The ID scanner on the gate is too much of a risk, so we jump the fence. That's a risk, too, naturally — Gabby's neighbours might be used to seeing me and Jason coming and going, but not to the point where they wouldn't phone the police on the two of us acting suspicious. But even in a rich part of London like this, the police will take their time responding to a call like that from a concerned neighbour. Whereas the ID scanner will grass us out to Gabby, who'll inform Owen — who can be back here in minutes.

We open the door and are greeted by a flurry of movement. 'Hello, Herb,' says Jason, catching the dog by its paws and walking him backwards into the hallway as I shut the door behind us. 'Oh, I've missed you, haven't I?'

It's the sort of thing people say to dogs after not seeing them for weeks, not a few days, but I can tell from Jason's tone that he really means it. The two of them always got on like a house on fire: he always was Herb's favourite of the four of us, and I got the impression Herb was his favourite too. When Gabby wasn't in it was Jason that Herb would stick to as he moved from room to room — his surrogate master.

'OK, boy, let me do my job,' he says, his voice serious as he places Herb's front feet back on the floor. 'Jason has work to do.'

I give Herb a stressed smile, then follow Jason further inside. It is strange to imagine this could be the last time we both see him. Our day-to-day lives have been tied up in Gabby's world for so long that it's almost impossible to imagine them disentangled.

'Do you need to be anywhere in particular to connect to the VPN?' I ask, glancing out the back window in the kitchen. Will is outside watching the front, but there's still a chance Owen might come back in through the back garden, possibly to surprise us. I take out my key, lock the door, and leave the key in the lock to trip him up – at least for a second – if he tries to use his own.

'No,' he says as I return to the living room, pulling his laptop and an ethernet cable out of his bag and setting up at his usual spot on Gabby's living room table. 'But it'll be way faster if I'm plugged into the router.'

It's an awkward trade-off – more speed in exchange for the ability to keep watch out the back – but speed seems more important right now. It's a calculated risk.

I move around the table to look over his shoulder. He's already found what looks to be a detailed schematic of the ILS office building, with comprehensive floorplans detailing where all the cameras are, suggestions for where guards should be stationed, and which areas have restricted access.

'Is she in there?' I ask. Being here is one step closer to getting Beth back safely, but the need to actually see her alive is overwhelming.

Jason seems to understand that. 'Gimme a sec,' he mutters. 'There are no cameras in Pascal's flat, don't think his paranoia would allow for it. I'm just figuring out which cameras in the main office she would have passed and when as they took her in.'

'It would have been around 10.30,' I tell him. 'Yesterday evening.'

He nods and types in something else. A window containing a greyscale corridor appears, people coming and going in jumpy staccato steps. They're just regular office people, dressed in various interpretations of the phrase 'smart casual', looking perfectly normal.

'This is now,' Jason says. 'God, it's this busy on a Saturday? Pascal really is a boss from hell.' Then he types in something else. The lighting changes, the regular workers vanish, and I see her. My incredible, smart, beautiful, funny friend Beth is being manhandled by some thug through the corridor of the ILS building, her hands zip-tied together behind her back. Rage and relief surge inside me simultaneously – relief that I know where she is, rage that a fucking pesticide company think they can get away with doing this to her just because she came across some documents they didn't want her to have.

I take a deep breath and let it out, channelling the rage into something more focused and keeping hold of the relief like it's a warm and precious liquid. Then I recognise the man holding her. 'It's him,' I say. 'From the meeting.'

Jason nods. 'Tommy Mitchell. Pascal's personal bodyguard.'

'That has to mean she's being taken to Pascal's flat, right? Not some other part of the building.'

Jason hits some more keys and brings up an image of the security checkpoint outside the door leading to Pascal's penthouse – and Beth being manhandled through.

'The flat itself is a black box,' he says. 'No cameras – or if there are, they're on a different network. Once she's in there . . .'

Anything could've happened. But there's no use thinking like that.

'Double-check they didn't take her out again later, OK?' I tell Jason. He nods. 'Great. And how long until you can sort everything we talked about?'

Will and I had run him through what we needed while we were still outside. Ideally, we'd want Jason to get both of us onto the fingerprint system that blocks all the internal doors, take out all the cameras, and find us a point of entry – with that fire door on the roof looking the most promising.

Jason leans back and cracks his typing knuckles, before getting back to it. 'The internal fingerprint scanners look easy,' he says. 'Whoever set *that* system up was an idiot. Cameras I can fuck with a bit by uploading a virus to their systems to take them offline when we really need it, but once their security notices it's only a matter of time before they can get them back up.' He looks at me anxiously. 'I don't know what I can do about that fire door Will was on about, though. I can disable the alarm, but you still won't be able to open it from the outside.'

'Don't worry about it,' I say. 'Just focus on what you can do.'

The other thing was getting more serious weapons. Legally speaking, even the guards on Pascal Robertson's penthouse checkpoint *shouldn't* be armed, but I'd noticed a pretty suspicious bulge beneath Tommy Mitchell's jacket the

225

last time we were in the building, and a single small-calibre pistol can only do so much. Chances are, we'll need some serious gear if we want to get to Beth.

I phone Will on my way down to the firing range. 'Any sign of Owen?'

'*All clear,*' he replies. '*As long as he doesn't suspect something's up, I should be able to see him coming a mile off.*'

'Great,' I reply, jamming in the code of Gabby's highly illegal basement arsenal and pulling back the shutter. 'I'm in the armoury. What do you want?'

'*Well, what have you got?*' Will asks.

'Oh, baby,' I say, looking at the assortment of rifles, shotguns, and submachine guns. 'Telling you what we *don't* have would probably take less time.' I slip a sheathed knife into my pocket and a couple of automatic pistols into my bag along with a flashbang, but I'm just thinking about the practicality of getting an AR-15 across London without owning your own car (prognosis: unlikely) when I hear a crash from upstairs.

'OK, Will – eyes on the house,' I say, 'he must have come round the back.'

I put my phone on speaker to maximise the mic sensitivity and slip it into my pocket – it's not quite the high-tech system we'd use to let Jason provide backup on missions, but it should at least give him some oversight of what's going on inside. Then I run up the stairs as quickly and silently as I can, slowing down as I come out into the hall. A quick glance backwards tells me that Owen must have smashed the pane of glass in the back door and reached in to turn the key. And we were so sure he hadn't spotted us . . .

Suddenly, the calculated risk of not working in the kitchen is looking a lot less calculated.

★

'Come crawling back, have you?' I hear Owen say as I creep closer to the living room doorway. 'Bit of a stupid move, mate, if I'm being honest. Gabby wasn't *too* fussed about you disappearing off, you know. She'd guessed what you found, and figured you couldn't hack it. You know what she said? Fair play. That's Gabby for you. Always championing the ethical stance. But sneaking back in without telling anyone . . . That's a bit shady, Jason. People could get the wrong idea.'

Owen pauses, and I think I hear him cock a pistol.

'It's a shame, though. I always liked you, mate. I don't know if you got that, but when it's just two lads working together, you feel a sense of brotherhood, don't you? So when Gabby told me I might have to kill you, I wasn't happy about it, that's for sure.'

'You *don't* have to kill me,' Jason pleads. 'Just let me leave.'

I take that as my cue. 'Drop it, Owen,' I say, holding up the assault rifle that I happened to still be carrying when I heard him upstairs. It's not the most practical weapon, given the circumstances, but it sure makes a statement.

Owen glances in my direction, keeping his silenced pistol trained on Jason's head. He laughs when he sees what I'm carrying. 'All right, Maisie. What are you gonna do with that, then? Fire it once and hope that if everyone in the borough calls 999 at once it'll blow up the switchboard?'

'Want to risk it?' I ask.

Owen shrugs.

'Looks like we're in a stalemate, then,' I say, playing for time until Will can find a way to break it.

But Owen just smiles. It's a sickening, evil grin that makes me even more repulsed than I already was that I once — however briefly — found myself swayed by his lumpy, bodybuilder physique.

'We're not,' he replies.

If his comment didn't give away what was coming, his glance over my shoulder did. But I call his bluff, ducking and charging towards him rather than looking around to see the man lurking behind me. It's another calculated risk: if I'm wrong, Owen puts a bullet in Jason's head.

If I'm wrong, the guy behind me shoots me in the back.

But if I'm right, it's because I'm acting on the basis of several assumptions. One, I'm assuming Owen is at least as smart as old Cyril Hargreaves, RIP, who once helpfully told me that even silenced pistols are pretty loud. Two, that for this reason Gabby will have told Owen not to use it in her house even if it costs him his life. Gabby, as the proud owner of both a vast illegal arsenal in her basement and a reputation she wishes to keep spotless, does not want police sniffing around where they shouldn't. Three, that for the same reason, the ILS goon behind me won't have a gun either. Four, that Owen is capable of sticking to Gabby's instructions.

Of these, four feels the ropiest.

But I'm right.

No one fires a shot and I barrel into Owen's chest. I let my own rifle hang from its shoulder strap as I grab the wrist of his gun arm hard with both hands, digging my nails in until he drops it. Owen is bigger than me, so I don't have much hope against him in a wrestling match, and he brings in his free hand to grab me by the neck and pin me against the wall in a powerful chokehold – my head cracking into it so hard that blood fills my eyes and plaster dust gets in my mouth, assault rifle pinned uselessly – and painfully – between my ribs and the wall.

'I might feel bad about Jason,' he leers, 'but *you* will be a pleasure to kill.'

There's another puff of plaster dust and a heavy thud, then the other man has Jason pinned to the wall beside me in a perfect imitation of Owen's move. Owen leans in so close that I can smell the coffee on his breath. 'You don't know how long I've waited to do this. Swanning around like you own the place, always up Gabby's arsehole. Well! That turned out well for you, didn't it?'

He's gloating because he thinks he's got me, and you know what? Maybe he's right. My hands scrabble uselessly at his elbow around my neck and black spots accumulate in my vision. All the while Herb whimpers in the background and Will remains nowhere to be seen.

Then finally, I hear Will's voice. Except it's not in person, just tinnily audible from my pocket: 'Maisie, there's another guy out the front – armed. I'll try and get the jump on him, but it's going to take a while. Play for more time if you can.'

Owen reaches into my pocket and pulls out my phone. 'Ha!' he says, hanging up and throwing it on the floor. 'You've got your new boyfriend from the ball, have you? Some use he'll be.'

But his reaching for my phone momentarily eases the

pressure on my neck. I take a gasping breath, and as my strength surges back, I pull a hand free, rip the knife from my pocket, and sink it into his leg.

'You bitch!' he shouts, raising his gun as I dart away.

I carry my momentum into a kick and knock it out of his hand. Well, that's what I intend to do – actually, Owen just goes crashing to the ground, dark blood gushing from his leg and pooling around him on the floor. Must have hit an artery, I think, feeling a little detached.

I turn again to check that the other man really isn't armed. He's not, like I predicted, but by the time I see him he's already in the process of running, far enough that I won't be able to catch up. Jason is dusting himself off, looking at me with the startled expression people do when they see me kill someone. He's also gone a little grey, though I'm not sure if that's from what happened to Owen.

Then Will comes in. 'Sorry, Maisie. Had to take care of that guy outside. Don't think anyone saw, though.'

Then he notices Owen on the floor, face white, surrounded by what looks like an ocean of blood. The room goes silent the way it tends to around death.

'We should get moving,' Will says quietly after a moment.

That snaps me out of it. I pick up my phone from where Owen threw it. It's no use getting sentimental – Owen was a bastard, same as the rest of them.

'Did you see any sign of the police?' I ask Will, unstrapping my assault rifle and placing it on the sofa. Owen was right, in a way – that sort of firepower is more trouble than it's worth. The pistols in my bag will have to be enough.

'No, but it's probably safer to go out the back,' Will replies.

'Come on, Jason,' I say, noticing he hasn't moved.

'Is that it?' he asks. 'We work with this man every day and you're happy just to leave him?'

Really? Jason has heard me kill countless people over the radio, or watched it on CCTV. Is it actually being in the room that makes the difference? Or is it different when you work with someone, even if they're a bastard?

Normal people would know the answers to these questions, I realise. Actually, that's wrong. Most normal people wouldn't even ask them.

No time for that now, though. 'Come on, pack up your laptop,' I tell him gently. 'How much did you get done?'

Jason is still for a moment. He closes his eyes, breathes, and seems to make a decision.

'Fingerprint system on the internal doors, and the virus for the cameras,' he says, as he throws his laptop in his bag. 'I think I should be able to silence any fire alarms, but I didn't get much further on the external doors.'

I nod. It'll have to do – assuming we get out of the mess we're in currently.

Owen's leg starts to buzz.

I'm not sure why, but for some reason I reach down and gingerly lift it from his pocket.

'Gabby's calling,' I say when I see the caller ID.

21

Gabby calls again as we hop the fence – going out the front seemed too dangerous, given all the commotion we've caused – and then again as we're escaping through Highgate Cemetery. Only it's not Owen's phone she's ringing this time. It's mine. I ignore it, trying to focus on acting casual.

I'm not going to lie, this is the absolute worst I've felt after killing someone. I don't think it's because it was Owen, though maybe that's part of it. A bigger concern is the sound of sirens in the distance – and the knowledge that for once, I'm operating without the cushion that comes from being on the Gabby Hawthorne side of history.

Are you a hitwoman, Maisie, or a vigilante? she's asking in my mind. *Because you know what the difference is, don't you? Hitwomen get paid, while vigilantes get caught.*

'Can't you get Removals to, you know . . .?' I hiss at Will, when the sirens get noticeably louder. If this sort of thing happened when I was working for Novum, I could at least be confident in Gabby working tirelessly behind the scenes to grease some palms over at Scotland Yard.

'This isn't contracted,' he whispers back. 'What I do on my own time is none of their business.'

'Gig economy bastards.'

'Yep,' Will agrees. 'But at least they let me choose my own gigs.'

I've got no comeback to that one. He's right and he knows it.

'Do you think she knows?' Jason whispers, jogging to keep up, when Gabby phones again. 'That we . . . you know.'

'Probably,' I say, glancing around. Will nods in agreement.

And soon everyone else in the country will, too, I think, *unless we get our act together.* We're already getting some concerned looks from some of the historic cemetery's paying visitors, darkly curious about the two men and a woman who all seem to be having the worst days of their lives. Well, except for Will, now I look at him. He is, as ever, remarkably unflappable. Which probably makes us just look even stranger.

The sirens get closer. Again. Gabby calls me. Again.

'Maybe you should answer it,' Will says. 'See what her angle is.'

I don't want to. Then the sirens *stop*. Which is worrying, since it suggests the police cars are no longer moving.

'Fine.' I duck down a quieter alley between some less well-maintained tombs. 'Hi, Gabby,' I say, affecting to sound as unflustered as possible, just on the off chance she genuinely doesn't know anything. 'What's up?'

'*Maisie, darling,*' she says, and God it's *weird* hearing her voice again after everything that's happened. '*I'm struggling to get a hold of Owen. You wouldn't happen to have any idea where he is, would you?*'

'Oh no, I don't,' I say, leading the three of us into a dark hollow beneath some trees, towards what I hope to be a climbable fence out of here. 'Sorry – why, has something happened?'

But she has to know, doesn't she? Except the more I hear those soothing, honeyed tones, the more convinced I am that somehow, *somehow*, she doesn't.

'*You know I'm not one to worry,*' she says. '*But he was managing something for me in the house all day – we've been in communication near constantly – and now he's gone quiet, and my neighbours are calling me to say they heard some strange noises.*'

'Could be anything,' I say, thinking of his stretched-out form on the floor, the deep pool of blood soaking into her lovely cream carpet.

A sigh, like white noise through my phone speaker. Then, when Gabby replies, her voice is ice cold. '*Please don't lie to me, Maisie,*' she says.

Fuck. I should have known it was a mind game. Why did I let myself fall for it? Rule number one, with Gabby Hawthorne, it's *always* a mind game.

'*I have to say, I'm a little disappointed,*' she continues when I don't reply. '*Not with the fact you killed Owen – you and I both know he probably had it coming – but with the fact you were so stupid about it. Do you honestly think I could have lived somewhere like that for twenty-five years and not been friends enough with the neighbours that they phone me* directly *when they see someone climbing over my fence?*'

The ground feels like jelly beneath my feet. It's partly what Gabby's saying; partly the fact we've come through the trees far enough to confirm that the fence is low enough to jump – but there's a police car creeping slowly down the road on the far side of it.

'Shit,' Will breathes. Now even he's looking flustered. He darts another way and I follow him, but if the walls were ever closing in, they're closing in now.

'*I know there's been a lot going on lately,*' Gabby continues in my ear. '*But please, Maisie, give me one reason why I shouldn't just let you and Jason get arrested and face the consequences for the nonsense you've pulled. And yes, I do have that kind of influence. Or did you seriously think it was just your excellent skillset that was keeping you safe all these years?*'

I've only got one chance, and I have to take it. It's a gamble based on the fact Novum apparently wasn't involved in Beth's disappearance — because seriously, why buy out a hitman agency, and then use your own bodyguard to stage a kidnapping? Unless . . .

'I want to come back, Gabby,' I tell her.

'*Forgiveness is earned,*' she replies. '*So earn it.*'

She suspects I have something, I think. *Something she doesn't.*

'I will,' I tell her. 'Because we're not the only ones who have been keeping secrets. Pascal has been hiding something from you. There is a flaw within ILS that is going to tear it apart. I can show you — if you let me come back.'

Gabby pauses, and I can tell from the sharp inhale of breath that it's the answer she was hoping for.

'*And that's what you truly want, is it?*' she says finally. '*To come back? To earn my forgiveness and go back to how things were?*'

'Yes,' I breathe. 'I understand why you did what you did. But ILS . . . Well, you'll see when I bring it in to you. You should know, I only ever wanted what's best for Novum. For our mission. I'm sorry it's ended up like this.'

Another long silence.

'*Meet me at the ILS office,*' she says finally. '*Just you. You'll have to go through all of their security, so don't think about trying anything. Bring whatever it is you have for me — and let's hope for your sake that it's good.*'

'So . . .' Will says when I've hung up the phone. And maybe I'm just imagining it, but the sirens already seem to be fading.

'We have a way in.'

22

I arrive at the ILS office building alone, undisguised, and unarmed, as Gabby requested.

I can't say I care much for the architecture. Five storeys of white marble in a pretentious example of Edwardian Baroque, complete with ornamental columns, angular, protruding lintels above the windows, and shield-carrying angels carved ostentatiously into the stone near the top. Then there's the big black overhanging glass cube of Pascal Robertson's luxury penthouse, like an alien spaceship that's come in to land. It always struck me as strangely disproportionate, and having seen Will's satellite photograph of the roof I understand why – it must have been built off-centre to allow access to the rooftop fire escape from the rest of the office.

Somewhere inside there is Beth. I'm going to get her back.

The glass front doors of the building slide open ahead of me as I approach, and the security guards look up warily as I step up to the metal detector. There are four of them in total, two on each side of the doorway, all wearing the same nondescript uniform as the men who ransacked my flat last night. Where are those men now, I wonder. Have they been signed off with their injuries? Or are they being forced to work overtime to make up for their blunder? Would these guys have any idea? And do they even know about the twenty-eight-year-old woman that their boss has kidnapped upstairs?

I step under the metal detector. It goes off.

'Pockets,' a guard grunts, gesturing towards a plastic tray. I tip my phone and USB stick containing the documents Beth received from Gainsbury into it, then try again.

This time it's all clear.

As I get my first proper look at the reception area, I see someone waving at me from just inside the security barrier. It's Steph, heels clicking on the marble as she crosses the lobby floor. 'What a weekend,' she says cheerfully. 'And it's only Saturday. You and Owen really made a mess of things at the ball, you know. It might be a while before either of you work your way back into Gabby's good books.'

Either of us? So either Gabby hasn't told her about the fact I've just killed Owen, or Steph's been taking classes from her about how to fuck with people's heads, constantly leaving them guessing about who knows what and what's even real.

She notices my plastic tray emerging from the scanner and scoops up my phone and USB stick before I can get to them. 'I'll be taking these,' she says. 'Sorry, Maisie. You know what Gabby's like – I can't take any chances.'

We bypass the reception desk where last time we picked up our temporary entry passes and head straight to the gates. She taps an ID card on the reader and poses so her face will be picked up by the face scanner, lets me through, then follows behind.

'Where are we going, then?' I ask politely, not taking her bait. I'd been hoping that Steph might be less intolerable now that our workday rivalry, each vying for Gabby's affection and approval, has so definitively come down in her favour. Apparently, she's a sore winner on top of everything else.

She looks back at me and grins as she leads me to the lift. 'Oh, you don't know, do you? I always forget Gabby never got around to bringing you in on the whole merger situation.'

As if. But I don't rise to it.

'I'm so excited for you to see it, actually,' Steph continues. The red LED floor counter on the lift is ticking down slowly – too slowly. 'Pascal has gutted a whole wing of the fifth floor and turned it into our little Novum HQ. It's about time we had a *real* office, don't you think? It's good marketing to say a company started in someone's living room, but no one actually wants to *work* in one for too long. Hunching over Gabby's dining table was horrible for my posture. After you, please,' she adds when the lift finally arrives.

I notice a guard has peeled off from the edge of the foyer and is getting in with us. Steph does her best to ignore him, but a little flicker of annoyance gives her away. Buying out a hitman company to serve as your protection, but not trusting them enough to move around the office without a silent escort? It seems like I was right to think it's not all happy families just yet following the acquisition.

'Sounds great,' I say without much enthusiasm.

As we exit on floor 5 – the guard staying put – I take a second to map out the building in my head. The floor is split into two by a central corridor, each wing seemingly belonging to a different department. From where we are, I could take the central staircase up another flight to get to Pascal's flat, while the fire escape staircase ought to be accessible through the wing to our right.

'Come along, Maisie,' says Steph – leading me to the left.

She scans her thumb to unlock a set of double doors, pushing one open to reveal a largely empty office space. 'When this is finished, it should be incredible,' she says, holding the door open for me to enter. 'We'll have soundproofed firing ranges with moveable targets – actually, the whole place is already soundproofed, but it'll be *extra* soundproofed – plus a sprung dojo for weapons practice, and a far better technical setup for whoever we hire to replace Jason. It's going to be *magnificent*.'

Ah, a slip-up there. Steph's so excited by the interior design that she's forgotten to pretend that Jason's absence isn't due to his sick aunt.

So far, though, I can't see Steph's vision. The room we enter is just an empty space with an ugly grey carpet and a few desks scattered around as if at random, the wires of multi-sockets trailing haphazardly between them.

And Gabby.

She's leaning on one of these desks, her trademark suit looking freshly pressed, not an ice blonde hair on her head out of place, illuminated from behind by refracted sunlight through those unearthly bulletproof windows.

'Come, Maisie,' she says when she sees me.

I come. Behind me, I hear the swinging shut of the door Steph was holding open, and the click of the safety being

240

taken off the pistol I didn't clock she was wearing. I don't give Steph the satisfaction of looking around, but I can feel the gun's presence behind me like a magnetic pull. Guns have a power like that. And, as Steph helpfully reminded me, the noise won't get far.

'Take a seat,' Gabby says.

A single office chair – black plastic, blue cushions, no wheels – has been placed in front of where Gabby is standing in the centre of the empty floor. It strikes me as the sort of chair you might tie someone to before you execute them, if you were that way inclined. Nonetheless, I take it.

Gabby leans forward. 'Now, Maisie. Would you mind telling me what on Earth you've been playing at?'

If you were to ask, being honest, what percentage of me just wants to grovel right now, I'm not sure what I'd say. A significant chunk, certainly. I can almost see a version of myself sobbing: *I'm sorry, Gabby. He led me astray. I didn't know what I was doing. It took me too long to understand how right you were all along. I am not worthy of you. Forgive me.*

Would that Maisie mean it? Or would she just be trying to play on Gabby's vanity? Maybe there's no difference. Maybe it would work.

I can see a version of me who would get down on her knees and beg.

But I'm not her. Not anymore.

'Why did you do it?' I ask, tone level. 'Why sell the company to ILS?'

Gabby leans back, appraising my response. 'I've been telling you all along, Maisie. ILS are an excellent partner for us. They're exactly the sort of partner who can help us reach the goals I founded Novum to achieve. Pascal has promised us complete independence, as long as we don't act in opposition to his main endeavors. In that sense, nothing has changed. But integrated as a larger whole, Novum and ILS together can open up a world of possibilities.'

As Gabby speaks, Steph edges into my eyeline, giving me a good view down the barrel of her pistol. She looks comfortable with it in her hands: relaxed, natural. Is it just posture, or has Gabby been training her? Yet another thing I've been left out of.

'You founded Novum to make a difference,' I say. 'Not to prop up your failing charities. How much did you make from the sale, anyway? Or from the dirty contracts you had Owen do behind my back?'

Gabby gives me a quizzical look. 'Oh, do you think this is just about money?' She laughs. 'Well, I suppose I can't blame you for getting the wrong end of the stick. No, Maisie, I wanted to work with ILS because they really are what they claim to be: the vanguard of an eco-friendly, technology-driven agricultural and industrial revolution, which Novum will be at the centre of. We founded Novum to make the world a better place. Pascal is *building* a better world. With their unwavering support we will be able to achieve far more than we could ever imagine. That's all I wanted, Maisie. With every decision I made regarding Novum, I just wanted what's best for the world and for women like you.'

'Even if it means the deaths of innocent people?'

Gabby laughs. 'Agent Perseus has been telling you sob stories about his brother-in-law, has he? Sean Davies was an unfortunate casualty, but whether he realised it or not, he was standing in the way of progress. ILS were in a delicate position – the defection of their top scientists would have ruined them before they even got going.'

I stare at her, unspeaking. Is this really the woman I spent seven years trusting with my life? Were these really the ideals on which Novum was founded? It was easier to accept that she had lost her way for money. Maybe she did – more and more, I realise, that I can't trust a single word that comes out of her mouth.

'When did you plan on telling me?' I ask.

For the first time in the conversation, Gabby falters. 'I hope you understand why I had to broach the subject slowly.'

'When, Gabby?'

She smiles at me sympathetically. 'Oh, Maisie. You always were the moral centre of the operation. You had such a strong vision of what Novum could be – and what I could be. It was what made you so good at what you did, but because of it, I was worried you wouldn't understand. I needed to make sure you were in the right mindset when I told you, and all this Agent Perseus business was just too much of a distraction. As soon as that was wrapped up . . .'

She's lying. She's lying, and she isn't even giving me the courtesy of telling me a good fucking lie. A lie that makes sense. I'm nothing to her, I realise. Just a tool. A pair of hands with which to hold a knife or a gun. How long has this been the case? Since we founded Novum? Or worse – since she hired me?

I think of the application I wrote for her mentorship programme, stressed out of my gourd and increasingly drunk the deeper I got into it. I never did go back and read what I wrote that night, during a predrinks, party songs blaring – I was too embarrassed by what I might find. What did Gabby think, really, when she found that in her inbox? Did she see the promise of a diamond in the rough, like she said? Or did she see a weak and vulnerable young woman – someone she could mould into whatever shape she needed?

'So,' Gabby says, as businesslike as ever. 'Now that you know where we stand, would you like to help us? Or would you prefer to keep throwing your silly little tantrum and getting in my way?'

It's not impossible that the best thing to do here would be to lie. But I can't lie. 'No,' I say. 'I don't want to be part of this.'

Gabby laughs again. 'Well, good. Because it's too late for that, anyway. I know I said on the phone that Owen had it coming, but killing one of your colleagues really is crossing a line. But if you aren't even going to pretend that you want to come crawling back, Maisie, why *are* you here?'

I stare at her, scrutinising every muscle in her face for a sign that she already knows the answer to that – that I'm here to rescue Beth, the journalist her new boss has kidnapped. I know I have a bad track record with falling for Gabby's mind games, but I am *certain* by now that she doesn't even know Beth's here. If she did, and she had a whiff of our connection, she would have found some way to lord it over me, and she wouldn't have sounded so genuinely curious when she asked that last question. And if she doesn't know about Beth, how much else doesn't she know?

'Pascal Robertson has a secret that will destroy ILS if it gets out. It's what he had Owen kill Sean Davies to protect. Right now there is a journalist upstairs in his flat, who *he* abducted because she discovered his secret – and I'm willing to guess he hasn't told you.'

The way her eyes widen as I speak suggests I've hit the nail on the head. 'And what is that information?'

'It's on the USB stick Steph took from me, but it's password-protected. I'll tell you the password if you let me go.'

Gabby laughs. 'Maisie, you must understand that you don't have much of a negotiating position here.'

I don't. But all I'm gambling is that checking the USB stick will distract Steph enough that I can make a run for it. That, or if I can play for time long enough . . .

'OK, but it's not *just* a USB stick,' I tell her. 'I've set up an online server with a dead man's switch. If you don't let me go, it'll be sent automatically to every media organisation in the country, and all ILS's competitors – including the competitor who took out all the hits against them through Removals. Someone out there *really* hates ILS, Gabby – someone with power. And now, if ILS go down, they'll take Novum with them.'

I'm bullshitting, naturally. I probably should have done all that stuff, but I'm going to be honest, with everything else going on, I didn't think of it. Will and I had been hoping for a better way in than, well, whatever *this* is, and Jason was already at his limit, doing as much as he could in the time he had.

Gabby doesn't even react enough for me to gauge if she's bought it. She just holds out a hand for Steph to pass her the USB stick, then holds it up to the light, letting its aluminium casing glimmer in the recessed downlights embedded in the ceiling tiles. She's trying to look sceptical, even ironic, but there's a power-hungry gleam in her eyes. However much she's trying to act as if she's OK with playing second fiddle to Pascal Robertson, I can tell that it irks her. If there's one thing I'm sure I know about Gabby Hawthorne, even now, it's that she doesn't play second fiddle to anyone without a fight.

'Well, well, well,' she says, laying the flash drive on the desk beside her. 'So – what is this incredible piece of information that I should spare your life just to get a glimpse of?'

'Verdicure. It'll make the world infertile.'

Gabby holds my gaze for several seconds without speaking. The she laughs – and not just in the way she was laughing before. She throws her head back and howls, putting a hand on the desk behind her for support. I've never seen her laugh like that, and even Steph shoots a concerned glance in her direction, though she doesn't look away for long enough that I can use it to my advantage.

'Come now, Maisie,' Gabby says once she's regained her composure. 'What do you take me for? You'll have to do better than that.'

She *knows*? But that doesn't make any sense. I'm still certain Pascal didn't let her in on the plot to kidnap Beth – but does that mean there's something else he's trying to hide, which we've missed? Unless . . .

'Pascal doesn't know you know, does he?'

Gabby sighs. 'Pascal doesn't know what he has. As far as he's concerned, the long-term consequences of Verdicure are simply a liability. All he cares about is making money, and he's worried that the Achilles' heel in his wonder chemical will stop it from rolling in. He hasn't been around as long as I have: he still believes in the media and the regulators and Parliament and all the little lies people tell themselves to soften the reality of the sort of the world they live in. Might makes right, doesn't it, Maisie? Money and bullets – you understand that. Furthermore, while Pascal doesn't really care about those so-called negative effects as long as they don't affect his bottom line, he still has no vision for the *positive* consequences of his happy little accident. But I do.'

'What?' I ask. My hands appear to have clenched into fists.

Gabby looks disappointed. 'See, Maisie, *this* is why I didn't bring you in on the ILS project. Your sense of morality is so short term, no vision for the greater good. You have no problem at all removing undesirable elements from the human population on an immediate basis, do you? We must agree that this is frequently justified, or else you wouldn't have kept coming to work every morning, given your temperament. What Verdicure offers is simply a logical progression. The world cannot support its current population, and Verdicure can solve that without you or I having to raise a finger. It's already the top-selling pesticide around the world – especially in, shall we say, developing markets. It's only a matter of time before it gets into the soil and its effects become irreversible.'

I look at Steph, who's still pointing her gun at me. 'You're OK with all this? Genocide? Population control?'

Steph shrugs. 'It's a brave new world,' she says.

'Exactly right,' Gabby agrees, pushing herself from the desk to stand, looming over me. 'Maisie, the way you put it sounds so 1930s. We are on the cusp of something great. I was hoping you might come around to my point of view, but alas . . .' And here she gestures to Steph. 'I'm afraid I might have to let you go.'

At that moment, I hear footsteps approaching the door behind me. It's the moment I'd been waiting for – the reason I'd been spinning the conversation out for as long as I had. Because if I know one thing about Pascal Robertson, it's that he's a suspicious man – paranoid, even. And if there's one thing a paranoid man doesn't like, it's three women in a room, with the door closed, potentially talking about him . . .

'You have no right to be here,' Gabby snaps over my shoulder as the door opens.

'I'll go where I want, thanks,' says Tommy Mitchell. 'Pascal's getting curious about your visitor.'

23

As Tommy comes into the room, Steph glances to Gabby for guidance. It looks as if she's suddenly getting second thoughts about the whole 'pointing a gun at Maisie' situation, which is interesting, isn't it? It's almost as if shooting me for her boss is one thing, but shooting me in the presence of someone who reports directly to her boss's boss is another. Gabby, meanwhile, has slipped Beth's USB stick into her palm, blocking Tommy from seeing it. Which is *also* interesting. It's an action that suggests that what's on that stick is not quite as worthless as Gabby made it out to be.

'Honestly,' Gabby snaps. 'I am speaking with *Novum* employees in the *Novum* suite of offices. Surely between the two of you you can figure out who this is? You only met Maisie last month.'

'He knows who she is,' Tommy growls, stepping past where I'm sitting. He's armed, too, but his gun is just one more lump beneath a shirt already made lumpy by his bulletproof vest. 'He wants to know why your other employee is pointing a gun at her.'

Steph looks abashed, Gabby apoplectic. I'm having a moment of clarity.

Ah, I think. *I should've thought of this sooner.* I was so fixated on whether Gabby had made the wrong choice throwing her lot in with ILS that I didn't stop to consider how Pascal might feel about buying a hitman company that now employs a grand total of zero hitmen. Well, one, maybe, if you count Steph, but given how her aim has wandered in the confusion following Tommy's entrance, I wouldn't – not yet, anyway.

'We are having an *internal dispute,*' Gabby is yelling, but before she's finished speaking I've taken advantage of the distraction to close the distance with Steph and kick the gun from her hand, sending it skittering across the carpet tiles down to the other end of the room.

'You idiot,' Tommy growls as he reaches beneath his shirt. 'What did you let her do that for?' Then the blue and black chair I was sitting on crashes into him – because I've hit him with it – and he staggers sideways. He's only winded, but it gives me enough time to dash to the fingerprint scanner by the edge of the door, which I prod with so much force that I worry it'll break. But it doesn't. The door opens.

'How the fuck . . .?' Tommy yells, perhaps realising that I was never as trapped as he thought I was. If he'd known I'd been added to the fingerprint system, maybe he wouldn't have been so cavalier about letting me hit him with a chair. But by the time he's processed this I'm already gone, slamming the door behind me and leaving him to scan his own finger if he wants to pursue. From there, it's out into the corridor, past the central staircase leading up to Pascal's office, and onwards, through the next set of fingerprint-locked doors, into the opposite wing. It turns out to be some kind of lab, replete with stark white countertops, liquids bubbling away under fume hoods around the edge of the room, while my path through the centre is obstructed by a wheeled hydroponic setup similar to the one Archie Henderson had with him on stage moments before his fateful death. It seems like so long ago now. A man in a lab coat emerges from behind him as I dash for the door in the opposite wall. 'You shouldn't be in here!' he shouts, throwing up his clipboard in protest.

'Neither should you!' I retort, shoving a silver trolley stacked with microscopes in the direction of the door, hoping it'll trip Tommy up when he inevitably follows me through. 'It's a Saturday, for Christ's sake! Go home!'

The crashing sound from behind me as I throw myself against the far door indicates that the microscopes did their thing in delaying Tommy, but the gunshots as I slam it shut behind me suggest he doesn't have Steph's squeamishness about shooting me to death in pleasant company. But even though I can sense him gaining on me, I'm not dead yet – and the door to the fire escape staircase is in sight. I throw myself through that one, too, then start dashing up, three bare concrete steps at a time. By now, Tommy is hot on my heels – I see him come through the door just as I turn back on myself for the second flight, forcing me to duck for protection behind the thankfully also concrete banister as bullets fly overhead. One of them obliterates the casing of an emergency light fixture, sending shards of translucent white and green plastic flying – but the exit onto the roof is in sight.

'There's no use running,' he says, a little out of breath but getting closer.

With Tommy about to round the corner, I creep upstairs

silently, my eyes set on what appears to me now to be the most beautiful phrase in the English language: PUSH BAR TO OPEN.

'Even if you make it out there, there's nowhere to hide. You're trapped. Unarmed. Pathetic. Just give up now and all this can be over.'

One more step. Then another. Then, just as I hear Tommy about to round the corner at the half-storey landing, I reach up for the bar and *PUSH!*

And I am *so* happy to discover that the sign wasn't lying to me. Under the weight of my hands the bar makes a lovely tactile crunching movement inwards towards the door panel. Then, just as promised, it swings open.

As the door opens, a hail of high-calibre gunfire rains over my head. I duck back down and twist around to see great chunks missing from the wall right where Tommy was standing. Tommy, though, is a pro. He saw what I was doing, twigged what it might mean, and took cover – back down the stairs and round the corner, out of Will's firing line.

But I don't care about that, because Will has just stepped into the building.

'Heya, Maisie,' he says. He crouches down beside me, adjusting his shades with one hand, passing me a spare machine pistol with his other – along with a precious little trinket in the shape of an earring. 'I heard you had company so I thought I'd make a louder entrance.'

'Jesus fucking Christ, I could kiss you right now,' I whisper. Then I wrap one arm around his shoulders and draw him towards me, almost pulling him off balance.

And OK, yes, there's a man with a gun just down the

stairs from us, and it wouldn't be unfair to say that this is neither the time nor the place for a romantic gesture, but on the flipside, never in my life have I placed so much faith in another human being to be there for me and then had them pull through like this. Trapped inside the office building, cut off from the outside world, I had no way at all of knowing if Will Thomas was going to be there like he promised he would be when I pushed open that door. He could have been arrested climbing up a drainpipe. He could have been caught lurking on the rooftop by someone on Pascal's team. He could have simply decided that, with everything that has been kicking off lately, the ILS offices were too hot to handle, not worth messing with even for the ludicrous sums that someone is offering via the Removals job board for Pascal Robertson's head on a metaphorical platter. He could have just fucked off home – but he didn't. He was there. And as a result, Tommy Mitchell didn't turn my back into Swiss cheese the moment he realised he was safe to do so. Is it weird that this is the most romantic thing a guy has ever done for me?

But we still have to figure out how to get past Tommy. We lock eyes for a moment, then Will slips a flashbang from his pocket and shows it to me, pulling a 'Shall we . . .?' face.

'Just the one, right?' I whisper back.

He nods. Not ideal, then. Better to save it if possible.

But if not, we seem to be in a stalemate. The switchback design of the stairs is such that in order for either lot of us to get into a position where we can shoot the other, they'd have to open themselves up to getting shot. It's a situation that massively incentivises waiting for your opponent to get impatient, but Tommy should know he has time on his side, since if and when the police show up, he could probably explain his position as a security guard doing his job – with the institutional backing of ILS to argue his case that carrying firearms isn't *that* illegal, all things considered. We, on the other hand, would be fucked.

'How much is he paying you?' Will calls down to Tommy. 'Enough to be worth the risk?'

No reply.

'There's a pretty big bounty on his head, you know. We're already going three ways but we wouldn't mind cutting you in as a fourth. What do you fancy?'

Silence.

Then Tommy speaks. 'Oh, piss off. He's a top bloke, Pascal, no matter what people say.'

I look at Will, who shrugs. It was worth a try.

'*Tommy, what's happening?*' comes a voice I recognise over the tinny speaker of a walkie-talkie. It's Pascal Robertson. '*The cameras have all gone down. Where are you?*'

Nice work, Jason. Just when we need it.

I remember the earring and slip it in, pressing the hidden button to activate it.

'*Afternoon, Maisie,*' says Jason through my earpiece. '*It won't keep them forever, but I'll do what I can to keep it offline.*'

And I could *almost* kiss him too – in a platonic friend sort of way.

'*Tommy, come in,*' Pascal repeats.

'All right, boss,' Tommy replies. 'Some mess this is. The girl's just brought in a friend. They're camping by the roof exit – the two of them together. What do you want me to do?'

'*Don't worry about them. Can you get back here safely? All the noise has tipped off the police — they're sending an armed response unit. If you're inside my apartment when they come I can keep you out of it, but if they find you themselves . . .*'

'But the intruders . . .'

'*Don't worry about them,*' Pascal snaps. '*All sensitive employees are to lock down in here and keep my penthouse secure. Novum are inside already: if the intruders are still out there when the police arrive then good — they can deal with them. If not, we track them down later.*'

Will and I glance at each other as we listen carefully for what Tommy does next. There's a shuffling sound as he edges out of cover and gets to his feet. Then the door to the fifth-floor laboratory swings open and closed.

'Not thinking of backing out, are you?' I say as I get to my feet.

Will grins at me, taking my hands in his. 'Wouldn't miss it for the world.'

And maybe it's the adrenaline and the endorphins, or the fact I trusted him with my entirety and he still came through for me — or maybe it's how safe and relaxed I feel when I'm around him even when the bullets are literally flying overhead — but suddenly, in that concrete stairway, the thought of not kissing him becomes unbearable.

So we kiss.

★

Anyway. Here's the situation:

We've got a locked door that my fingerprint can't open,

one well-trained and well-armed bodyguard inside Pascal's flat (plus Pascal, Gabby and Steph), as well as three to five security guards in position outside it. Are they also trained and armed? Well, only a couple of the thugs I've encountered so far had real weapons, and none of them were particularly well trained. But as we run back down to the fifth floor and back up the other staircase to the sixth, Will and I run numbers between us on the most important question: how likely are they to have guns?

'They didn't last time I was here,' I say, starting us off.

'You sure?'

'I'm sure.'

'And if Pascal is hiding all his sensitive employees in his flat, whatever that means . . .'

'. . . then leaving a bunch of illegally armed mall cops loitering outside his door . . .'

'. . . would be pretty stupid, yeah. But then so is giving us free rein of a building full of all his stuff.'

'Unless he expects the police to get here, like, now.'

'But they haven't yet. Wait. I hear sirens.'

Lots of sirens. OK, scratch that part about the police not being here — though, if they stick to standard procedure, they'll still spend at least a few minutes outside assessing the situation before they bust in — then there's all the fingerprint-locked doors they have to worry about — but they're coming.

'Better assume they're armed,' I say as we come up onto the sixth-floor landing, just one bend in the corridor separating us from the security checkpoint. 'It's too risky. We should use the flashbang.'

'But then we wouldn't have a flashbang.' Will grins back at me, handing me the device in question for safekeeping. 'And you know how I feel about risk.'

And fuck he looks sexy as he runs round that corner, machine pistol in hand.

'Stop or I'll shoot!' yells a guard. Will's hands go up in the air. I guess I was right, then.

I step around the corner more slowly, my own gun drawn and ready. Behind the airport-style bag scanner are two men and a woman in the same black-shirt-and-trousers combo that all the ILS goons have been wearing, each pointing a pistol at Will – until they see me, that is, at which point one of the men decides to switch to the new target. I aim mine back at him for good measure. Not for the first time, I'm blown away by the scale of Pascal's security operation: the man is practically amassing a private army.

'OK, OK, OK,' Will says. 'No one has to get hurt here. All we want to do is get inside that door.'

'Pascal says who comes in,' says the woman, taking charge.

'And what Pascal wants he gets, does he?' says Will.

No response.

Then I notice the desks the guards are sitting at. And you know, I've seen inside a bunch of offices in my time, and during that time I've seen a bunch of desks. Usually, when people are allowed to feel *ownership* of their desk instead of being forced to keep moving, the desks they sit at tend to accumulate a sense character. You get a proliferation of knick-knacks: ornaments from people's holidays, funny A-fold calendars to count the days, mugs for tea with cute slogans, either bought from a store or specially printed by their colleagues or family to commemorate important events: birthdays, promotions, births or weddings.

Outside of hotdesking, the one place you don't see that sort of thing is in an army – even a private army. Believe me, I've seen where those people work, too. Armies don't want character. They want conformity. Allowing character allows for independent thought, which leads to independent action – or, worse, for loyalty *between* the lower orders, instead of *to* the top.

Pascal might be trying to build an army, but these desks are not soldiers' desks. These desks are oozing character. They've been sticking up postcards with cats on them, for Christ's sake.

'It's a pretty easy job you've got here, isn't it?' I say. 'On a normal day, that is.'

The woman blinks and looks at me, but keeps her gun on Will. 'Yeah,' she says. 'When we don't have to deal with pillocks like you.'

'You must scan, what, five bags per day usually? And then what do you do the rest of the time?'

She grits her teeth, unwilling to answer. But the half-drunk mugs of tea on each of their desks tell me exactly what they do with their time. They do what any group of colleagues would do when they don't have much to be getting on with: they sit around and chat. They get to know each other. They become friends.

I change my tack, looking between the two guys as well. Will is staying out of it, but I catch a growing smile out of the corner of my eye. 'Seriously, tell me,' I ask, 'how do you guys feel about working here? Good pay? Good benefits?'

'We look out for each other,' says the man with the gun trained on me.

I think it's supposed to be a warning — don't mess with one of us unless you want to face us all — but I don't take it that way. I smile. 'Good! And so you should. But what about—' I nod my head in the direction of Pascal's door '—the man in there? Does he look out for you?'

A flicker of doubt. That's a no, then.

'Thought not,' I say. 'He makes you carry these guns, doesn't he, even though it's not in your contract and you know it's illegal. And you've heard about strange things going on around the company. Colleagues of yours who've been sent out to raid people's houses. That's a bit odd. Then there's the woman he's got in there. Dragged in last night by your other boss, Mr Mitchell.'

'*I might not have cameras, but I'm on the police radio*,' Jason tells me over my earpiece, '*and guys — you've got a SWAT team making preparations to come inside*.' That's not great news, but it's not the worst, either. We've still got *some* time — the police don't know where we are, so they'll want to ensure every floor is fully sealed off and cleared before moving up — but we don't have *much* time. We need to get in that flat pretty pronto.

'And the police are coming,' I add, speaking quicker and quicker. 'Right now. So, OK, I know this might sound like a threat but trust me when I say that I really don't mean it like one, but the fact of the matter is, even though it's three on two and his gun is pointed at the ceiling, if any of you start firing, I'll be able to kill at least one of you. And that would be really sad, wouldn't it? Something you'd have to live with for the rest of your life.'

They're glancing at each other. I can tell I'm making progress.

'*Whereas*,' I continue, 'if you let us go in that flat, we only kill Pascal and Tommy, and you'll probably forget it within a week. Plus we can take your pistols with us to hide them from the police so you don't get in trouble.'

'And we can give you some of the reward money,' Will adds.

'That, too,' I agree. 'Some people *really* want the two of them dead.'

'Can't imagine why,' says the man facing me, prompting the woman in the middle to shoot him an irritated look. 'What?' he says back to her. 'She's right – they're a couple of pricks.'

'Well, maybe,' says the woman. 'But even if we wanted to open that door, we can't. There's a code, and we've not been told it.'

I glance at Will, then look between the three of them. 'Are you really telling me that all three of you have been sitting out every day here with nothing to do, and not one of you has been watching what numbers they've been pressing on that keypad every time someone tries to enter the flat? That you didn't even get curious?'

'No,' snaps the woman. 'Why would we?'

But the guy facing me looks thoughtful. 'I think I could make a pretty good guess,' he says.

'Good man,' says Will, grinning broadly. Then, as the guy walks over to the door, he leans in to me to whisper: 'Maisie Baxter, you are *incredible*.'

24

In the end, only two of the three guards take us up on our offer to dispose of their guns for them. The woman, who seems to be the most senior, says she'd rather take the risk of still having hers when the police get here than leave the two of us with all the weapons. I have to admit that's fair enough. Besides, a *fifth* gun between the two of us would just be cumbersome.

As it turns out, the guard who reckoned he could get us in through the door reckoned right. He inputs all six digits and then stands well back, leaving Will to do the honour of turning the handle while I keep my gun on the woman who's still armed. Sorry, sister, but you made your choice. There's a buzz and a flash of blue light above the number pad, then Will steps aside, leaving the door to slowly swing open. I think we both expect to be greeted by a hail of gunfire, but nothing comes. Just silence.

Well, not quite silence. Voices echo from the far end of the penthouse – definitely at least one man and at least one woman, though it's hard to tell if anyone else is speaking besides Gabby and Pascal.

'All right then, Mr Risk-Taker,' I whisper to Will after a second. 'I solved the last problem. Now it's your turn.'

Will takes off his jacket and flaps it across the doorway like a matador provoking a bull. It's a classic trick to get a would-be ambusher to reveal their position or waste their ammo, but it either doesn't work or no one's there. Nothing.

We exchange glances. I look at him and then towards the door, eyes narrowed in the timeless expression of *go on, then*.

Will peeks his head round the corner. 'Clear,' he whispers.

One by one we pass through the doorway into the lobby of Pascal's penthouse – Will first, facing forward, me second, facing behind. Once we're inside, I gingerly, gingerly, gingerly swing the door shut until the lock clicks into place.

'Some security system,' Will whispers.

'It pays to remember that parts of it have feelings,' I reply.

But as often happens on missions, the witty banter part of my mind has detached itself entirely from how I really feel. Actually, my heart is in my throat thinking about where Beth might be and how she might be holding up.

There are five doors off the corridor, two on each side and one at the end. 'We stick to the edges of the space to avoid sightlines from the far door, in case it suddenly opens: I take the right path, Will takes the left.'

'You are absolutely unbelievable,' Gabby is shouting from the far end of the corridor as Will tries the first door on his side. It's a gym, I see past his shoulders. No Beth. 'Sheer, rank incompetence. They could be here any moment and you have your bodyguard, what, trying to fix the camera system? Why?'

262

'I've explained this, Gabriella,' Pascal says as I try the first door on my side. It's a library. No Beth. 'Tommy is the only one who knows how the system works. If we hear them fighting the guards outside, he can ready himself. Until then—'

'Ah yes, your *guards*,' Gabby spits as Will opens the third door. It's a whiskey nook. No Beth. 'Where did you find them, guarding a McDonald's? Even nightclub bouncers are more ruthless. If you want people to kill for you, Pascal, it takes time. You have to *break* them first.'

My blood runs cold hearing her talk like that. Will looks at me, except it's more than that. He's checking up on me, I realise, but his eyes are flashing with anger.

Pushing my emotions down, I open the last door on my side. Behind it are bank after bank of blacked-out screens, which I imagine would provide an overview of every meeting room, corridor and cubicle in the building if it wasn't for Jason's stellar work in knocking them all offline. And getting up from the desk and turning, gun in hand, is Tommy Mitchell.

Without thinking, I fire.

He never manages to stand. Sparks go flying from the banks of screens as they weather bullet fragments and arterial spray simultaneously.

'Do you see what I mean!?' Gabby screams. 'All right, that does it. *Up. You* are coming with me. Steph – give me that.'

The door in the far end of the hall opens inwards, and through it walks Beth. A burst of relief rushes through me at the sight of her, tempered only by the sorry state she's in right now. There's no way to sugarcoat it: Beth looks a mess.

She is gagged, her clothes are ripped, her hair is spilling out of her usually slicked-back ponytail, and she's stumbling as she walks with her hands wrenched awkwardly behind her. I take in the matted blood along her hairline, the shocking red-blue-yellow of bruises across her cheek and chin that tell the story of what's happened to her over the last twenty-four hours. Then there's the gun to her head. Gabby, holding it, follows behind.

'Let her go,' I hiss, hate rising like bile in my throat.

Beth's eyes bug out as she sees me – and what I'm carrying. I hear her try to speak but nothing comes through her gag but muffled cries.

'Maisie, Maisie, Maisie,' Gabby says, pushing Beth forward into the hall. Steph comes trotting behind her, but there's no sign of Pascal – even when Steph closes the door behind her.

I catch Will edging towards her. *Don't!* I think.

Gabby sees him, too, because she turns to him and barks: 'Back! Or your girlfriend's friend here gets it. And put your guns on the ground – both of them. Who do you think you are, John Rambo? Don't be ridiculous.'

He takes a glance in my direction then does what Gabby says, placing each of his pistols gently at his feet.

'Back against the wall,' Gabby yells. He does it without question.

'Let her go, Gabby,' I plead.

Gabby doesn't listen. Instead she's gazing past me towards the mess of Tommy's body in the observation room. She takes a good long look at what's in there, then pulls an approving grimace. 'Oh, good, you *do* still have it in you. I was starting to worry that with this one doing your job for you you might have lost your taste for blood.'

'What do you *want*, Gabby?'

Gabby laughs. 'I could ask you the same question. Only, I've figured it out, now. It didn't take me *too* long to catch on that Pascal's mysterious woman was someone you knew – though I swear you told me she was called Bridget? Oh, Maisie, was that you attempting to trick me?'

'I never said that. You just never bothered to remember.'

Gabby looks unfazed. 'Is that it? Well, if you say so. But the one thing I *don't* understand, Maisie, is why you would even want to rescue her, considering there's no chance she'll ever want to speak to you again, now that she's seen who you really are.' She grabs Beth by the skull and forces her to take in the gore in the observation room. Beth squirms in her arms, trying to look away, but Gabby's grip is strong. 'She never did tell you what I had her doing all day, did she?' Gabby gloats in Beth's ear. 'Well, not *honestly*, anyway. That's the thing about people in Maisie's line of work – they do have a tendency to lie.'

'*That SWAT team has entered the building,*' says Jason. '*They're securing the ground floor now.*'

'I don't care if she accepts me,' I say – and it's true. 'I just want her to be safe.'

Gabby smiles. 'That's touching. Oh, Steph – if you want a gun of your own, just take Tommy's. Maisie, stand back, please, to let Steph pass.'

We both do what we're told. *Not too different after all, then.* Steph squats down and delicately picks up Tommy's gun between her thumb and forefinger, wiping some of the blood off on her skirt before she takes hold of it properly – and points it at me.

'Don't trust her,' I tell Steph. 'Whatever you do, don't trust her.'

But her face is a mask. *You have to break them*, Gabby had said, while Steph was right there. I remember now how Gabby broke me. I can see it for what it was. Endless gruelling bouts of self-defence training to normalise violence, then she just happened to show up late after arranging a meeting with a notorious record producer. One thing led to another, and before I knew it . . .

'Steph is coming along marvellously as your replacement,' Gabby says. 'I've thought I might need one for a while, after you started getting so finicky about accepting jobs. You were a good employee, but I never expected you to understand this ILS business. I had already written you off as on your way out.'

'*First floor secure*,' says Jason. '*And they're picking up speed*.'

'What has she made you do?' I ask Steph.

Steph's mouth spread into a lopsided smile. 'Oh, don't worry about me,' she says. 'I'm fine – promise.'

Beth struggles and my eyes snap back to Gabby. 'What do you *want*?' I shout.

'Now now, Maisie,' she says. 'Inside voice. What I want is to let your friend here go.'

What? 'Then do it,' I say.

'On one condition,' Gabby adds. 'I need you to do a job for me. You figured out that ILS bought Novum, didn't you? Well – how closely did you read the terms of sale? When I said that we would retain full independence, I meant it.

There are several strict clauses in the agreement that dictate the terms of Novum's position as a subsidiary. Another clause relates to my title: as well as leading up Novum, I am also, on paper, Deputy CEO of ILS as a whole. It's not a position with much power, I have to say, but it does have one important responsibility. Can you guess what it is?'

'If Pascal dies . . .' I begin.

'Yes,' says Gabby. 'I want you to kill for me one last time.'

My eyes lock with Beth's, so wide they're circular. She's terrified. I think of how terrified Jason had been to see me, when he thought Gabby had sent me to kill him. Like I was a monster.

'*Second floor, guys,*' says Jason.

'I'll do it,' says Will, seeing my hesitation. 'Let me kill him. It doesn't have to be Maisie.'

'It does,' says Gabby. 'Because I don't want *you* to do it. I want Maisie to do it.'

'Why?' I breathe.

'It's a win–win situation,' Gabby says. 'If we're all standing here like this when the police arrive, I'll simply blow Beth's head off and the blame for all the bodies in here will fall naturally on the armed intruders. Pascal, however, will remain President of ILS and will continue to run the company with the singular lack of vision he has shown thus far. But if you kill Pascal and then escape, Maisie, Steph and I can play clueless survivors of an otherwise successful home invasion. You three go home – together or apart, it's none of my business – while I keep the police occupied for as long as it takes you to get away. Then, when the smoke clears, I find myself the proud owner of the company that will usher in a new dawn for humanity.'

'*Third floor and speeding up*,' says Jason.

'But why me? Why not Will?'

'Oh, that. Because I want you to remember, Maisie: I made you what you are, and I have dirt on you that would make a statue weep to read it. Wherever you go after you leave here, you are and will always be mine.'

I lock eyes with Beth — I don't know for how long. I feel like I should be able to find a way out of this that doesn't give Gabby what she wants, but what that looks like, I don't know. Keeping Beth alive is the most important thing; then Will; and then me. Pascal undoubtedly deserves to die but after everything I've been through, the thought of killing for Gabby makes me sick.

'*Fourth floor.*'

'Fine,' I say at last. 'I'll do it.'

'First door on the right,' Gabby says. 'At least, he was when I left him.'

If the world would be a better place with the target dead, they should die, I remind myself as I walk to the door to the next room. That was always my philosophy. The client doesn't matter.

Four pairs of eyes and one gun barrel track me as I cross the hallway and open the door. I come out into another corridor and take the first right as instructed. It's a bedroom. Pascal Robertson is huddled on the floor in the far corner behind the bed, shielding his head with his hands.

If the target deserves to die, they should die.

Targets do that, sometimes. Huddle in on themselves. As a hitwoman, you regularly find that targets do not wish to die.

But if the target deserves to die, they should die. If the target deserves to die, they should die. If the target deserves to die, they should die.

I repeat it like a mantra as I blow Pascal's brains out.

'*Fifth floor secured,*' Jason tells me.

★

The police and I burst through opposite doors into the hallway at exactly the same time, exactly as planned. That was another calculated risk: that Gabby wasn't wearing an earpiece, and therefore couldn't possibly know the movements of the police with the same precision as Jason was able to give me, even without access to the building's cameras. As such, her threat to kill Beth before they got here had to have been a bluff: she had no way of knowing if she'd be able to do it in time, and even with Gabby's sway she probably couldn't get away with shooting someone right in front of them — or them rushing in while she's still holding the gun and the body.

I toss the flashbang into the centre of the room as I enter, shielding my eyes and rushing forwards. The scariest thing about flashbang grenades is that they look practically identical to explosive grenades, especially when you glimpse them rolling across the floor towards you, not far from your feet. If you *expect* to encounter a flashbang, you can take precautions. You can cover your eyes and ears and keep your gun trained on wherever you expect your opponent to be, firing as necessary even if you can't see your target. But if you're not expecting a flashbang, all you see is a grenade, and you're faced with making a split-second life or death decision on whether to run away.

In short, when I see the cops are backing out of the room, Gabby letting go of Beth, and Steph making a mad dash to Tommy Mitchell's side room, the flashbang has already done what I wanted it to. Then the grenade flashes and bangs, and OK, both of those are pretty scary, too.

'Beth!' I shout, though I can't hear myself over the ringing in my ears. Opening my eyes, I grab her by the shoulders and pull her into me. She is screaming through her gag, which is understandable, and I pivot quickly to drag her back with me towards the door I just came out of, sparing just one look over my shoulder to make sure Will is coming with us. I'm happy to find that he is.

Gunfire comes from somewhere, but I'm not sure from where, as the three of us dash unharmed into the next corridor and around the corner. Will's looking from door to door as we pass them, calculating something. 'These windows should still open from the inside,' he shouts over the din.

'And then what?' I yell back.

'Removals have a safehouse a few rooftops over,' he says. 'If we can get there . . .'

He sees the door he wants and slams his way through it into another bedroom, throwing open the ugly fishtank glass of the window as soon as he reaches it. Beth, meanwhile, has pulled off her gag. 'Maisie, what the *fuck*!?' she yells. 'What is going on?'

'I'm sorry you had to hear all that,' I say, as Will props himself up to perch on the sill.

'It's a pretty gnarly jump,' he says. 'Watch yourself.'

Then he's gone, leaping across the gap and onto the next rooftop. 'Think you can make it?' I ask Beth, pushing her up after him.

She takes one look at the drop and scrabbles her feet, almost falling backwards onto me. 'What!?' she yells. 'Um, no!'

I lean past her to perform my own assessment of the risk. Will's right: it *is* pretty gnarly. 'I think you can do it,' I tell her softly, hoping it's true. 'Just push as far as you can with your legs and reach as far as you can with your hands. Imagine you're a frog, OK? You'll be fine.'

There's a banging from behind us, out in the corridor. I leave Beth on the windowsill and pull over a cabinet so that it blocks the door, then add an armchair behind it for weight.

'Is that the police?' Beth asks, glancing at my improvised barricade.

'It could be,' I say. But my heart sinks when I see her expression. I'd been so set on getting Beth out of here with me that I hadn't stopped to question whether that's what she'd want, given the choice. 'Would you rather go with them?' I ask. 'You can if you want, but . . .'

She looks between me and the door. 'Be honest with me, Maisie,' she says. 'What are you?'

'I'm a hitwoman.'

'You kill people for a living?' Her voice is more curious than shocked. Is that surprising, after the twenty-four hours she's just had?

'If they deserve it,' I say. 'If it makes the world a better place.'

Someone bangs on the door. 'Police! Open up!'

'And what'll the police do if they find you?' she asks.

'Right now? Probably lock me away forever.'

'And if they find me?'

I glance towards the door. Something heavy has just connected with it. Probably a battering ram. 'If you're lucky, they'll help you get home. They'll give you one of those reflective blankets and maybe even help you find counselling.'

'And if I'm not lucky?'

'If you're not lucky, Gabby Hawthorne has talked her way out of the situation she was just in and has them in her pocket. She finds a way to implicate you in the killings of Pascal Robertson and whoever else. You go to prison.'

She takes another look at the gap. 'And if I go with you?' she asks.

'That depends on you,' I tell her. The battering ram collides with the door again, only this time hard enough for the wood to splinter. 'But you have to jump.'

Will is waving at us from the other side, urging us to make the leap. I notice Beth looking at him as if for the first time. 'Wait, that's him, isn't it? The guy from your photo?'

Despite everything, I feel a smile come to my face. 'He's amazing,' I tell her. 'I can't wait for you to meet him properly.'

Epilogue

Almost four weeks to the day after our madcap dash across the rooftops of London, I find myself on Margate Beach with Liv, Beth and Michelle, watching the tide come in.

It's a crisp day, cold enough to feel like autumn has arrived before summer even really got started.

We didn't realise until later, since both Beth and I had left our phones somewhere or other in the ILS offices, but Liv must have messaged us about her birthday at about the same moment as Pascal's brains were spattering across the floor:

I'm so sorry gals but I'm going to have to call it. The weather is looking absolutely pish for tomorrow – can we reschedule next month? Celebrate me turning 29 and 1 month? Xxxx

Which was a relief to discover, all things considered. Neither of us could have handled a heavy Sunday given the Saturday we'd just had, but flaking on Liv at the last minute would have caused further problems – especially if we couldn't think of any good excuses.

'So when did you decide to quit?' Michelle asks from the far end of our beach towel, leaning over Beth who has fallen asleep beneath the pages of a thick tome about Nicaraguan history. We're all wearing coats and some of us even have scarves, but it's dry and Liv has been wanting to go to the beach for months, so the beach it is.

'Oh, I don't know exactly,' I tell her. 'I think it was a long time coming. There was just a point where I realised what I wanted from the role and what Gabby wanted from me didn't line up anymore.'

'I didn't even realise,' says Liv from my other side. 'I thought you still loved it there. How did Gabby take it?'

'It was pretty emotional,' I say. 'For both of us really. But we knew it was for the best.'

'It wasn't because of all that business with – what were they called, ILS? Like, what was going on there? Was it really just bad timing or did she, you know . . .'

I laugh, because that's the thing – despite everything that had happened inside the ILS office, and everything Will and Jason and Beth and I discovered in the lead-up to 'what happened', as Beth has taken to calling it, very little made it out of that office and into the outside world. Three days later, news broke that its eccentric CEO Pascal Robertson had taken his own life following concerns that he'd ignored alarming reports of Verdicure's effects on human fertility – at least according to outlets aligned with one of the firm's well-established transatlantic competitors. Presidency of the company passed, via a mechanism no one seemed to quite understand, to one Gabby Hawthorne, who led the company on an apology tour, during which she insisted that she had categorically no knowledge whatsoever of this cover-up when she was hired for the Deputy CEO position just a scant few weeks prior. The product was recalled, the stock price plummeted, and Gabby resigned a few weeks later – bruised but not wounded in the public eye.

As for what went down between Gabby and the police, even I can't say for certain. True to her word, she had apparently managed to smooth things over. Maybe my flashbang even contributed to the innocent victim narrative she'd been going for.

'Probably good to get out when you did,' Liv says with an encouraging smile.

'Heyyy!' Michelle calls, waving to Arman, Sam and Will at the far end of the beach. They are on their way back from picking up ice creams for the seven of us, laughing at a story Will seems to be telling, if his wild gesticulations are anything to go by.

'They seem to be getting on,' I say. To be honest, I'm relieved: this was Will's introductory jaunt with the friend group and I had the fear that, while *I* saw him as sweet and charming and, perhaps most importantly, surprisingly normal, throwing him into harsh comparison against the steadfast normalness of Liv and Michelle would reveal some previously unseeable freakishness that, like a vampire in front of a mirror, would instantly out him as a murderer.

So far, though, that hasn't happened.

'You're looking happy,' I say as he hands me my 99.

'It's all this not working,' he says. 'Pretty nice, isn't it?'

True to his word, Will split Robertson's bounty three ways with me and Jason – minus some smaller cuts for our friends in ILS security – so we hadn't had to worry about work for a while.

'Pub, pub, pub,' chants Sam, pulling Liv to her feet.

'We saw a great-looking one just back there,' Will adds by way of explanation. 'Want to go check it out?'

I glance at Beth, who has just woken up enough to pull the book from her face. 'You go ahead,' I tell Will. 'We'll catch you up.'

He nods and jogs after Sam and Liv, who are already moving away.

'Sorry you ended up seventh wheel,' I say, helping Beth to pack away the towel.

'It's OK,' she says, giving me an awkward smile. I feel a sickly sensation in my stomach. The most difficult thing about the last few weeks has been handling my friendship with her. When we're around others we've been acting like everything's fine, but when we're alone . . .

Well, we're not even alone as much as we used to be. Once the dust had settled on our escape from the ILS offices, I got the sense that she wanted space to process who I really am, and because of that — and because, admittedly, I've been swept up with Will — I've practically been living on *The Narrow Escape* the past few weeks. We've still kept up our weekly film nights, but even they have felt stilted, both of us happy to use whatever's on screen as an excuse to not talk.

'How long do you think you'll stay out of work?' she asks.

It's a loaded question. I'm not sure how to answer it — only partly because I don't know myself. 'I'm not sure,' I say. 'I guess I'll see how things go.'

'And when you go back, will it be to the same . . . industry?'

I stop what I'm doing and look at her. I guess this is the conversation I've been avoiding, even subconsciously. 'I'm not sure,' I say. 'What do you think?'

'I think you need to do what's right for you.'

Great. A riddle. 'How about you?' I ask, trying to change the subject. Beth also quit her job after 'what happened', citing irreconcilable differences with her boss, Dominic Waters, as the reason for wanting out. 'Have you started looking for other jobs in media?'

She snorts, looking out at the steel-grey ocean. 'No way. I'm done with that. Documentaries are a nice idea, but in practice what can they do? At the end of the day you can only show what the studios and the networks are happy for people to see. Newspapers are the same.'

Then she turns to look at me.

'You know, I've been thinking a lot since what happened – especially having the flat to myself. I've been starting to think I was barking up the wrong tree. That maybe there is a virtue in a more . . . direct approach.'

I hesitate, not sure where she's going with this. After my years spent worrying about how Beth will react to my deep dark secret, is she really about to—

She leans in and whispers in my ear: 'I'm saying I want in.'

Acknowledgments

First off, a massive thanks to the wonderful Clare Gordon for everything. Thank you for believing in us and for taking the risk. Thanks, too, to Francesca von Krauland, Maren Landsnes, Imogen Gordon Clark, Lou Nyuar, Rhiannon Morris, Amy Cameron, and the wider team at HQ.

We wrote most of this book while living and working in Beijing and while there have had the pleasure and privilege of getting to know some incredible people. To the vibrant English-language writing community at Spittoon and the Writing Wizards, to those at CUGB for being there pint-in-hand when we were ready to crawl out of our writing cave, and to everyone else who has made us feel welcome so far from home: thank you.

To our friends and family who made home feel a little closer when we needed it: we love you all endlessly. Most of all thanks to our parents, Kathryn and Lloyd, Hannah and Rachael, Kez and Emma, Lauren, Cami, Holden, Max, Annie, Yas, Ollie, Chris and Katie, to Tina for the years of kindness and generosity, and to Luke and Carolina who were there right at the beginning on Mile End Road.

And finally, to each other. What an absolute joy to get to do this together.

Dear Reader,

We hope you enjoyed reading this book. If you did, we'd be so appreciative if you left a review. It really helps us and the author to bring more books like this to you.

Here at HQ Digital we are dedicated to publishing fiction that will keep you turning the pages into the early hours. Don't want to miss a thing? To find out more about our books, promotions, discover exclusive content and enter competitions you can keep in touch in the following ways:

JOIN OUR COMMUNITY:

Sign up to our new email newsletter: http://smarturl.it/SignUpHQ

Read our new blog www.hqstories.co.uk

𝕏 https://twitter.com/HQStories

f www.facebook.com/HQStories

BUDDING WRITER?

We're also looking for authors to join the HQ Digital family!

Find out more here:

https://www.hqstories.co.uk/want-to-write-for-us/

Thanks for reading, from the HQ Digital team

HITWOMAN

HITWOMAN

ELSIE MARKS

ONE PLACE. MANY STORIES

HQ
An imprint of HarperCollins*Publishers* Ltd
1 London Bridge Street
London SE1 9GF

www.harpercollins.co.uk

HarperCollins*Publishers*
Macken House, 39/40 Mayor Street Upper
Dublin 1, D01 C9W8, Ireland

This edition 2025

1
First published in Great Britain by HQ,
an imprint of HarperCollins*Publishers* Ltd 2025

ISBN: 9780008762537

Typeset in Bembo by HarperCollins*Publishers* India

Printed and bound in the UK using 100%
Renewable Electricity at CPI Group (UK) Ltd

For more information visit: www.harpercollins.co.uk/green

Praise for *Hitwoman*

'*Hitwoman* is funny, sexy, and strangely relatable.
I cheered for the protagonist even as she committed
multiple murders and loved the rom-com style romance.'
Tasha Coryell, author of *Love Letters to a Serial Killer*

'Who'd have thought murder could be such fun? This gem
will have you rooting for the delightful Maisie as she strives
to be the most ethical of assassins until she finds herself in
the crosshairs. A wonderful not so cosy crime masterpiece.'
Graham Bartlett, author of *Bad for Good*

'*Hitwoman* is the most fun I've had reading a thriller this
year! Elsie Marks has created a fun, funny, and fast-paced
romp that's pitch-perfect to take on vacation or read over
a weekend spent in bed. I never thought I'd be rooting for
an assassin until I was introduced to Maisie Baxter.'
Kellye Garrett, author of *Missing White Woman*

'Thrilling, fast paced, exhilarating . . . I was totally there for
every last word of it.' **Reader Review, ★ ★ ★ ★ ★**

'This is a totally bonkers book, and that is a such a good
thing.' **Reader Review, ★ ★ ★ ★ ★**

Elsie Marks is the pen name for Louisa Burden–Garabedian and Neil Weaving, a writing duo from the UK now living and working in Beijing.